THE CURSE
OF
CROOKED
RIVER

MICHAEL J. SUTTON

ISBN: 978-0-6455671-5-1

Hidden Road Publishing

Hidden Road Publishing recognizes the indigenous, aboriginal, and Torres Strait Islander peoples of Australia as the rightful owners and custodians of the land. We long for the day when true justice is achieved, when restitution is made, and when equality is achieved between the descendants of the landed aristocracy and the indigenous people dispossessed, exploited, and abused. Their voices, their stories, their witness needs to be heard.

The characters of Biddy and George are fictional, and care has been taken to depict their plight, identity, and place on the land with the deepest respect. The story of Australia's indigenous peoples is not fictional, their suffering is not exaggerated, and their misery is not whitewashed. We make no apology to the pastoralists who raped the land and the people, the church leaders who protected and enabled the abuse, and the governments who covered it all up. It is time for the truth to be told, remembered, and taught.

DEDICATION

To those who do not come home,
who linger, like ghosts on forgotten battlefields.

ODE TO THE PAST

This is the first historical fiction novel of Nathaniel Chambers, set in the Colony of New South Wales, in 1871 and 1872. The events of this book take place in real locations, some which can be visited, explored, and seen today. Gulgong still exists and one street remains as a memorial to the goldrush. It is worth a day trip from Mudgee. There is a sign that reads 'Home Rule' a few miles out of Gulgong, all that remains of a bustling gold rush town that represented the hopes and dreams of thousands of people eager to make their fortune. These days, the rustling of the grass has replaced the sounds of people carving out their form of civilization in the rugged Australian Bush. The Bush won. But if one stands on Red Hill in Gulgong on a cool afternoon, one can hear, ever so faintly the hustle and bustle of yesteryear, the cheers of joy, the sighs of tragedy, and feel the ghosts of the past walk by.

1.   HOME

Gulgong, December 1910.

Biddy was the first to see him arrive and the last to see him leave. But someone had to come. The land needed cleansing after all that blood. Years later, when she had young grandchildren, she would gather them around whenever there was a storm and tell them the story of that night. It was the night her world changed. It was the night the stranger rode into town out of the red cloud, like one of the horsemen of the Apocalypse, a rider on a red horse.

Her grandchildren were always interested in the way she described the horse, how it snorted red dust and dug its hooves into the dirt. They all quivered when she told them how the black eyes of the red horse met hers that night as she stood alone on the road. It was better that way.

The more she spoke about the horse, the less she had to say about the man. He was two-faced, one face was that of a bully, the other, the face of a homeless wanderer. She was glad to see him go. It was as if the land gave birth to him, and he had come for vengeance.

Revenge.

She had more reason than most to seek it. Mary used to say that Biddy was the last of her tribe. Mary didn't understand. None of them did. Biddy belonged to no tribe. Like the stranger, she had no home. Perhaps when they looked at each other that night in the dust storm, they recognized a common bond. The stranger was the only one to see Biddy as an equal.

Though he was not looking, he found her brother, George. It was all downhill after that day. A cacophony of screams matched only by the day they came for her family near Crooked River and slaughtered them like cattle.

Maybe that is why she was glad the man left. He brought justice but at a terrible price. But it was more than that. He unsettled too many

1

ghosts. In trying to save others, he tried to save himself, but sometimes the dead are best left alone. Some things said cannot be unsaid, and some things cannot be forgotten.

2. WHAT HAPPENED AT CROOKED RIVER

Early December 1871,
Crooked River, the estate of Mr. John Knox,
by the Cooyal Creek, near the town of Gulgong, NSW

His right hand still held the knife. Both hands were covered in blood, her blood, and his sweat. His left arm still felt her fingernails where she had grabbed him. Getting her onto the bed was difficult. She resisted. He needed the knife to cut the rope. Tied to the bed by her wrists and ankles, she writhed in pain, sweating profusely, her eyes darting frantically around the darkened room searching for help. None came. She kept calling out for her husband, pleading with him to stop the pain as it throbbed through her bloodstream, working its way to her heart. Out of pity, Jed went to a side table to collect her Bible.

'Leave it!' boomed the voice in the dark from the far corner of the room.

Jed was too terrified to turn around and so kept his eyes on the woman twisting and writhing in agony.

'For the love of God, Mr. Knox,' he pleaded despairingly. 'She is calling for God to help her, the least I can do is give her a few words.'

'You touch the Bible Jed,' spat Knox, 'and tomorrow at church, I will announce your death as well.'

'I am not taking any of that vile poison,' protested Jed.

'There isn't any left,' said Knox. 'But I will break you with my bare hands and say that you fell off your horse.'

With that threat hanging in the air, Jed moved his hand away from the Bible and closer to the bed where Mrs. Knox lay crying and moaning in pain. She was close to death. She looked up at him, her eyes frantic, staring at the knife, and in disbelief at all that she had heard.

'Shamus!' she cried out, lurching away from Jed in agony.

'What did she say?' demanded Knox, leaning forward painfully in his chair, but not getting up.

'Nothing, Mr. Knox,' lied Jed softly, not daring to utter that name.

Mrs. Knox stared at him, and her red eyes showed a sudden and acute awareness of the situation, as if then, only at the end, in her final moments, did she realise the awful truth. Suddenly, her body was struck with intense spasms of pain. Jed released his fingers on the knife and put it on the side table. He stood still, but in his heart, he wanted to help the woman dying in front of him. But John Knox was not a man for idle threats. He would snap his neck like a stick if he wanted to. There was nothing Jed could do.

Knox was a strong man, with thick shoulders, powerful arms, and an iron constitution, but his Achilles Heel was his back. His spine was in constant pain because he fell from a horse the previous winter, and nothing could abate the spasms that haunted his every step. But many on the land were strong and some of them were kind. Knox's weakness was jealousy. It had eaten him like cancer. His jealousy brought him to this awful night when he poisoned his wife out of rage in the belief that she had given her heart to another man. He had sat too long at the feet of his morbid vulturous sister-in-law, Henrietta Knox, who had filled his mind with her malicious gossip. He drank deeply from that well of bile, driven by his paranoia and deep insecurity that his wife was never in love with him.

Jed knew Henrietta and her friends were all pathological liars. Most of the troubles in Gulgong and Home Rule could be traced back to the insidious innuendo, slander, and accusations of three women on the Church of England parish committee. Mrs. Knox was a good woman, a kind woman, from a wealthy background who married Knox in Ireland when he was a kinder, younger man before greed overtook him and he became the violent brute Jed knew and feared.

But whatever that spiteful Henrietta said, Mrs. Knox loved her husband and would die devoted to him. Jed remembered what she would always say to him. 'Spare a thought for my dear husband Jed, and do not be unkind. He has a lot of responsibility in the town, and in his heart, he is a good man.' Poor Mrs. Knox. Jed knew that John Knox was far from good. He had strayed too far from the gates of paradise. He lived a secret and violent life, with Jed left to clean up the mess.

Jed consented to Knox's plan because he thought that the poison would not take long to work. He thought she would die peacefully without much pain, slipping away into eternity. Jed, in his fear, didn't realize he was speaking out aloud.

'I don't want her to be spared pain Jed,' explained Knox. 'I want her to suffer. She is an adulteress and a Judas. She betrayed me. I was her husband. Her life belonged to me. A wife must submit to her husband.'

Jed remained silent. His life was at Knox's disposal as well. Knox saw what he did to the prospector in '68. Testimony from a member of the landed gentry would lead to the gallows and so Knox made him a deal, his servitude for silence. It was more like slavery. With Mrs. Knox gone, to what levels of depravity would his Master sink? He feared for his life, but he had no choice at all. He also feared for Millie Thorpe, dear sweet Millie, with Mrs. Knox dead. What would become of her?

'Tomorrow, after church,' said Knox, 'go to Gulgong and kill the Irishman, as we planned.'

Jed nodded reluctantly.

'And blame it on Lee Peng,' he added.

'The Celestial?' asked Jed, surprised at this new turn of events.

'That's right,' replied Knox. 'Henrietta told me this morning that Murphy and he were seen arguing about something. It doesn't matter what it was. Henrietta said it looked bad. That's enough motive in this town. I'll get Henrietta and her friends to speak to Cooper and leave the rest to him. I don't want Lee Peng to tell anyone he sold me the poison.'

Jed sighed and nodded again. He looked down at Mrs. Knox who was in the last moments of agony. Her eyes were closed now, and her twisted, strangulated body was still spasming, but the movements were fewer. Shamus and Lee Peng were both innocent. Shamus ran a hotel on Herbert Street in Gulgong, with his sister Mary. It was popular with the thousands of miners who had come to the district in search of gold. Lee Peng was a Chinese migrant, a Celestial, as they were called in those days, brilliant at business, both legitimate and illegal, managing a market garden by day, and a little illegal distillery tucked away in a secret gully or cave somewhere. All Mrs. Knox did was innocently talk to an old friend, but now she was dying, and Jed was to kill the man she simply called a friend.

Jed often wondered how many men Knox had killed over the years. It was quite possible that the estate of Crooked River was littered with shallow graves containing the bodies of all the people who had crossed John Knox in one way or another. But John was the churchwarden, a devoted member of the Church of England, and a respected pastoralist. The funeral of his wife would be well attended as everyone would come to lament the loss of a great woman, taken away in the prime of her life by an unfortunate snake bite, or that was the story Knox was going to spin.

As Jed was thinking this, Mrs. Knox cried out in pain, her chest heaving off the bed trying to reach for something. Her eyes flickered and she strained forward, but fell back, dead. Jed sighed deeply. 'Thank God,' he said to himself. In the silence, Jed thought he heard something move in the hallway outside. He rushed for the door and opened it. Millie was standing there, her face white, her eyes fearful.

'How long have you been here?' asked Jed. 'I thought you were in town tonight.'

I didn't hear anything Jed,' protested Millie. 'I promise you. I really didn't. I didn't hear a thing. I was just startled by the noise.'

Her face was white, and she was shaking. She looked at the corpse of Mrs. Knox and then at Jed, her eyes wide open. She saw Knox rise to his feet, with his rifle in his right hand. As soon as Millie saw the gun, she ran down the corridor and down the back veranda. As she ran, she begged Knox for mercy.

Knox tried to follow her, but Jed stood in his way and tried to stop him. 'For the love of God,' he protested. 'She is only a child!'

Knox pushed him away, storming after her, with his gun.

When he reached the back veranda, he could see that Millie had climbed back on her horse and was riding off into the distance. Knox lifted his rifle in her direction and fired. He could hear Millie cry out in pain, and he knew he had hit his target. He grinned broadly. He had always hated the girl. She was his wife's choice for a maid, and she cost money. Shooting her saved him the trouble of paying her. He turned to Jed who was standing next to him.

'I think it is a mortal wound,' he boasted. 'She's riding in the direction of Eliza. Make sure she doesn't get to tell Chambers what she saw.'

'You want me to kill her?' asked Jed, horrified.

'I hit her good Jed,' said Knox with a smile. 'She won't last long. You are putting her out of her misery if you would like to justify it to yourself, but if you don't kill her, then you are a dead man.'

Jed looked back at the farmhouse where Mrs. Knox lay dead in her bed, and then up at Knox. 'What will I do with the body?' asked Jed resigned to his fate as the executioner.

'Get rid of it, of course,' said the old churchman. 'Bury the bitch by the river with all the others.'

3. A STRANGER IN TOWN

Early December 1872 Home Rule, near Gulgong, NSW

The soil struck her face like a whip. The red soil twisted around her, like an unfurling snake, spitting in her eyes. The dust storm had come out of nowhere suddenly, engulfing the town like a whirlwind. The sky darkened, as she tried to untie her horse from the wooden railing in front of the hotel. A strong rush of wind struck her and so she took refuge behind her horse. She regretted her decision to leave town the moment she stepped out onto the dirt. Her horse could have told her what was coming. He sensed the danger and longed to be under shelter while the storm clouds gathered, and the wind rose. Tied to the railing, he watched as the miners and townsfolk scattered and took refuge in their frail, hastily built wooden dwellings. The horse longed to be back home out of the wind, but he knew Biddy too well. His mistress was not the kind of girl to let a raging storm get in the way of a day's business, so he waited patiently in front of the Canadian Hotel until his mistress emerged.

Biddy untied the knots and looked up into the sky. She could see nothing. The wind was hot, unrelenting, and unforgiving. As far as she could tell, she was the only one left on the street. Everyone had taken refuge inside one of the many buildings or tents. It amazed her how quickly the town of Home Rule was built. Six months ago, there was nothing but paddocks and a stream. Now, there were pubs, hotels, boarding houses, restaurants, trading houses, and lots of tents. Even the miners, who slaved away every day for flecks of gold, had scampered like mice in a barn for cover. Mary had offered to let her stay for the night, but Biddy needed to go back to her homestead. There was work still to be done. After all, it was only a storm, not the end of the world.

Biddy led her horse out onto the middle of the street and was about to climb up and ride home, when she saw something in the corner of her eye, lurking at the edge of town. It was in the darkness, where the storm seemed to rage the fiercest as if trying to decide whether to allow the traveller to pass. The land often seemed disturbed by the presence of the miners, their hundreds of shafts stabbing the earth, and their desire to recreate an English village in every gully, leaving forests desolate. Droughts had come and gone, ferocious hailstorms had fallen from the heavens, and bushfires had scorched the earth, but nothing could budge the resilience of the people who had made the country their home. They were like ants on an anthill, an assortment of miners, shopkeepers, refugees, and farmers, all trying to carve out an existence in the middle of a land that didn't want them there.

Biddy knew the land more than most. She was born here, the product of a brief liaison between a settler and her mother around the year 1830, give or take. Her mother never spoke of it but raised Biddy with all the love a mother could give. Biddy used to live with her mother, and younger stepbrother George, on the edge of town. Her mother refused to reveal to her the identity of her father, but Biddy always had her suspicions. There was a farmer who showed pity for their family and brought them food from time to time. She would sometimes see the farmer in Mudgee or Gulgong. He would tip his hat and say hello to Biddy and her brother. She had always suspected that he was her father. Why else would he acknowledge her existence?

Only a few spoke to her in the town. Most of them didn't know her, as they were from all over the world searching for gold. The locals ignored her, but they were polite about it, most of them anyway. No one accepted her for who she was. They only saw what they wanted to see. Even her best friend Mary had only time for half of her. She tried to ignore the other as if it did not exist. Biddy didn't mind. It was as it was, and Mary had her own crosses to bear. Mary was like a sister to her. Biddy did most of her trading with the Celestials from China. They were kind to her. They too understood the hate for they also experienced it firsthand. The settlers hated the Celestials more than they hated the Aborigines.

Biddy kept her eye on the edge of town. There *was* something there. It was as if it was waiting to gain permission from the storm to enter the town. It appeared to be a man on a horse. The red soil covered the horse and rider completely. The horse was snorting loudly, trying to expel the dirt that afflicted it, digging its hooves into the ground angrily, while the man sat still in the saddle, his face wrapped around with a towel under his hat so that only his eyes were exposed. The horse walked slowly into town, toward the place where Biddy had just left, the Canadian Hotel. It was the largest building on the street, and it was as good a place as any for this weary traveller to stop. The man groaned heavily as he dismounted, but he did not tie up the horse. He reached into the saddle bags, pulled out what seemed to be some food, and fed it to the horse. He stroked the horse's neck and spoke to her for a while. Biddy could not hear what he said, but there was something about the man. There was something that stirred in her, something familiar. Had she met him before? She decided to retrace her steps back to the Canadian to find out.

When she reached the hotel once more, the man had finished his conversation with the horse and was tying a rope to the railing. Biddy stared at the man. He finished what he was doing, turned, and looked at her. She could only see his eyes. His face was covered by the towel, and it was covered in red dust.

'Am I at Home Rule or Canadian Lead?' asked the man his voice muffled.

Biddy thought his voice sounded familiar which was deep, resonating, and calm. 'This is Home Rule,' she said finally. 'Canadian Lead is further up the road in the storm. This is the Canadian Hotel, and this is the street to Gulgong.' She pointed down the main street but realized the man was not looking.

'Do you know a man by the name of Johnson?' he asked. Biddy thought for a moment. Johnson? There were a few. It was a common name. She had met a miner by that name only a few weeks before. But the most well-known Johnson in the area was a solicitor.

'You mean the solicitor?' she asked.

The man nodded. 'Where can I find him?'

'His office is in Gulgong, Herbert Street.'

'Thank you,' replied the man, walking to the door of the Hotel. He looked back at Biddy. 'Are you coming or going?' he asked.

'I was leaving,' she said.

'Well, thank you for your help,' he said, and he bowed to her.

He bowed. This was enough for Biddy to stay. No one had ever bowed to her.

'Who are you?' she asked.

'Nobody important,' he replied, unwrapping the towel from his face, and then folding it up neatly. The storm had begun to subside, and the dust began to settle. The light from the hotel windows burst out onto the road, providing sufficient light for Biddy to see who the man was, but when the cloth was removed from his face, she could not believe her eyes.

The man standing before her was one who was dead. She had seen his corpse the year before. She held Mary in her arms as she cried uncontrollably in complete despair and loss when she told her that her beloved had been shot. Biddy didn't believe Constable Cooper's story that it was an accident. Mary's fiancé had been murdered. But, like most crimes in country Australia, the local police simply covered it up, to protect the farmers who paid for everything.

So did the priest. He lied. He knew what happened. He was there. Blackwell. The paedophile. He only came to Gulgong because he liked the children and women. She saw it in his eyes and the way he licked his lips in front of his yellow teeth and stubbled chin. For Blackwell, everyone was for the taking, especially the young. She had several times eluded his groping hands. Everyone knew. But he was a Mason and so was everyone of importance in the town. The townsfolk of Gulgong tried so hard to find a priest for their services, but none of the priests from Sydney or Melbourne could tolerate the rural life, with the flies, the filth of the town, the sweat of the miners, and the paucity of civic life. The tiny congregation of wealthy farmers who built the Gulgong church building the previous year, tolerated Blackwell because they needed a priest to preside over their Protestant Mass. Miss Dove and the other private school teachers managed to keep Blackwell at bay, but not all children were under their protection. Biddy was half-European, so she had to fend for herself.

Blackwell was not the only one. Biddy's only memory of the Church of England was a series of abusive encounters with violent men. Biddy sat in terror as a child at the Wellington 'mission' as the priests taught her about their version of God. She wondered what God would think about his priests trying to have their way with the children. Perhaps he didn't know. Perhaps her ancestors were right, and the land was cursed. From what she could tell, the Protestants also had a special hatred for Catholics, and had a particular taste for their children, if they could get their hands on them. She was told that the Catholics were all damned anyway and being Irish, twice damned. One less Romanist in the world the better, they said to her. Biddy never understood that.

As for the dead man standing in front of her, she suspected that

Knox, who hid behind his religion to commit the most grievous of sins, was responsible for his death. He was a monster. She did not believe the 'snake story,' that his wife was bitten by a snake and died at home. Nor did she believe the story that Millie ran away. Biddy knew fake tears when she saw them. Were all the people in the town of Gulgong mad? Maybe they all knew, but the fear of Knox and what he would do kept their tongues still. His demented sister-in-law with her forked tongue was famous for ruining the reputation of many in the town. Even Blackwell feared Knox, probably more than the God he pretended to believe in when he brought out in the bread and the wine every Sunday, waving his hands around as if to swat one of the dozen flies swirling around him, and then telling everyone that God was there.

God had left long ago. Why would he inhabit a house of blood? Why would he condone such hypocrisy? No, God had left Gulgong long ago, and Mudgee, and Bathurst. Every river and hidden valley contained the bones of her people, murdered by the priests and the farmers, so they could till the land in peace, make their money, and build their homes. Then on Sunday, they would wipe the blood of Biddy's people off their hands, get dressed, go to church, and talk to God about how good they were, how much God approved of them, and how much better they were than everyone else. Then once the church service was over, the killing would begin again. Now they had run out of aborigines to kill and so they were killing each other.

No, this man was the dead reborn, come to bring vengeance on all who brought blood to the land. This land was cursed. Her land. Her people's land. So many proud voices had been silenced, so many songs had been forgotten, and so many memories filled her eyes with tears.

The man heard none of this. What he saw was a beautiful woman with striking features and long black hair, dressed in work clothes, staring at him, speechless, her mouth open and her eyes a mixture of surprise and horror. He knew why she was surprised. He was too tired to argue but stood there for what seemed like an eternity. He realized that this would be the reaction everyone was going to make, so he needed to come up with the right thing to say.

'But you are dead,' protested Biddy with tears in her eyes. 'You died.'

The man stood there looking at her. He was tall, with broad shoulders, middle-aged, with what was once red hair but was now, going white around the edges. His eyes were blue, and they sat above a narrow nose and a rather large mouth surrounded by red-tinged stubble. He did not say anything. He turned to enter the hotel.

'I can assure you, I'm very much alive,' said the man.

'You can't go in!' Biddy said, grabbing his right arm. She then released it, realizing she had crossed a line, and apologized quickly.

'Why am I not allowed in?' asked the man gently, turning away from the door. He spoke to her without a harsh word, just like Mary.

'There is a woman in there, my friend Mary, who was in love with you. I cannot pretend to understand who you are, or how you came to be here. Maybe you are a ghost, but if you go into that hotel, you will bring heartache to the woman in there I care about. She will see you and her life will be forever changed.'

The man paused and laughed softly.

'Why are you laughing?'

'I do not mean any offense to you or Mary,' said the man. 'It just never occurred to me that my brother had a life here. He was as hard as a rock. I never imagined that a woman, or anyone for that matter, softened that cold, dead heart of his.'

Biddy was shocked. His brother? It was impossible.

'I'm Nathaniel,' insisted the man. 'Henry's twin brother. Nathaniel Chambers. You can call me 'Nate.' Most do if they aren't calling me something else.'

Biddy smiled for the first time that night. 'I have never met a twin before,' she said. 'God is amazing, to create two people the same.' She reached forward to touch his cheek instinctively. He did not stop her. Her finger touched his pink skin. It felt warm. She smiled and withdrew it.

'You look exactly like him,' she said, still smiling.

'When we were young, people used to say that. Sometimes we even tricked my father, but he never liked it.'

'I'm Biddy,' she said quickly, offering her hand.

'Pleased to meet you,' said Chambers, shaking her hand firmly. 'As for your friend Mary, maybe you should go in and prepare her for my entrance. I don't want to cause her, or anyone in this town, any grief by my visit. I'm simply here to sell the farm and go back to China.'

'China?' asked Biddy. 'Is Australia not your home?'

'No, China has been my home for most of my life, since I was a young boy.'

Biddy smiled nervously. It was the strangest thing a white person had ever said.

Suddenly the door swung open. In the light Chambers could see a tall, slender woman, perhaps the most stunning woman he had ever seen. It had to be Mary. Henry always went for the beautiful ones. She looked at Biddy angrily.

'What are you doing standing outside? Why don't you come in?'

She turned to Chambers and looked at him. She tried to speak, but her eyes wavered in absolute horror, and she fainted into his arms.

4.   NATHANIEL CHAMBERS

The Canadian Hotel, Home Rule

Chambers could feel the eyes of all in the hotel staring at him. He had not received this much attention since the time in Shanghai when he and his friend Ward started a brawl over that Italian woman back in '61. Chambers wondered if this night was going to go the same way. He was standing at the bar, slowly drinking a glass of water. Chambers had carried Mary into a back room where she was with Biddy. A thin, weedy man with a long beard and high eyebrows had poured him some water in a glass on the bar. He stood glaring at him, in front of several bottles of whiskey and rum. Behind Chambers were half a dozen tables, each full of men sitting silently, all staring at him, some bemused and others angry. They were probably miners, and a few farmhands, all taking refuge out of the dust storm that had followed him to Home Rule only to run out of energy and die down once he arrived. It made his entrance more dramatic. At the back were a few Chinese men sitting together, likely owners of some of the stores in Home Rule.

Chambers drank his water, and reached for his flask, pouring a little of his own 'whiskey' into the cup.

'Do you want some?' he asked the bartender. He shook his head but didn't speak.

'More for me then,' said Chambers and drank it slowly. His whiskey was only dark tea but had the same colour as liquor, but it made people more relaxed if they thought he was slowly getting drunk on whiskey.

'You're Henry's brother!' said a loud voice behind him. Chambers didn't move but kept drinking.

'You look exactly like him,' said the man, joining him at the bar. 'I thought I saw a ghost. You literally scared Mary almost to death. Poor Mary. I'm Jed Barton. I'm a good friend of Mary's.'

Chambers turned to face him. He could see immediately that this man was no close friend of Mary's, though he wanted to be. Jed's anxious, longing eyes told him everything he needed to know. Jed was in love with Mary. It was as clear as glass. He had eyes that seemed to bulge out of his sockets, a tuft of blonde hair, a clean-shaven face, and he reeked of whiskey. He kept looking over to the door through which Chambers had carried the woman, followed by Biddy. But Jed stood outside. He dared not go into that room. Chambers could see the longing in his eyes, this unrequited aching. This was important. Jed was the spurned suitor. Mary went for cold, dead Henry, with no charm, no wit, no personality. This Jed must have known something about Henry. Perhaps Jed knew something about the day his brother died. Perhaps he was responsible or had his hand in it. Lots of murders were committed by spurned suitors or jealous lovers, especially the quiet ones. He would have to be careful. He could be talking with his brother's killer.

'I see you like whiskey,' said Jed.

Chambers smiled but said nothing.

'I try not to drink too much,' said Jed nervously. 'Mary doesn't like me drinking too much in here, I tend to go a bit crazy.' He laughed to himself.

'Nothing wrong with a good bottle of whiskey,' retorted Chambers.

Jed's eyes lit up. 'You are absolutely right,' he exclaimed loudly. 'I work hard all day and that's a fact. I work for Mr. John Knox. I'm his station manager, and that is, I can tell you a position of reputation, there is no mistaking that. Nobody can deny it. I work hard, and a man deserves a good drink at the end of the day, at least that.' He stopped speaking abruptly, his eyes trailing off again to the shut door.

'I've come to Gulgong to sell my brother's farm,' said Chambers, sipping from his 'whiskey.'

Jed looked up, genuinely surprised.

'What's the matter?' asked Chambers.

'John Knox owns your brother's place now. Your brother sold it to him a few days before he died.'

'Well,' replied Chambers, quite surprised. 'I have a letter from a solicitor called Johnson who told me that I inherited Henry's estate, which included his farm called 'Eliza,' named after my late mother.'

Jed shook his head. 'No, I'm sure there was at least a handshake. It could all be settled if we could find Blackwell. He was the witness,' replied Jed, running his hands through his hair, with a frustrated expression.

'Who's Blackwell?'

'The priest, Andrew Blackwell,' piped up another man, who joined them at the bar. He extended his hand.

'Joe Mitchell,' he said. 'I'm from Bathurst, and I am a retired policeman, an active local citizen.'

'Active busybody if you ask me, Joe, you haven't solved a case in years,' spat Jed.

'Well, I'm not asking you, Jed,' retorted Joe.

Chambers shook his hand and introduced himself.

'What brings you to Home Rule?' he asked the policeman.

'I'm standing in for our local detectives who are working on a case in Mudgee. As of yesterday, we are officially looking for Blackwell, the Church of England priest.' He stopped and asked the bartender for whiskey.

'He's gone missing,' said Jed. 'He was last seen on Sunday, riding off towards Home Rule. Gone without a trace. Not a word to anyone, as if the land swallowed him up.'

'That isn't good news,' sighed Chambers. 'I received a letter from someone called Johnson, a solicitor in Gulgong that I inherited my brother's farm. I've come to sell the farm and then return home. I don't expect to be here long. Blackwell, according to Jed, was the last man to see Henry alive.'

'That's right,' replied Joe. 'I'm sorry about your brother. We all are. It was a real tragedy and a great loss to the district. You sure look like him.'

'He says a lot more than Henry too!' added Jed. 'Your brother was a quiet one. I guess that's why she liked him.'

'Who?' asked Chambers.

'Mary,' said Joe. 'She fell for him the moment she laid eyes on him. Quite the story around here.'

Jed looked uncomfortable talking about it. He pulled out a pipe from his pocket and stuck it in his mouth.

'I think the best thing to do is to talk to Johnson when his office opens on Monday. I am sure it will all be settled. It will be pretty straightforward. I did hear something about the farm being sold. It was from you Jed, but if Chambers received a letter from Johnson about the homestead, then maybe it isn't as clear-cut as John Knox thinks it is.'

'Who is John Knox?' asked Chambers.

'He owns the adjoining estate, Crooked River, said Joe. 'He, your brother, Blackwell, and one of my number Constable Cooper, were all good friends. His death hit them all pretty badly.'

'I am only saying what Knox told me,' Jed insisted. 'I didn't know about any solicitor. I just heard that Blackwell said that Henry told him that he'd sold the farm. Mr. Knox said the same at the funeral.'

'What was he going to do?' asked Chambers.

'I really don't know,' said Jed nervously, his eyes looking longingly towards the closed door.

'Yes, you do Jed,' said Joe. 'He and Mary were going to get married. He was going to go and help run the Shamrock and Thistle in Gulgong and make it really something,' said Joe, smoking his pipe.

'Makes his death more tragic,' said Chambers.

'And a complete mystery too,' added Joe.

'What do you mean?' asked Chambers. 'Are you saying his death wasn't an accident?'

Joe pulled out his pipe and sighed. 'The local doctor, a man by the name of Smythe, ruled it an accident, and I suppose we must take his word for it. It is just that Gulgong hasn't been blessed with the best of the medical profession. Smyth is new and he had a bout of pneumonia, and then dysentery until he could assume full duties. The last doctor is in prison for manslaughter.'

'Henry accidentally shot himself, is that right?' asked Chambers.

'That's what the doctor said,' said Jed. 'It's terrible news to hear, but that's what the doctor said.'

'That doctor is a bloody liar!' a woman shouted so loudly everyone in the hotel could hear. Her voice ended all the conversations, and everyone stopped drinking.

The three men turned to see Mary standing there, with Biddy by her side. Mary walked to the bar and Biddy went to sit down at a nearby table.

'Jed, do you want a drink? Joe?' she asked.

'I will have a whiskey,' said Joe.

Jed said that he had already drunk enough for one night, but Mary still poured him a small whiskey. He looked surprised.

'It will calm the nerves, Jed,' she said. 'I suppose this is the time you stop talking about me,' said Mary, glaring at Joe with contempt. 'I can speak for myself.'

'I am sorry Mary,' apologised Joe. 'I was just informing Mr.

Chambers about the situation.'

'What situation?' Mary asked angrily. 'My situation? Henry's situation? He was murdered, he was killed as plainly as anyone could see, and the police did nothing about it. Where were the famed local detectives, Hannan and Powell? Not interested in another 'Irish Problem?' This rubbish about the 'accident,' you know as well as I do, that Henry knew guns better than anyone in this district. He wouldn't have shot himself. You know we were getting married, and he was moving to Gulgong to be with me.'

She turned to Chambers with a furious look on her face. She had been crying. 'So, you are the brother, the prodigal son back from the dead, literally, good enough to take his money and mine, but not good enough to write.'

'You know about the brother?' asked Joe, very surprised.

Mary nodded.

'Gave me a real shock back there at the door didn't you, probably planned it that way,' she said angrily. 'Yes Joe, I know about the brother, Henry told me about his *twin* brother. He only mentioned you when he was drunk. He told me all about his father's favourite son.'

Chambers said nothing. He put his whiskey flask back in his pocket. There was more anger in the hotel than fury in the storm he had just come from. He was better off outside in the wind.

But Mary had only begun.

'Spent most of your life in China,' she spat at him. 'China, of all places? Henry told me you married a Chinese girl, of all people. You even dress up like a Celestial, eat their food, drink their wine, and live their life. Well, we have plenty of Celestials here, even a few in the brothels. You can take your pick if you have the fancy, there are more Chinese in Australia now than cockroaches in a barn.'

Chambers stood to leave, but Mary grabbed his arm tightly.

'What is this Chinese girl of yours like?' she asked angrily. 'Is she small and petite, do you have little bastards running around, little half-castes!'

'That's enough!' ordered Joe.

Mary stopped, letting go of Chambers, her face half angry, half ashamed of what she had said. She looked astonished as if she did not know what she had just said. She was surprised at her anger and venom which gushed out of her like a waterfall after a storm. She turned her face away. She was just angry. Her man had been murdered and his brother was not there to help. Instead, he was making his fortune a thousand miles away.

Chambers turned to see the whole hotel looking at him. He knew that look. He had seen it in Shanghai and Hong Kong, and whenever the truth slipped out. He had committed the unforgivable sin. He had made his bed with a Chinese woman. In their eyes, he had sunk lower than even the darkest heathen. He didn't blame them. Their anger and prejudice were simply based on fear and ignorance. He was like them when he was young before he climbed aboard the Nemesis in '41 and received a good dose of reality. Before the Opium War, he held the same worldview as his father and his grandfather before him. After the Nemesis, he realized the simple truth behind the Empire: the people who ran the world only had the largest cannon, nothing more.

Right at the back of the hotel, three Chinese men huddled at a table together. They probably knew Mary quite well, but her words would have hurt, regardless of their friendship. They were not miners. He could tell from their clothes. They were too well-dressed. They wore suits. Lambing Flat put paid to that. Chambers was in Young in 1861 during the riots. He was looking for a man then, a man who could have saved lives. This man escaped one hell in Taiping China only to find it resurface in Australia. What a mess that was. A complete mess. He was glad to leave Australia after the riots. He swore he would never return. He only came back to sell his brother's farm. He glanced at the Chinese Australians. They looked like storekeepers. They made more money selling mining equipment to the miners than the miners made from gold prospecting.

He called out a greeting to them in his Chinese dialect. The one who seemed to be in charge came over and said hello. Chambers said that he needed a place to stay for the night and that he was keen to have some soup and rice if they had some. The man laughed out loud and said that was the strangest request he had from a European in years. They talked a little about China, but the man knew that the sooner Chambers left the Hotel the better. He was not welcome there. The man introduced himself as William Fung. Both men bowed to each other politely and turned to leave.

'Jed,' said Chambers. 'Go and tell Mr. Knox that I will go and see Johnson about Henry's estate on Monday. I will stay at Eliza until the matter is resolved. As for his death, my brother was prone to bouts of intense depression, even as a young man in China. That he shot himself is no surprise to me.'

He turned and looked straight at Mary. 'Sometimes you just never really know someone,' he said. 'No matter how close you are to them.'

He nodded to Joe and to Mary and left the Canadian with Fung. Biddy watched him go amazed at what she had witnessed. The others did not see it at all. She laughed to herself. There was in God's world a white man who saw everyone the same. Skin made no difference to him.

'I couldn't understand a word they said,' blurted out Mary embarrassed.

'It's like the Devil's language,' said Jed.

'He speaks fluent Chinese,' reflected Joe. 'Like he was born there.'

'He was,' said Biddy, walking over to them. 'He was born in China.'

5.   FUNG'S DREAM

William and Sarah Fung's Boarding House, Home Rule

Mr. and Mrs. Fung lived in several rooms at the back of their storefront on the main street of the town of Home Rule, next to a small boarding house on one side and a coffee and pie shop on the other. Fung's wife Sarah was of Scottish descent, and she ran the boarding house for those wanting a place to stay for a night, or a few days. Fung also sold tents which were popular. After a series of gold rushes in and around the vicinity of Gulgong from 1870 to 1872, the discovery of gold along part of the old Canadian Lead led to the discovery of what the miners called 'Home Rule,' referring partly to agitations in Ireland at the time, but mainly to anger over elaborate and excessive government regulations regarding mining practices.

In May of 1872 gold was discovered at Home Rule and almost overnight a town was born. Fung, or William as he was called, had his main base of operations in Mudgee where his son and daughter lived. His dream was to build and run an oriental tea house in a respectable part of Sydney, but he felt a strong attachment to the country and kept postponing a move to the city. The Coffee and Pie shop was simple, with his wife preparing meals she had grown up with when she lived in Scotland. None of the Fung establishments served liquor (as he was a teetotaller) and his boarding house was a popular haunt for Congregational and Methodist evangelists who had been active in creating congregations in the town.

Fung was a Christian or rather, had converted to Christianity, as he felt he had to thrive in polite Australian society, though there wasn't much of it in Gulgong or Home Rule. He spoke with an educated English accent, dressed like a good Englishman, wore the right clothes, and could read and write English fluently. Originally, he was an interpreter, arriving in Sydney in 1850 and making his way out to the rural hinterland of the colony of New South Wales. He sought peace and quiet, but he needed to make a living. By chance or the providence of God, as he would often say, Fung happened to meet a local farmer in the area, who needed an interpreter for a shipload of labourers he had brought over from China to work on his farm. The labour was needed because all the men had gone to the gold rush. This farming family had been in the area since 1828 and they made their fortune in sheep and cattle. Their homestead was at a place called Guntawang. This family epitomized the landed aristocracy, and they were the heart and soul of English civilization in a rapidly changing land.

William and Sarah sold household items, tents, pots and pans, and cutlery as well as all the tools required for mining gold. As such, they did a roaring trade. Most miners who came to the goldfields to make their fortune during the 1850s onwards never made much money. Most eked out only a scanty find and lost that in gambling, vice, or alcohol. The miners used to make fun of the pastoralists, telling them that gold was a fast way to money, but the pastoralists predated the goldfields and continued long after the last leads ran out.

The miners all had gold fever. William knew madness when he saw it: covetousness. A look in the eye, a glint, a licking of the lips, the boastful dreams for the future, everyone was going to make it big and settle down, become rich, richer than anyone imagined. The idea of persistent, hard work made no sense to them. The gold was there for the taking.

William had seen the greed in China, where he was born. He saw it in the eyes of his older brother who only prayed to the gods to advance himself, and in the eyes of his merchant parents who used their position in society to enrich themselves. There was nothing wrong with money, William always said but you can't eat gold and money is heartless. Maybe it was this sentiment the old farming patriarch at Guntawang saw in 1851, or maybe it was the boldness and adventure he saw the day William reined in a wayward horse that broke out of the stalls and almost trampled some guests who were visiting the Rouse estate. In a few years, William was a member of the Masons and courting a young Scottish girl whose parents lived on the outskirts of Sydney.

William had come to the colony of NSW like Chamber's brother, Henry but he was haunted by a desire to do good. He had a moral compass, a moral core. For William, a man knew the difference between right and wrong and he had the freedom to choose. He didn't learn about morality from the Church of England. That he knew from being born in China. The Church of England taught him little by way of moral substance, even though he had been baptized. He knew that all the church cared about was appearance and what looked good. The heart, motivation, initiative, and intention, none of these mattered. He had not seen hypocrisy in full bloom until he joined the church. He saw gross hypocrisy there. He knew that Jesus would have been horrified by the wealthy hoarders of his English Church, happy to cast away every doctrine, but not part with one-hundredth of their wealth. He felt more at home with the Masons, who reminded him of the secret societies his father joined in China.

Maybe the late Richard Rouse saw that moral code in him as well. Integrity. It was in short supply in the bush, but without it, towns would perish. Many did. Most were scoundrels, criminals, deviants, squatters, bushrangers, or opportunists. In the eyes of many, William was just another Celestial, a foreign import. Fung was more Australian than most of them. William didn't care. He had his wife, whom he loved, and two wonderful children. Most importantly, he was away from the madness of China. To William, Chinas was a land torn apart. It was like suitors seeking the affection of a dishevelled and despairing woman, who ended up selling parts of herself to ward off further invasions of her pride and dignity.

His brother was on one of the Chinese junks that were blown out of the water by the Nemesis in 1841 at the start of the first so-called 'Opium Wars,' and his parents died during a subsequent battle with the British. William would say that England only won because they had more powerful cannons. He had no love for the English, but they ran the world and so he came to live in a little part of England, New South Wales. Rouse told him to get a trade and excel in all that he could do. He told him that the world was not a perfect place, but it was the one God gave them, and that William needed to make the most of it so he could give something back. His wife convinced him to go into business, and so he did.

William knew who Chambers was but never told him. He was content to play the role he was good at, the role of the ignorant, but well-meaning Celestial. The name 'Chambers' kept appearing over the years for those who kept their ears open, as did a few foreigners who made their reputation in China one way or the other. Infamously, he was one of Ward's men, the instigator of the Ever-Victorious Army in

Shanghai, and was there when Ward was mortally wounded. He also served with General Charles Gordon, or 'Chinese' Gordon, as the English press called him.

Some said Chambers was incredibly wealthy, others said that he lived the life of a pauper. He had survived numerous attempts on his life over the years and presently was involved in a long-running feud with a former Taiping warlord who had been under the protection of the great Manchu General Zeng Guofan. William was grieved to hear that the General had died that year, which meant China would continue its slide into oblivion. That Chambers had arrived at Home Rule was bad news, because he was not there to settle a matter of inheritance. He was there for blood.

William never liked Henry. He had no moral core. His opinion changed like the hot wind that blew across the land or the dew that sat on the grass in the morning. It was gone by midday. He suspected that Knox murdered Henry in December 1871 to steal his farm. Joe Mitchell, also a good Mason, agreed with him. They had spoken about it a few times. John Knox was not a Mason, which was a blessing for the Lodge, but he could never work out why. Maybe it was because Knox was Irish, or simply because everyone knew evil when they saw it. If families like Rouse ensured a strong town, people like Knox were like termites in granite, there was nothing they could not pull down if their hearts so desired.

Knox had been held in check by his wife, who was probably poisoned by her husband. Since that fateful two days, she died, along with four other people. Too much blood. One death could be contrived as an accident, but not five. Their deaths must have been connected. Henry's farm was next to Knox's, and he was dead that evening. Knox's servant vanished. The next day, in Gulgong, Mary Kelly's brother Shamus was murdered, allegedly by one of William's employees, a successful young man by the name of Lee Peng.

Poor Lee Peng. William had turned a blind eye to Lee's illegal still. It was a harmless enough indiscretion in a town drowning in booze, and it also showed ingenuity. Lee was supposed to marry William's daughter who lived in Mudgee. It had all been arranged.

Since those fateful two days a year ago, there was not a night when William did not sit on his back porch, smoking his pipe, and ponder what might have happened. Then, out of the blue, Henry's brother turned up. Of all the foreigners who might come to Home Rule, it had to be Chambers. It was unlikely that any of the pastoralists knew of Nathaniel Chambers, not even Rouse's grandson, named Richard after his grandfather, who inherited Guntawang. He knew about horses, farming, and business and rarely asked William about China. William also thought it unlikely any of the newcomers to the Bush knew of Chambers either. People in Gulgong were too busy salivating over the gold, chasing women, or getting drunk. There was more vomit on the streets of Gulgong than horse manure. Sarah and a few other members of Home Rule's upper class tried to cultivate a sense of propriety around town. He didn't begrudge her efforts. She meant well.

Outside the polite little circle William was trying to create, Fung saw the rubbish of the Empire, the refuse and garbage spewed out by the English criminal justice system, convicts, and criminals. They strutted around town with all the airs of English nobility, but they stank, wore all the wrong fashions, and had all the wrong manners. The majority were Catholic Irish, a few English poor, a splattering of Scots, and Welsh, a few Americans, and Swedes, some New Zealanders, and poor Germans. There was rampant promiscuity, drunkenness, and violence. The popular joke in Gulgong was that the brothels went up before the first shaft went down. The pubs and hotels followed quickly. William saw himself above all of that and longed for a nice respectable tea house for the right sort of people, people like the Rouses and others. But the best he could do was Home Rule and Gulgong. If he made enough money, he could move to Sydney, and open a tea house there for all the gentlemen and ladies of high society. It was his dream.

William and his wife often discussed the problems of country life over the evening meal, with a nice pot of tea brewing. Sarah was a Presbyterian and was not welcome at the Church of England, so William never went, not that they had a building to attend in Home Rule anyway. There was a brief time when all the religions gathered at a Union Church in Gulgong, but that did not last long. The Methodists and Congregationalists arrived first, and the Catholics quickly built their church. The Church of England existed primarily for the landed gentry, not the people, and most wealthy farmers had chapels on their estates. It was difficult for the landed aristocracy to contemplate the radical idea of a church for ordinary people.

The Protestants hated the Catholics, but everyone on the goldfields hated the Church of England. It represented the law, and the law was always against the town and the miners. Most of the people avoided the Gulgong parish, and since wealthy farmers were the only ones who were welcome, it was rarely attended. The demands of farm life were exhausting even for the best of them. A local private school rented the property for classes. Most could not tolerate the people in charge, namely John Knox, his brother Tom, and his extended family and social network. If God in his kindness took Knox and his friends to heaven, or hell, or anywhere, that might give Gulgong a chance. William was always amazed at how superficial the men of the Church of England were, how they all behaved impeccably on Sunday, but then reverted to their normal selves as soon as the priest gave the benediction. It was as if God gave them time off for the weekly punishment of attending the services. It deeply upset him.

In China, the gods were part of life, everything was related to family, obligations, and fate. He raised it with the Rouses from time to time. They would smile and give their answer. But he liked Sarah's the most. She would lean across the table, press him on the chest, and say 'the problem is here, my darling. It is the heart. A little water sprinkled on the head of a wee babe makes the babe wet, but the babe is still a babe.' He let her love for God infuse their children, while he taught them as much practical wisdom as he could, to prepare them for life.

6   THE MONKEY KING

William and Sarah Fung's Residence, Home Rule

William's house reminded Chambers of his father's ancestral estate in England. He felt the atmosphere as soon as he stepped from the shopfront to the house through a large, thick wooden door. It was as if he moved up the class system with one step. There was a small hallway for boots, cloaks, and umbrellas, and then the room opened. Maybe it was the carpet, the neatness, the preciseness of the ornaments, or the softness of the light in the room, and the hundreds of neatly packed books on the wall. It was devoid of anything Chinese, stripped of all senses and smells of the Orient, nothing to indicate the land of Fung's birth. He perused some of the volumes on the wall and noticed some familiar editions, smiling to himself. William had probably read more of the English classics than he had.

'I remember a story about a monkey,' said Chambers, pretending to look for the Chinese classic. 'He is a kind of spirit and travels across China to India, in search of Buddha's scrolls.'

'And what are you searching for Mr. Chambers?' asked a woman standing at the door to the dining room. She was in her mid-40s, with long reddish hair, piercing eyes, and a furrowed brow.

'Just a bed for the night would do fine,' he replied. 'I appreciate the kindness of your husband inviting me. I was not welcome at the hotel.'

'Well,' said the woman. 'We have a little boarding house next door if that suits you. But, before that, we would be honoured if you would be our guest. I am sorry. It is only mutton stew, some potatoes, and onions. Nothing fancy.'

'Thank you,' replied Chambers, bowing to her politely. He could see that she was visibly upset. He wondered if it was because he was there.

'We do not bow to friends Mr. Chambers,' she said, allaying his concern.

Chambers smiled.

William entered the room, ushering Chambers into the dining room.

'We can talk about the Monkey King later Mr. Chambers,' he said politely in polished English. 'I am sure you are quite famished by your long journey through the Bush. Did you begin in Sydney?'

'Yes, about ten days or so ago actually,' replied Chambers sitting down at a small table in the middle of the room. 'I stayed with an old friend there, and then made my way here through Mudgee.'

'How is Mudgee?' asked William, sitting down opposite him.

'I think jealous of what is happening out here with the gold rush,' said Chambers looking around him. The walls were covered in portraits and paintings, most of them of England or the ancient European past. His eyes found a family crest, a few photographs of Mr. and. Mrs. Fung, a few mirrors that gave the room more depth, and a small, wooden cross. When he saw the cross, he didn't want to look at it. It offended him immediately and, in his mind, saw red flames. He turned his eyes away quickly and looked at the table. Fung noticed this. Sarah came in and sat down at the table.

'The Church of England service is at Gulgong on Sunday morning. You should attend,' said Fung directly. Chambers could see that his wife was also puzzled by the statement.

'Most of the important landowners attend,' qualified Fung. 'You might find someone who would like to buy your farm.' Chambers smiled and thanked him. Mrs. Fung smiled and went back outside to the kitchen.

'Do you attend a Church of England service in China?' asked Fung, persisting with his questions.

Chambers smiled again.

'There are a few churches in Shanghai, but none in the mountains, where I have spent my last few years.'

Chambers looked at the beams on the ceiling. They were strong and well-built.

'I am impressed by the great architect of the universe,' he said. 'I love the foundations of the world, how things are built, how they are made, what holds them together.'

'I see,' said Fung staring at him understanding what he had just revealed. 'We also have a Masonic Lodge, very informal, but most people of importance attend if you wish to avoid the Church.'

Chambers nodded. So, Fung was also a Mason. 'Is Knox in the Lodge,' he asked.

'You are very direct Mr. Chambers.'

'As are you, Mr. Fung.' William smiled.

His wife entered the room with the plate for her husband. She went and brought Chamber's meal and then her own. Fung said a prayer of grace and Chambers politely observed it. It was his first proper meal since leaving Sydney.

'I am sorry I do not have any whiskey,' said Mr. Fung.

Chambers reached into his pocket and pulled out the flask.

Mr. Fung became very stern. 'This home does not have any alcohol,' he said, breaking his very polished accent.

Chambers smiled. 'Trust me,' he said, handing him the flask. 'You might be surprised at the taste.'

His wife was horrified that her husband took the flask in his hand.

One Chinaman to another,' said Chambers. 'Even the Monkey King pretended not to be an immortal.'

Fung smiled, took the challenge out of politeness, held the flask to his mouth and sipped it. He laughed. 'You are more Chinese than I am,' he said, turning to Sarah. 'It is tea! This is an old trick.'

She sighed in relief.

'Everyone in the Hotel assumed you were a whiskey drinker,' said Fung.

'And they thought I was partly drunk,' replied Chambers. 'I try not to drink. I cannot afford the risk. In my line of work, it is too dangerous. You cannot go into battle drunk.'

'Are you a soldier Mr. Chambers?' asked Sarah.

'I used to be,' he replied. 'These days, I live in the mountains with my wife.'

'What part of China?' asked Fung, leaning forward on the table, handing him back the flask.

'A day's ride to the west of Nanking, deep in the mountains.'

'You left your wife there and came to Sydney?' asked Fung. Chambers nodded. Sarah looked at him with a puzzled expression, but Fung ignored her.

'What is she like, your wife?' asked Sarah genuinely.

Chambers smiled. 'When I met Mei, she was graceful and kind. Her family's village is tiny, you would miss it if you were not looking. But the mountains, they are beautiful, and the air is fresh, and the way the mist rises in the valley is something I would never get used to.'

'You left her there in China, and came to Sydney,' asked William again, trying to clarify. 'She did not come with you to Sydney?'

Chambers shook his head. 'No,' he insisted. 'She is still there, in the mountains.'

There was a long pause. Fung looked at Chambers and realized he was not being honest. Chambers' wife was dead. He would tell Sarah about it later. No man would leave his wife in the mountains and come to Sydney, for any reason. It was simply too dangerous. Fung listened to Chambers chattering with Sarah about life in Home Rule. He looked at Chambers trying to understand him. After the dreaded Taiping were defeated, chaos reigned across the nation, or what was left of it. A man like Chambers, weary of war, and deeply acquainted with the human heart, could easily find a new life tucked away in some obscure mountainous area, but he would only emerge from such a paradise if there was no reason for him to stay there.

The three of them spoke a little more until Sarah took the dishes to the kitchen and the two men retired to the porch to smoke. Chambers raised the subject of John Knox.

'You need to understand something about Gulgong,' said Fung. 'That place is full of tribes, just like it is in China. In the beginning, Biddy's people were here. The farmers came and exterminated them. This was back in the '20s and '30s. There were lots of massacres, and their bones were used as fertilizer for the crops. Even now, Biddy's people keep dying. Her brother George went missing about a year ago.

'Home Rule didn't exist last year. It is less than six months old. Gulgong began in 1870. Aside from some of the old farming families, everyone is here for the gold. It brought John Knox here. He arrived in 1868 or '69. He pretends to be a farmer, but he makes more money from gold claims on his land. He was originally from Ireland, but he is a Protestant. I thought all Irish were Catholics, but some are in the Church of England. Knox represents the side of chaos. Rouse represents order. The two men despise each other. Knox and Rouse, two families, two ways of life wrestling with each other for the soul of the land.

'I will tell you the truth Chambers if you have the stomach to listen. I believe Henry's death had to do with a woman. What would we not do for a woman? My Sarah is my sun and my moon, she is my life, your wife in China, she is everything to you, I can see that. Mrs. Knox used to apologize for her husband all the time, his anger, and his paranoid jealousy. She was a remarkable woman, but for whatever reason, she ended up marrying Knox.

But there was another suitor at the time. His name was Shamus Murphy. He was wealthy also, but Mrs. Knox chose John Knox and never thought she would see her Shamus again. As life would have it, Shamus fell on hard times and migrated to Sydney. He opened a hotel there but came out to Gulgong last year and had a nice little place on Herbert Street. One day last year, Mr. and Mrs. Knox were in Gulgong getting supplies when she met Shamus quite by accident on the street. They had a polite conversation. She was happy to see him. He was happy to see her. John Knox even invited Shamus to Crooked River for dinner. But some doors should never be reopened, some friendships die for a reason, and I am afraid, John Knox became drunk with jealousy.

'Biddy said the land is cursed. Maybe she is right. There is darkness here. There are little spaces of calm and peace around, but out there, in the dark, something lurks in the Bush. The big towns with all their lights and hustle and bustle stifle the dark, but out here, in the silence, there is always the spectre of evil tempting men to do the worst things possible. You might have sensed it in China, during the war, a lingering atmosphere of evil. It wanders and finds a home to settle in, and then begins to infect people. Maybe it was awoken by the lust for gold, I don't know.

'After the dinner at Crooked River, there was a terrible and public row between John Knox and Shamus Murphy in Gulgong. I was there getting some vegetables from our garden. I could see everything Chambers, how the evil had spread, even after one year. There was Knox, constable Cooper, Knox's station manager Jed Barton, the priest Blackwell, and a few others.

'A month later, Mrs. Knox apparently died of a snake bite, but no one in town believes that. It was the night your brother died. The next day, Shamus Murphy was stabbed behind his Hotel, the Shamrock and Thistle. He died in Mary's arms.

'One of my employees, a man by the name of Lee Peng, was blamed for the murder and was arrested by Constable Cooper that afternoon due to the testimony of three false witnesses who saw them arguing. Lee Peng had spent time in prison as a boy in China, and I am sure that you know what kind of nightmares that poor man had. When

Cooper told him that he was going to be locked up, Lee ran blindly across the road and was struck by a stagecoach. He died a few hours later in my arms.'

Fung stepped onto the dirt and looked up into the sky.

'The so-called 'testimony' that convinced Cooper was simply malicious gossip from John Knox's sister-in-law, Henrietta Knox. Lee Peng worked for me. What is more shocking is that on the day of the murder, Lee Peng was not in Gulgong where he was supposed to be, where he usually was, but he was on a stagecoach coming back from Mudgee. I told this to Cooper, and he just laughed. He said he could not trust the word of a 'Chinaman,' even me.'

Chambers remained silent.

'That is the difference,' said Fung. 'Old Richard Rouse would have believed me.'

He turned to Chambers.

'I wanted that boy as part of my family,' he said emphatically and angrily. 'He needed a new life here, away from China, away from the old ways, a life of business and opportunity. We have a future here. Under England, there are laws that protect us. English justice, not the cruelty of the warlords or the brutality of the brigands. Lee Peng was doing well. He made his family proud. His father was a distant cousin of mine. His mother is still in China. His father was killed by the Taiping in 1862. Lee was there the day they killed him. You know what I am talking about. You have lived in China. Lee's mother married again after the war to a former soldier. He raised the boy as a father ought, and then sent the son to me.'

William kicked the dirt angrily. 'He would have made my daughter happy.'

He looked despondent and sighed. Chambers looked up into the sky. It was clear and he could see the moon. He said nothing. He knew that no words could comfort another man in such pain. Fung's agony would last a lifetime and he needed to face it alone.

7.   ELIZA

Henry Chamber's Farm,
by the Cooyal Creek, between Home Rule and Gulgong

The next morning, Chambers set off early for his brother's farm. He paid Mrs. Fung a fee for staying at the boarding house, even though she did not insist upon it. She refused to accept it, so he left it on the small cabinet beside his bed. He had spent the night mostly awake, thinking over all that Fung had told him, but more importantly, why he had told him. He knew that Fung was a man much like himself, hidden behind layers of politeness and formality, ever careful to hide his true feelings. During their long conversation, the polite façade of William Fung broke only twice. First, there was the astonishment over the flask of whiskey, and second, when he spoke about the death of his future son-in-law.

What Fung said about Knox did not surprise him. Every town he had ever lived in had someone like Knox. He realized long ago that life played itself out again and again in different places, with different people performing the same function, in a kind of drama. China, London, Gulgong, and Sydney, the names changed, but the people did not. There was always a man like Rouse, a man of the establishment, the old order. They were dignified and strong. There were always the people in the middle, like Fung, and his Scottish wife. Every place had a man like Knox and the parasites who attached themselves to his position. For Chambers, there was also another common feature, no matter the place, even though he sought always to elude it. This was death. This seemed to haunt Chambers, as he sought to play his role which was to avoid what needed to be done, as long as possible, because the cost was always going to be too high.

But Fung had hidden many secrets from Chambers. He knew that. This was also not new. Wherever he went, Chambers felt the truth of the matter was always there, ready to be revealed at the right time. The more he sought it, grasped for it, and lunged for it, the further it slipped from his fingers, and it would only emerge at the end when it was least wanted.

It was duty that kept Chambers in China at least in the early days, duty to his father, to the family name, and to the Queen. Other motives came in over time, but he was never motivated by money, though he had certainly come from it. As he rode his horse slowly along the dusty street, the motive for everyone there was plain to see. Near the town of Home Rule, men were sluicing by Cooyal Creek and digging shafts on every inch of open paddock. Little red flags stood unfurled everywhere announcing the discovery of gold. He had heard about the Gulgong gold rush that really took off in 1871. Leads spread out from the road like snakes in the grass, and men came and went, all scurrying around like ants on an anthill. Miners nodded an acknowledgment as he rode past, and he remembered a few faces from the Hotel the night before, but most kept their faces down and were walking fast, carrying various kinds of tools, or sacks over their shoulders. Chambers wondered how many had bought their tools from Fung.

Long ago, Chambers had lost interest in discovering gold. It gripped him like a disease in 1854 and it almost cost him his life. He fled to China to find peace but was sent back again in 1861 and wondered then if the old lusts would stir. He went incognito, looking for a man he had been asked to find. He pretended to fossick and found he needed to do so to avoid suspicion of being a government agent.

In 1854 he felt the addiction to gold run through his veins. In 1861 he discovered the violence of gold. Many were robbed, beaten, and killed for their finds. Men who boasted about their finds often ended up dead, and he had no intention of dying. In those days, the gold fields were full of Chinese who knew how to work together, and as a result, they found more gold. This infuriated the illiterate English poor who had come in search of quick fortunes from Sydney and Melbourne. The English settlers fought amongst themselves like rabid dogs. There was enough to go around, but the English wanted it all for themselves.

An old miner told him once that gold made all the filth and mud worthwhile. Chambers did not agree. Being alive was the greatest treasure a man could hope for. He was caught up in the race riots of '61, but eventually found the man he was looking for, his brains smashed out and his belongings strewn in a shallow dry creek bed. A prince among his own people, he was virtually stripped naked and left to rot by the side of the road by men driven mad by gold, what little there was. Now, after ten years, he was back again, and the nation was still in love with gold. But was it love, or just an addiction they could not shake?

Fung was right. Maybe there was a curse on the land and gold was the enticing illusion, to draw men and women into the darkness that lurked outside the town. Something was wrong. He could feel it. He could sense it. Maybe the storm the night before was trying to tell him something, but the air was still, the sky was blue, and everything remained calm.

The last place he expected to be was Australia. He had been fighting General Wei Li, the renegade bandit and former statesman, in the mountains near Nanking with some of Zeng Guofan's men when he received word from Shanghai that his brother had been shot. There was some confusion over whether the shot was fatal. Chambers turned his horse around to the coast. Despite their estrangement, Henry was still his brother. When he arrived at the military post, he was given the complete message. Henry was dead. A solicitor by the name of Johnson from a town called Gulgong wrote to him that he inherited Henry's house and estate. When he arrived in Shanghai, an old friend had in his possession the letter which had arrived in China. It sat unopened on some official's desk for months until, quite by chance, his old mate found it while searching for his own mail. He passed the original message on to a businessman, who passed it onto an associate, who eventually told Chambers.

Now he was back again. The Celestials had been largely forced off the goldfields now, thanks to the organized mob violence of the past, and were slowly being marginalized in society, though men like Fung were making their mark. Fung was wrong though. The problem was not Knox, nor Rouse, but gold. The town of Gulgong might have had some semblance of civilization, but it didn't fool him. It was a testimony to man's lust for gold. It was not a farming town, relaxed, quiet, seasonal, or stable. This was a mining town. The worst scum of the earth came here, all for a shiny metal.

Chambers turned aside from the main road and followed the map Sarah had drawn him. He rode up a long bush road that meandered and rose and fell. He went across what he guessed might have been Cooyal Creek and thought he may have been lost when he finally found an old sign hammered into a tall gum tree. It read 'Eliza.' It was his mother's name. This was the place. Henry was her favourite.

The path had been dug out of the bush and led around a large, open paddock, on which was a small homestead, with a veranda that encircled it. There were fruit trees of various types near the house and an overgrown English-style hedge. Beyond that, the Bush stood ready, ever advancing towards the house, eager to reclaim its lost territory. The land always wins in the end, he thought as he saw all the decay of what was left of his brother's sojourn. There was a small stable for a horse, and an equally modest barn for hay, and farming tools. What struck Chambers the most was the silence. He could hear nothing, no sounds from the sheep, cows, bulls, horses, or even the singing of birds. Johnson had written to him to say that Henry's estate included a sizeable flock of sheep, some cattle, and a few horses. They were all gone.

He dismounted and took the horse to the stable. He gave the horse an apple from his pocket. He found a small pond of water behind the house. He drew some water for the horse to drink. He took off the saddle and then turned his attention to the house, where his brother had lived and died. He walked around to the entrance of the homestead and up the rotting wooden steps to the front door. The wooden steps creaked as he walked. He tried the door. It was unlocked. That surprised him. He had assumed he would have to get in through a window. Johnson had written to say that Eliza would be under the responsibility of a caretaker, but the homestead was empty. There was no sign of anyone. He opened the door and stood there.

This had been Henry's home.

For some reason, he did not feel able to cross the threshold. There were many things about his brother he never knew. They rarely spoke after their mother's death. Henry retreated to Australia and Chambers stayed with the family. They had not spoken in decades. Yet, for some reason, Henry left the farm to him. Why didn't he leave the farm to Mary? They were getting married. Maybe he died before he could alter the Will. Maybe Johnson the solicitor would know more about all of that, and why he named his estranged brother the sole beneficiary. Poor Henry.

Fung was right. A murder had been committed.

His brother was many things, but careless with guns, he was not. Their father had taught them how to hold a rifle when they were boys. Henry was always the better shot. He rarely missed his target. Their father called him 'Robin Hood' as he always hit his mark.

The idea that a marksman would accidentally shoot himself was absurd. Chambers knew as he stood on the threshold that if he took a step inside, he would not stop until he found an answer to the riddle surrounding the death of his brother. He looked back at the stable where the horse was eating and drinking. He could turn around, get back on his horse, go to Knox and resolve the matter as gentlemen. He owed his brother nothing. He was also dead, with nothing to say and no last words. None of this was his fight.

It was also tragic what happened to Fung's future son-in-law. He knew the pain his mother and stepfather would be feeling in China. Fung was not only to bring the young man into his family, but he was responsible for Lee Peng while he was in Australia. He was under his care and tutelage. It was awful enough that Lee Peng died tragically under the racing hooves of a horse, but his last moments were filled with dread following false accusations.

It also would have reminded Fung of his real place in his adopted land. He could wear the clothes of an Englishman, convert to his religion, drink his tea, and speak with his accent, but he would never be anything more than an outsider. He needed to carve out his own world with the people he loved, like Sarah and Lee Peng and his beloved children. Australia was not his world, they were, and this made the death of Lee Peng more acute. With the boy's passing, William had lost part of his soul and he would never be whole again.

Chambers knew all about loss. He knew all about grief. He could not get over the death of his wife in the mountains of China. There was not a day or an hour in which he did not see her face and hear her accusations ringing in his ears. He felt awful guilt about his failure as a husband to protect his wife. He felt deep, abiding loss within every part of his soul, and was drowning in a reservoir of anger, guilt, and sadness. He was in no fit state to do anything but grieve in his own way and in his own time. He was responsible in a way, for all of it, and wanted to make sure he suffered for his sins, even if he carried them around in his heart for the rest of his life.

No, he didn't owe his brother anything.

But Henry was still a Chambers. He was his mother's son. He owed it to her memory. He owed it to Eliza. Chambers took his first step into the house, but as his boot hit the timber, he knew death had come with him.

8.   THE LOCKET

'Eliza,' Henry Chamber's Farm, beside Cooyal Creek

Henry's homestead was small and modest. From the front door, a corridor ran through the house to the back. There were four rooms, all the same size, and out the back, there was a stove and kitchen in a separate building. There was also an outhouse in a small, wooden structure about one hundred paces away. The cottage did not seem to be old, and most of the furnishings, what was left of them, were new. It was clear from first glance that someone had already gone through the house and had first pickings of what they thought to be valuable, leaving the barest furniture and household items behind. Portraits were missing, leaving faint shades on the wall where they had hung, drawers to cabinets were open in the bedroom, and garments had been thrown around the floor, some of the bedding was gone, and most of the China in the cupboard had been taken. Chambers walked out to the back and into the kitchen. There was scarcely a cooking implement left, and the pantry had been emptied. The house had been ransacked, stripped of value, until only the naked walls remained, empty. This angered Chambers. His brother had been shot, and the locals fought over the spoils.

In the bedroom, Chambers saw that a small wooden cross hung over the bed. It was covered in dust and nailed to the wall, so that was probably why it was still there. The family Bible was gone. Chambers knelt to find some clothes that had been tossed on the floor. He picked up a piece of clothing laden with dust. He sneezed loudly. When his eyes refocused, he saw that it belonged to a woman. As his eyes surveyed the rest of the clothes, he realized that they all belonged to a woman. They were discarded, tossed aside, and exposed in the room. Mary had not been in this house since Henry's death, otherwise, none of these items would still be there.

Chambers found a painting of Eliza, his mother in the dining room,

39

on the wall, a portrait of no value, and so it was probably left behind. Her stern face stared out across the room, probably mirroring Chambers' anger at what had happened in this house. There was a bare table, a few chairs, and a huge cabinet probably too heavy for the thieves to lift, open, and remove. The table had been moved to the wall so that unwelcome visitors could take the carpet. It was the same in all the rooms.

Chambers found what he needed to prepare a simple meal. There was enough. He had been in worse places. He found a few pots and pans, plates, and cutlery. There was no firewood left so he would have to cut up a fallen tree. He searched for an axe, which he found in the barn. He swung the axe over his shoulder and walked off to find some wood. His travels took him up a little rise, to the end of the back paddock. It fell slightly into a gradual gully that led to the creek, which flowed past. On the other side of the creek, he could see another homestead of a far hill, with smoke rising from the chimneys. That must be Knox's estate Crooked River, thought Chambers.

He spent the morning chopping wood from the trunk of a huge gum tree that had fallen across the middle of the paddock. It took most of the morning to carry the chopped wood to the kitchen, start a fire in the stove, and boil some tea he had in his knapsack. There was nothing in the pantry that he could use, though there was some soiled flour on the bench where a sack might have been. He sat on the back porch, looking out across the paddock. The sun was shining brightly, and Chambers tilted his hat so it would not hurt his eyes. The tea quenched his thirst and renewed his strength, though he craved a little bread, and maybe a morsel of meat. As he was thinking this, he saw something glint in the sun, in the middle of the paddock. He put down his tea and went to have a look. There was something half-buried in the dry grass. He knelt to see what it was.

It was a locket, a woman's locket, with a broken chain. Chambers dug it out of the red soil. It was scratched and covered in dirt. He wiped it on his shirt. Chambers held it in his hand. It was a fragile thing. The broken chain hung down. On the face was the shape of a diamond underneath a floral design, and each side of the diamond was edged by two large palm branches. The back had a different design, with a little flower surrounded by two arrows. It was quite beautiful. He opened it and expected to find two exquisite portraits on either side, but it was empty.

The locket reminded him of his mother, Eliza, a brief flashback to his youth, just an image of his mother wearing a locket, the smell of lavender, and bright lights. He must have been young. This image often came to him. He could not remember the place, or the occasion, just a locket, his mother's face, and the smell of lavender.

He was alerted suddenly by a voice behind him. He turned around. It was Mary Kelly.

She was wearing a long, blue dress, suitable for riding, and her hair was tied at the back. The anger she had expressed the night before was gone. She was instead rather inquisitive.

'What have you found?' she asked.

'A locket,' he said, holding it out. She walked over and he placed it in her hand. She gazed at it carefully but didn't open it.

'The chain is broken,' she said sadly. 'It is a shame, such a nice chain.'

'Is it yours?' asked Chambers.

'No,' said Mary, not looking up. 'I do not wear these kinds of things. They get in the way. Henry wanted me to wear one, he even bought me one, but I have never let a man put any on me, even a necklace. I have never felt comfortable wearing anything like that.'

She handed the locket back and looked at him. 'I see you have the stove on, I assumed you were out the back. Henry always was. He rarely spent time in the house, except when I came.'

She turned to walk into the house, but Chambers grabbed her left arm.

'It is not as you remember it,' he said gently. 'You need to prepare yourself. It is worse than even I imagined.' She looked at him angrily, and so he released his grip.

'I have not been back since that night,' she said. 'It will be like a knife in my heart, but it has been there many times since I held my Henry in my arms.'

'Do you have some flour?' he asked changing the subject.

'In a knapsack on my horse,' she replied. Chambers thanked her.

'I will leave you alone if you like,' he said. Her eyes said that she wanted him with her, but she told him that she would be fine by herself. He stayed in the paddock for a few moments while she walked back to the house. Chambers went and found her horse. He discovered she had brought enough supplies for at least a week. He took the sacks of food to the kitchen and went back and attended to the horse, leading it to his horse in the stable. He left the saddle on. He made sure the horse had access to water and some hay. He went to the kitchen, took out the flour, and with a little water, kneaded it into small balls, placing them with a sprinkling of salt into the oven. He looked at the vegetables sitting in the sack and pulled them out. There were a few turnips, potatoes, some maize in a smaller hessian bag, and some salted pork.

He went to the creek to get some more water for the pot, and when he returned, Mary was standing on the back veranda, holding onto one of the wooden beams with both hands. She looked drained and her eyes were red. Chambers went back into the kitchen and waited until the water boiled, preparing tea in two cups. When he emerged from the kitchen, she was sitting on the back steps, her eyes bright red and her hair untied. Chambers gave her a cup and sat down next to her.

They did not speak for a while. The aroma of freshly baked bread wafted through the kitchen. He took out the cakes of damper and they burnt his fingers. He managed to locate two plates that had not been smashed on the floor and took some bread out to Mary, placing it next to her. Chambers quickly ate the damper. It was hot and satisfying. Mary turned to him, smiled faintly, and began to pick at the bread, eating pieces slowly.

'Would you like some soup with the bread?' she asked abruptly.

Chambers said that it would be very agreeable to him. She stood up and went into the kitchen. Chambers took out the locket again and looked at it. It was not Mary's, nor his mother's, so to whom did it belong? What was it doing outside on the paddock? He stood up and started to walk around the property.

As he walked, his heart went out to Mary and the tragedy she had experienced. He thought of his brother and how he must have died, being shot at home. There were too many questions. His brother's gun was also missing, and the house had no ammunition, nor a medicinal cabinet. He had been carefully looking for signs of blood in all the rooms. He had not found any. Was he shot outside? He wanted to ask Mary, but he felt he should wait until she was comfortable to speak. The sun was hot, and Chambers sat on a branch of the large tree he had been chopping up with his axe earlier, lost in his thoughts.

'Soup's ready!' she shouted from the edge of the kitchen.

Chambers looked up and realized his wanderings had taken him to the edge of the creek. He walked back. Mary had prepared some soup for him in the dining room, to have with some more bread that she had baked. She knew her way around the house as if it were her own, that much was clear. She had obviously stayed often. Mary had found enough utensils for the meal and some bowls, and she sat opposite him at the table. She said a quiet prayer of thanks by herself, and they began to eat.

'It is good, thank you,' said Chambers, breaking the silence.

Mary smiled. She sighed deeply. 'It is the first time I have been here since Henry's death,' she said quietly.

'You did not come for the wake?' he asked. 'Did they have a wake?'

'I am not a member of the Church of England,' said Mary. 'I am Roman Catholic.'

'I am not sure I understand,' said Chambers. 'You were going to marry him.'

She looked at him as if she were about to say something, but she just smiled. 'They did not allow me near the coffin, nor at the funeral, and they would not allow me near the house for the wake. It was organized by Knox and his family. They said it was Henry's dying wish. Johnson would not even allow me to get my things.'

'Have you been in all the rooms?' she asked, her face turning red. Chambers nodded.

'All those clothes are mine. They were deliberately thrown around by someone who hated me, probably Henrietta Knox, John Knox's sister-in-law, a hideous, spiteful, vindictive woman. She married above her station, more of a chambermaid than a lady, but she married Tom Knox, the older brother of John. He is a toad of a man, slothful, and corrupt, like his brother, but everyone in town looks up to them as pillars of the community, such as it is.'

'Was Henry religious?' asked Chambers.

Mary laughed. 'Henry? He kept up appearances. Mr. Rouse asked him to attend divine services at the Church of England. Henry tolerated them from time to time, but he didn't believe in God.'

'But there is a cross on the wall,' said Chambers.

Mary smiled. 'I put that there,' she said. 'I had a little statue of Mary as well, but that's gone, probably smashed outside with all the crockery. Henry kept taking the cross down, and I kept putting it back up, until one day, I nailed it to the wall. Henry just laughed.'

There was a long pause.

'It is a horrible way to die,' said Chambers. 'It is truly awful. They are images that you never forget. One never sleeps soundly again.'

Mary looked up surprised. She looked up at the cross with Jesus hanging there. She was puzzled by what he had just said. 'Are you talking from experience?' she asked slightly bemused.

Chambers nodded. 'I have seen it. Nothing prepares you for the sight of it. I have not slept soundly since then. I don't go to church, but I feel sorry for Christ, and what they did to him. They wanted him to suffer. I understand that now. They wanted him to experience pain, and anyone who is strung up on a cross will not die without it.'

Chambers looked away from Mary and ate the rest of the soup. After dinner, Mary said that she would like to stay the night as it was too late to return home by horse. Chambers said he would sleep on the back veranda. He went to the stable, apologized to the horse for keeping the saddle on, took it off, fed and brushed both horses, and had a conversation with them about the day's events. When he returned to the house, he found a blanket on the veranda, a pillow, and a few other rugs laid out for him. He saw that the lamp in the bedroom was on, but he did not go in. Within moments, he was asleep.

Mary took off her blue dress and stood in her room silently in the dark. She looked at her bed. All that remained was the skeleton of the frame, a testimony to how she felt, and how empty her life was since Henry died. She did not even feel his presence, and even her memories were too painful to relive. She felt unsafe in the house. She took her blanket, wrapped it around herself, and went out to the back veranda and found a place to sleep further down near Chambers. She nestled up against the wall.

It must have been near midnight when she woke with a start. There was a noise. She looked over and realized Chambers was having a nightmare. He kept calling out in his sleep and speaking Chinese, tossing, and turning. He was in a state of unconscious terror. Mary did not know what to do. She began to weep softly. She did not know for whom or why, but eventually her tears exhausted her, and she too fell asleep.

9   SPECULATION

Chambers woke early, not that he really slept. He rubbed his eyes and face. Every night, he had the same nightmare, not that it was an actual nightmare, but rather the replaying of the same set of events again and again in his subconscious. He and his fellow villagers were returning to their small valley after failing to catch some fleeing bandits, only to find their homes burnt and everyone, every single person, man, woman, and child, dead. Chambers and the other soldiers had been lured out of the valley by a clever ruse, and their enemy had come in when the defences were weak.

Every dream was the same. He dismounted his horse and ran to his home, only to find it smouldering, and then he heard the shouts and the wailing from his friends, as they learned what had happened to their families. In his dream, he too followed their gaze and looked up to the hillside, and there he saw his wife dead, hanging on a cross. Chambers got up quickly. He did not want to think about it again that day. He had failed to protect her. He failed to keep her safe. He failed as a man in his most fundamental duty. There was no redemption for him, no forgiveness for such a transgression.

As he stood up, he realized that Mary Kelly was fast asleep next to him on the veranda. He looked at her while she slept. She looked comfortable and calm, and he wondered how she ended up on the balcony, and why. She was, Chambers knew, a beautiful woman, not only physically. There was a spirit of authenticity inside her, a deep quality he found appealing, not so much in a romantic way but in the way she held back her feelings. Like Fung, she had a depth to her that was seen in her actions and speech.

Like Fung, Mary was an outsider. He had wondered the night before why she had come. She could have come to the house any time in the last year. She chose not to. Something held her back. It was probably fear. Chambers suspected that the food and supplies were her way of saying sorry for the way she treated him at the hotel, but he decided he would say nothing about their first meeting.

Chambers went to the creek with a bucket and drew some water for the tea. He put some more wood in the fire and was able to start it. The flames started to rise on the stove, and so he put the pot on with some tea. Mary soon stood at the entrance to the kitchen, barefoot in her flimsy nightgown, her long red hair around her shoulders, and the blanket wrapped around her.

'Good morning,' she said sleepily with a smile.

'Would you like some tea?' he asked.

She smiled and nodded slightly.

'I did not sleep well,' she whispered. 'Tea would be nice.'

He handed her a cup. She took and walked over to the steps, sitting down. Chambers joined her. The air was still cool, and the sun had not yet risen high in the sky, so Mary tightly wrapped the blanket around herself.

'Sarah told me that I should apologise to you for the other night, in the hotel,' she said sipping her tea.

'I said some horrid things about you, and your relationship with your wife in China, horrid things. Sarah said she was shocked when her husband told her what I said. I don't remember saying them. I remember seeing you, and then a feeling of deep anger coming over me, like a raging fire and I honestly do not recall saying anything. Besides that, I am not good at apologising for anything.'

Chambers looked out across the paddock where he found the locket the day before. 'I did not leave because of what you said,' he replied.

'Then why did you leave?'

Chambers did not answer immediately. Surely, she knew the reason why, he thought. She had lived with the Fung family and would have known Sarah's struggle, being married to a Chinese man. Sarah would have had the same stares and prejudice, the same criticism, and the same troubles. He had done nothing wrong in marrying Mei in China. He had committed no sin before God if he even existed. He was accepted by her mother, by the town, and by her friends. They were happy to have another man work the fields. How he loved the work, after all those years of fighting. He had been fighting the Taiping for close to two decades. The land had been purged of men. Millions had died. Crops failed because so few people were left to till the ground. Mixed marriages were common in the now defunct East India

Company, even encouraged, and in the treaty ports of China he knew men who married local women. He left the hotel because of the looks he received from the men in the hotel when they discovered he had married a Celestial. How dare this filthy rabble judge him, he thought. Who made them God?

'I left because the townspeople of Home Rule passed judgment on me for marrying a Celestial. It amazes me how Sarah survives in this town if this is the attitude of the people,' he blurted out finally.

Sarah turned to him and stared into his eyes. They suddenly widened, as if she remembered what she had said. She turned her face away in shame.

'I have always been jealous of Sarah,' admitted Mary. 'I have been jealous of their marriage and how happy they are together, she and William, we all call him that, it is his English name. They have lovely children. My life, on the other hand, has been one disaster after the next.'

She stood up and walked down the steps, looking out at the paddock.

'I came to Australia five years ago with my husband and brother. My family was involved in the fight for Irish independence since the famine of the 1840s when the English let us starve to death. My late husband, Thomas Kelly, was involved in the Republican movement, secretly at the time. In 1868 we had to leave Ireland and so we came here, to the Colony of New South Wales. Tom was a man of property in Ireland, and was involved in politics, but when he came to Australia, he succumbed to gambling. We lost most of our wealth very quickly and so we gathered what we could and ran a hotel in Bathurst for a while. My husband died there. He drank himself to death.'

'Did you come up with the name of Home Rule?' interrupted Chambers.

'It seemed appropriate given what the government always tries to do, which is take away our freedom. But no, I didn't invent the name. It just seemed good at the time.' She smiled to herself. She turned and looked at the house.

'He was a bully, my Mr. Kelly if you understand what that means. He blamed me for all his misfortunes in life. I was the reason we left Ireland, not the English or their crimes against us, but me. I still do not sleep well. I fear the night, as it was when Tom came out with his fists flying. Shamus tried to protect me, my brother that is, but he was not always there. I was glad in a way that my husband died, I know it is an awful thing to say. God forgive me. Shamus and I went to Gulgong last year to take over a new Hotel that had lost its owner. I met Sarah and William, and they were very keen for me to marry again. They tried ever so hard,' she blurted out, laughing to herself. She turned to face Chambers.

'Then, in August last year, Shamus and I went to see Joey Goughenhiem perform at the old Cogden Assembly Room in Gulgong. It was lovely to hear some Irish singing and it lifted my spirits. That night, I met your brother. He was polite and kind. I do not want to sound critical of him, now that he is dead, but a woman in my position does not get to choose among so many suitors out here in the bush. Henry was a widower. He was depressed, and I needed a man. I tried to shine some light on his life. He soon proposed. I accepted immediately. He wanted to leave the farm and start anew. Your brother was drowning in a life of bitter regret and sorrow. His wife and child had died of pneumonia. He felt responsible. He wanted a new start. Shamus proposed the idea that we could work at the Shamrock and Thistle together in Gulgong.

'In early December we had chosen a date for the wedding. We were both excited. I was falling in love with him, which I did not think possible. The night Biddy told me that he was dead, I rode out here. His body was in the barn covered in a blanket. He had been shot in the head. Half of it was missing. Mr. Blackwell, the priest, tried to prevent me from viewing the body. He said it was too horrible. He was right. That memory is seared in my heart. Blackwell said that Henry committed suicide. He said that they were talking about the wedding and drinking whiskey when Henry stopped in the middle of a sentence, excused himself, and left. A few minutes later, Blackwell heard a shot.'

Mary sat back down on the step next to Chambers.

'Regret eats away at you until there is nothing left but holes and hollowness, enough for the wind to lift you into the air. I thought Henry had moved on from all of that, but he was still drowning, all the time I knew him. I knew that Blackwell didn't tell me the whole truth, but it didn't matter. Henry was still dead. It wouldn't have changed anything. My Henry, my protector, was gone. I thought I was in hell, but the next day I fell truly into the abyss. I spent the night of Henry's death with friends in Gulgong and returned to the Shamrock and Thistle late the following morning. Shamus was kind and supportive.

He said that he needed to go out for supplies, but a few moments later, he staggered into the hotel through the back door. He had been stabbed. He was covered in blood. He died in my arms.'

'Did he say anything?' interrupted Chambers.

Mary looked at him, her eyes quivering. Chambers knew fear when he saw it. She shook her head.

'He said nothing,' she replied, closing her eyes.

'How did Lee Peng get mixed up in it all?' asked Chambers.

Mary sighed, running her hands through her long red hair.

'Henrietta Knox, Mr. and Mrs. Clarke, and Bert Palmer claimed that Lee Peng was seen arguing with Shamus the day before. They were always arguing about something. They were like two boys, my Shamus and Lee Peng. I found out later from William that Lee Peng had been called away to Mudgee at the last moment on the day of the murder when William twisted an ankle on the front step of his store in Home Rule. He was not there to kill my brother. That didn't stop Constable Cooper from trying to arrest Lee Peng that afternoon. Poor Lee Peng. The stagecoach to Mudgee was racing along Herbert Street and he didn't see it coming. For some reason, the thought of being put in prison terrified him. He ran blindly onto the street and was struck down by the horse and carriage and died later that day in a lot of pain, his body broken.'

Chambers put his hand on her shoulder. 'Come with me,' he urged, standing, and walking out across the paddock. Mary tip-toed with him, as she was not wearing any shoes, the blanket wrapped around her.

'Henry was not killed in the barn,' exclaimed Chambers.

'What do you mean?' Mary asked, shocked.

'He died here, or he was shot here.'

'Where you found the locket?'

'Yes.'

Mary knelt and surveyed the grass.

'Henry was shot at night. There was a woman here. It was not you. It was not Mrs. Knox because she was dying on the farm across the creek. It was some other poor creature. It was night. It was probably cloudy.'

Mary nodded.

'I remember that night. It had rained earlier that day. It was still raining slightly in the evening and so you are right, the moon was probably hidden.'

'Henry was a good shot. He always was. He was better than I was, better than my father, and there was no one who had more respect for guns than he did. He was a Chambers, whatever he was, he would not have taken his own life. His honour would have held him back. It was probably what kept him alive, that and his fear of dishonouring his family name. He was going to marry you. He would not have dishonoured you, Mary. No, he didn't take his own life.'

Chambers looked out to the Knox farm. 'His death had something to do with the death of Mrs. Knox that night. Fung said that the servant girl of the household was missing.'

Mary nodded. 'Her name was Millie. A sweet, fragile little thing, not more than fourteen years old. She is still missing.'

Chambers sighed. 'She is most certainly dead,' he proclaimed solemnly. 'I bet a year's wages that the locket is hers.'

Mary started to cry. 'So much death in two days,' she murmured softly.

'It was a moonless night,' suggested Chambers, looking over to the creek. 'Henry comes out after drinking with Blackwell. They must have been planning the wedding. Something brought him out in the dark. It must have been this Mille coming across the creek, or across the paddock, but there must have been a loud enough noise to startle the two men in the house. Maybe there was a shot? I don't know.

'Henry meets Millie here. Henry is shot here. It was dark. Was it intentional? Did Millie shoot him? No, it was his farm, she would have known that. Was she likely to carry a gun? Fourteen you say. Frail, fragile Millie, using a gun? No, that's not it. Why did she leave the Knox farm in the middle of the night, the night Mrs. Knox died? What made a young girl flee across the paddock? What made her lose her locket? It must have been precious to her. She wouldn't have left it behind.'

Chambers looked in horror at the creek, then the paddock, and turned back to the house. He helped Mary to her feet and held her shoulders.

'I believe she was buried here somewhere. I swear to you Mary Kelly I will find out who killed Henry and they will face the full force of the law. There will be a trial and a conviction, and those responsible will be punished. Now, please go and get dressed and ride into Home Rule. Get Biddy and tell her to come here. She knows the land more than anyone. I need her eyes. She can see things Europeans do not see.'

Mary looked up at him. 'I do not understand, why do you need her?'

He held her shoulders tightly. 'Out here somewhere, in the dirt, is the body of Millie. She was killed here and most likely buried here. Blackwell has vanished. I suspect he's been silenced by Knox. It all comes down to the locket. They forgot it. They missed it. They were improvising. It was not intentional. It was not planned. Maybe the death of Mrs. Knox was, but everything afterwards was a series of unplanned disasters. I promise you. We will find Millie and shine light into all the darkness here. Henry's name and yours will be restored.'

10.   KNOX

Chambers was by the creek when he heard Mary call his name. He ran up the back steps, through the house to the front veranda. He found Mary dressed, with her hair pulled back. He could see the whites of her knuckles as she held onto one of the wooden beams of the veranda. Her face was red, suggesting to him that the conversation had already started, and it had not been a polite one. At the bottom of the steps, there were several men on horseback. From the way that Mary was staring at one of them, he knew he was looking down at John Knox.

He had a round, weathered, and wrinkled face, white hair, a deeply furrowed brow, and a small, tight mouth. He was quite a large man, with a stomach that flowed over a tight belt around his waist. He wore a cravat around his neck and a straw hat sat on his head. Chambers saw Jed Barton on the horse to his right and nodded an acknowledgment. Jed nodded in reply.

'Both of you are trespassing on my land. I don't take kindly to squatters!' shouted Knox in a large voice, leaning forward in his saddle.

'Your land?' asked Chambers, surprised.

Knox nodded. 'That's right. My land. Your brother sold it to me.'

'I received a letter from a man named Johnson who acts as a solicitor in these parts, and he told me that I inherited the homestead. That is why I'm here.'

There was a pause. Knox leaned forward again as if in pain. Chambers suspected that Knox was uncomfortable in the saddle.

'Jed told me this last night. I can tell you that it was a surprise. When Johnson wrote to you, he was not fully acquainted with the facts. The original Will was obsolete once the sale was organised. It was done to pay for costs associated with the marriage to Mrs. Kelly.'

Chambers turned to Mary. 'Do you know anything about this?' he asked her.

Mary replied that it was the first time she had heard about it.

Chambers reflected on the state of the house. It could explain why it had been stripped. Henry could have sold it to Knox. It was all quite possible.

'Did Henry have any money when he died?' Chambers asked Mary.

'I don't know,' Mary replied. 'I don't think so,' she said ambiguously. She seemed confused.

Chambers walked down the steps to where Knox was seated on his thoroughbred. He extended his hand in greeting. Knox hesitated for a moment, then lent down and shook Chamber's hand. Knox was wearing gloves.

'I am Nathaniel Chambers, Henry's brother. I'm glad to make your acquaintance Mr. Knox.'

Knox said nothing.

'I'm not one to doubt the word of a gentleman,' began Chambers. 'If you say that you bought the farm from Henry, then who am I to argue the point?'

'That is good to hear,' replied Knox sitting back in his saddle, greatly relieved.

'I suppose I should go and see Mr. Johnson in his office. What day is it?'

'Saturday,' called out Jed.

'Well, tomorrow, I'll go to church, and see Mr. Johnson on Monday to collect the money, and I'll leave for Sydney. If I could stay here for two more nights, I would be very appreciative. I was unaware of the transaction between you and Henry.'

Knox looked down at him with a scowl on his face.

Chambers could see a man of unrelenting hate. His eyes lifted to see Mary on the steps, still holding tightly onto the railing of the veranda. Chambers could see he despised her as well.

'It sounds reasonable,' said Jed to Knox trying to act as the mediator. Knox glared at him angrily.

'I will see you at church tomorrow then, Chambers. I am the Warden, and I will be happy to introduce you to everyone,' said Knox, tilting his hat.

He looked with contempt at Mary, turned his horse around, and moved off down the path, with his men following him. Mary and Chambers watched them go until they passed through the gate at the entrance to the property. Chambers had seen the look in Mary's eyes before. She had the same look in the eyes of hundreds of people over the years. He knew terror when he saw it, pure, undiluted, terror. He turned to Mary who was still holding onto the veranda.

'What did Knox say to you?' he asked.

'Nothing I care to repeat here, nothing he has not said before.'

Chambers walked up the steps. 'What do you mean?' he asked, looking at her. She tried to smile, but it could not hide her deep discomfort. She turned her face away from him.

'You do not understand, someone like Knox does not have to say anything.'

Chambers understood. Knox breathed violence. He knew he was a murderer the moment they met. Not only was he a killer, but he enjoyed it, he relished it, and he was satiated by the sufferings of others. It was some event in his past that corrupted him when he first got a taste for blood and drank regularly from that foundation. Chambers had seen it all before. As soon as he shook Knox's hand, he knew everything he needed to know about the man. He could fully imagine the kind of church this Warden would run, and the kind of god this man believed in. A god of fear, death, and retribution, a god who has been beaten into submission, and cast out of heaven.

'Do you think Henry sold the farm?' asked Mary, trying to change the subject. Why would he not have told me?'

Chambers laughed.

'It might have been a gentleman's agreement, a handshake, an understanding. I doubt very much an actual contract was signed. I suspect Knox craved this farm. It is quite possible that Johnson simply didn't know about the deal and sent me the letter anyway, but it could explain why there is no caretaker, and all the animals are gone. I was told that my letter was found entirely by accident by a friend of mine. If he did not find it, I would still be in China. I did not receive a second letter from Johnson correcting the mistake, so I suspect that he and Knox have an arrangement. Then, out of the blue, Henry's wayward brother turns up, the one who married the Chinese woman, expecting to inherit the property.'

'I am sorry,' interrupted Mary. 'I said some horrid things to you the other night, about your wife and your children. William told his wife and she insisted upon an immediate apology. She gets enough criticism from other people; she does not need it from her friends. She also demanded that I come and apologize to you. I have no right to judge you and your wife and family. It is not my place to pass judgment. If it was anything, it was out of pure envy.'

'Why were you jealous?' asked a surprised Chambers.

'You've found happiness in a wife, family, and home, all the things that have so eluded me the last few years. I just lashed out at God and my anger hit you instead.'

Chambers looked at her. She was genuinely apologetic, her eyes red. He wanted to reach out and wipe away her tears, for there was no need for an apology. He felt a stirring of compassion for her and her life, but he refrained.

'Thank you for your apology,' he finally said. 'Let's put all of that behind us, and focus on the tasks at hand. I'm convinced that Knox has overplayed his hand. If there was a sale, where is the money? You see a bully in Knox. He is indeed that, but he gets others to do his work for him. He wants to keep his hands clean so he can go to church and be a good Churchman, a good Warden, and he can blame things on one of his hired men, like Jed Barton, with his shifty eyes. I've met Mr. Knox a hundred times before. I feel my life is going in circles. The faces change but the story is the same. Knox is a liar. Come Monday, he'll offer me money to leave town. He will also try to stop me from asking any more questions about that night.'

'How can you be sure of all of this?' asked Mary.

'Listen, Mrs. Kelly,' said Chambers. 'May I let you in on a little secret? Everyone is the same. High, low, rich, poor, Chinese, European, it all makes no difference. People are the same. Once you work that out, life is a lot less complicated. Look into your own heart from time to time, almost nothing surprises you.'

'I don't understand,' replied Mary confused.

'Knox is improvising,' stated Chambers. 'If there was a legitimate sale, he would be able to produce the deed. Even if it was some handshake agreement, which I very much doubt, where is the money? Surely it would have been given to you, you were going to marry Henry. No, everything that happened that dark night a year ago is connected. The original crime might have been well planned, but it did not go properly, and Knox and his men have spent the last year covering their tracks. Blackwell has vanished as well. That is why I need Biddy. You don't realize how valuable she is.'

'She is a good friend,' replied Mary.

'I am sure she is, but that is not why I need her. She has one advantage over you. She was born here, Mary. She lives and breathes the land. She is the land itself. She's someone who does not fear the land but rather sees it as an extension of herself. She knows everything about the area, I knew that when I met her two nights ago. She was the only one on the street. Only a local would be out in that storm. She is part of the land. In China, I quickly learned that the local people know everything. They are a reservoir of knowledge and wisdom. I have been here for two days. My eyes are clouded by prejudice, sadness, and regret. I need her eyes and her wisdom. She's perhaps the only one in town who can find out the truth about my brother, and your Henry.'

All right,' said Mary, 'I will find her. I cannot promise that she will come here, but I will go now. In fact, I know she will not come. She is a free spirit and works for no one.'

Chambers sighed with disappointment. He knew he had no right to ask for her help. He had been in Australia before. He knew how the English treated the Aborigines, but he had no choice. His investigation was based on hunches, suppositions, conjecture, and speculation. He needed Biddy and felt that somehow their lives were intertwined in some way but at that point, it was all too elusive. As he was thinking this, Mary went back into the farmhouse to retrieve her belongings.

'Would you like me to ride with you back into town?' Chambers asked, thinking about finding Biddy on the way. She stopped in the hallway and then walked back out onto the veranda.

'It will only confirm in everyone's minds what Knox and his men will have already said. But thank you, maybe we can go for a walk together one day.'

Chambers smiled.

'I only came to apologize,' replied Mary. 'I've not been here since Henry's death. I'm too scared to be so close to the Knox estate.'

While she was gathering her belongings, Chambers put the saddle on her horse and led it out of the barn. The sun was beating down on his head. It must have been about noon when Mrs. Kelly shook his hand in farewell and rode down the path towards the town of Home Rule.

11.   ROUSE

After Mary had gone, Chambers set to work. He made a thorough search of the entire property. He searched the barn and the stables, and all the rooms of the cottage. He did not know what he was looking for, but he knew that he would know if he found it. He kept thinking of Mary and the look of terror in her eyes when Knox turned up and how she held tightly onto the veranda, her knuckles turning white. She dreaded the man.

But there was something more than fear. Maybe he had hurt her, threatened her, or poisoned others through what he had said. Chambers knew that what people said about others could do more damage than an actual act of murder itself. Carefully chosen words, insinuations, malicious gossip, and accusations, could kill more effectively than a knife to the heart, or a knife in the back. Chambers had been on the receiving end of this more than once in his life, especially when he was around the English, with their class pretentiousness, and deep-seated racism.

Knox sat in the Bishop's Chair at the little Church of England building in Gulgong, ruling over his domain. Everyone hung onto his every word. But how far did his power extend? Knox was not landed gentry, but a squatter from Ireland, an Irish Protestant, a strange combination, not exactly English, and not really Irish. William Fung alluded to the fact that there was an older English landed aristocracy in Australia. Knox, for some reason was not a Mason. What did they think of this new Irish bully? How long had he held reign in Gulgong? It could not have been long. The town only came to life a few years before. What made Knox want to hurt other people? Was he a sadist? Did he derive pleasure from the suffering of others? Or was he simply hiding something that no one knew, a dark secret?

Chambers had met people like Knox all the time in China. Most did what they did for a specific reason. Few, even the mad ones, were ever insane. Only one or two were genuinely crazy. They were the ones who thought they were the Messiah or the Son of God, and the result was always genocide. The rest had clear reasons for their actions, which were often veiled from others. This drove them to do what they did, but because it was hidden, others saw only the anger this produced, not the fear or sickness that was behind it. William said nothing negative about Knox's wife, so her death must have destroyed him. Whatever happened that fateful night, Knox was a broken and angry man. Chambers knew that if the puzzle was to be solved, he needed to work out what really happened that terrible night one year ago, the night Henry was shot.

Henry.

How little he knew of him.

Henry left China because of their mother's death. It was not his father's fault. He had no control over life and death. Henry should have known more than most about the frailty of life, living a life of privilege among the poor. Disgusted with his father, Henry left China in 1840, moving first to England, then to the colony of New South Wales, then to Queensland, and back to New South Wales. Chambers was surprised that his brother had moved back to New South Wales and that he had decided to become a farmer. The last he heard was that Henry was blackbirding in Queensland in the sugar cane plantations, making a small fortune. What a hypocrite, thought Chambers, condemning his father for working in China, and then running a plantation based on slave labour.

Henry was like that. He just never grew up. He never changed. It was not the way life was supposed to be. The stupidity and rashness of youth needed to be tempered by the realism of life, and the vagueness of morality. Henry died a man with the heart of a boy who still feared the wrath of his distraught and long-dead father.

Chambers found himself in the bedroom, where Mary had tried to sleep the night before. Was it really Knox that kept her away from here, thought Chambers? Did she also fear Henry? Did he carry his anger with him from his youth, all the way to Gulgong? Was she on the receiving end, a single woman surrounded by violent men? Mary's reaction when she accused him at the hotel, was that just about China, or was she angry with Henry as well? Maybe the house was already bare before they laid Henry in the grave. Maybe there was little to be scavenged in the first place. Maybe this spartan, empty house was all that there was.

A noise alerted him. It came from out the front of the house. It was too soon to be Biddy unless Mary had galloped all the way from Eliza and back to Home Rule. Chambers walked to the entrance of the homestead, and out onto the veranda. There was another man on a horse. He was tall, dressed in a neat grey riding suit. His thoroughbred was impeccable and obedient, well presented, as was her rider. The man had a neatly trimmed beard, a high forehead, and a narrow nose, above two piercing eyes. Chambers walked down the steps to greet him.

'Chambers,' said the man, dismounting. 'Allow me to introduce myself. My name is Rouse.'

The two men shook hands.

'What a beautiful horse you have here,' said Chambers admiringly.

Rouse smiled from ear to ear, as if Chambers had said the right thing. Chambers walked to the other side of the horse, and then back again, patting the horse on the neck. 'Simply beautiful,' repeated Chambers.

'I came about horses actually,' said Rouse. 'Your brother ran horses in our local races. He owned three. When he passed away. I took it upon myself to come and fetch them until the estate was settled. I was horrified to discover that no one was taking care of them.'

'I appreciate that Rouse,' said Chambers. 'It was good of you. It is only fair that you keep them, it is the least I can do for the kindness you have shown them.'

Rouse smiled again. 'Absolutely out of the question Chambers. Out of the question. I kept them on behalf of the one who would inherit the estate. I had assumed that it was Mary Kelly, Henry's fiancé, but for some reason, according to Johnson, the Will stated that the entire proceedings of the estate went to you. We can sell the horses at an auction, and I will bid for them. I'll make sure you get a fair price.'

Chambers looked at Rouse. It was very decent of him, he thought.

'You must come to Guntawang,' he added. 'It's the family estate, recently rebuilt. I have the horses there. You can see how they run. You might not want to sell them.'

'I intend to,' replied Chambers. 'But thank you for the invitation. I intend on giving the proceeds of the sale of the horses to Mary Kelly, who was engaged to my brother. It is only fair.'

Rouse paused and looked at him seriously. 'I did not think such a man existed out here in the Bush,' said Rouse. 'That is honourable of you. How she has been treated since your brother's death has been nothing short of a crime.'

'Henry had the facilities for cattle and sheep, but I don't know what happened to them,' said Chambers changing the subject. Rouse became quite serious. His smile vanished.

'I took the horses because on the day of the Wake, a few days after Henry's death, there was no sign of any of the cattle or sheep. I asked Jed Barton about it, and he said that Knox took them.'

'Knox came just before you; and told me that the land and the estate was his,' replied Chambers.

'It is possible,' said Rouse. 'Knox has never mentioned it to me directly,' running the fingers of his left hand across his forehead. 'I met your brother a week before he died, and he gave me no indication that he'd sold the farm. Quite the opposite. He was excited about something. I assumed it was his upcoming wedding. But looking back Chambers, it might have been something quite different. I have seen that expression on the faces of many men around here, especially when they have found some gold, or had some luck on the horses. Come to think of it, I do believe that this expression was the one on your brother's face.'

'Could he have discovered gold somewhere?' asked Chambers.

'I don't know for sure,' replied Rouse. 'It is entirely possible, though I don't believe that he ever prospected, or dug for gold. This land has already been surveyed and there doesn't seem to be any lead here on Eliza, though gold was found on the Knox estate, not much, but sufficient for a few claims, enough for Knox to live well for a while. Henry had a sore back which really caused him pain. I think he must have been thrown from a horse in Queensland, and the wound never quite healed. You could easily see it, especially if he needed to reach down for something. I think he was in agony. Mining requires much of the human body, and lots of twisting and turning in confined spaces. That would have been impossible for him.'

Rouse patted the neck of his horse. Chambers went to the barn and took another apple from his knapsack, and threw it to Rouse, who caught it. He gave it to the horse, who devoured it quickly.

'I did not know your brother very well. He had not been here long. He came just before old Tom Saunders found gold at Red Hill. I think Henry thought the area might be a quiet place, but last year, the town grew from a few hundred to well over ten thousand. This place was quite rundown and was owned by one of the men who used to work for my father. We did not see much of your brother.

'I often invited him to church at St James in Guntawang. I wanted him to be involved in setting up the new church in Gulgong last year and general civic affairs, but he wanted nothing to do with the town. I did not pry. We all have our reasons. William Fung told me that Henry had been widowed before he came. He lost his family in Queensland.'

Rouse was amazed at the remarkable similarity in facial features between Henry and his brother Nathaniel. It was uncanny, as if there was only one man with two different personalities. One of his men had been in the Canadian Hotel the night Chambers turned up and told his boss about the stern rebuke Mary Kelly gave him. William Fung told him much the same, as well as his anxiety that Chambers might want to find definite answers to the question of what really happened that night, the night Henry died.

Rouse had his suspicions about that night, which he kept to himself, but he did not want to get involved. The town of Gulgong already had enough problems. Blackwell had gone missing, which was a blessing in disguise. He was a most unpleasant individual. He had the blessing of the bishop and was related to someone important, so Rouse had little power to unseat him. There were so many problems with the mines, not least the disputes between miners over boundaries, claims, and rights. It was all fine when there was only Adams Lead and Black Lead, but now there were dozens of new Leads being claimed as well as the new, competing townships of Canadian Lead and Home Rule.

He especially disliked the name of the town as he knew that some of the miners were sympathetic to a free Ireland, especially Richard Noble, the owner of the Royal Hotel in Gulgong. He had ties going back to the Eureka Stockade in 1854. Rouse also felt uneasy around Mary Kelly because of her late husband's ties to the Irish republican movement.

The last thing Rouse wanted was political instability in Gulgong. He was glad that Brown, the local Commissioner, and the local police, were good at their jobs. They had plenty to do. Gold brought more crime than flies in summer. Bushrangers plagued the road from Wallerawang to Gulgong, and especially the road to Mudgee. There had been some grisly murders of late. It was these murders that deprived Gulgong of its two detectives, Charles Powell, and Robert Hannan, now in Mudgee hunting a vicious murderer. Two of the other constables were down sick, one at death's door, due to pneumonia, which left the town in the hands of Constable Cooper, who was in the pocket of John Knox.

Rouse had invited Joe Mitchell from Mudgee to look at the situation to see if a case of official corruption could be laid at Cooper's feet. Rouse was also concerned about stock prices, horse prices, wool prices, his overseas investments, and the weather, as well as all the domestic duties of a man of his position.

All this chaos was due to gold. It was simpler in 1865 when there were only a few large pastoralists and an uneasy truce with the remaining aboriginal tribes. But greed had come to Gulgong. It brought Knox and Henry Chambers, Shamus Murphy, Lee Peng, and Mary Kelly. It even kept William and Sarah Fung, even though he had advised them to move to Sydney and pursue their dreams in a much safer environment. Rouse looked at Chambers. The last thing he wanted was for this man to stir up old wounds or unsettle the waters with all his questions. He knew it was selfish.

'I thought Henry would have been married in the church,' said Chambers.

Rouse shook his head. 'Your brother was not religious, as far as I know. He was also marrying a Roman Catholic, so he could not get married in the church. Knox saw to that.'

'So where were they going to marry?' asked Chambers.

'A few of the farming estates have their own chapels. I heard that one of them was going to allow it, but I don't know any more than that.'

'Fung said you have lost the priest. I was hoping to speak with him.'
Rouse nodded.

'Blackwell was never the same after Henry's death. He was there that night. He was sick for most of this year from one thing or the other. He avoided everyone. Other priests from Mudgee conducted services, not that anyone would attend. I have tried to interest others in our church, but it has a reputation unfortunately as a centre for malicious gossip and so most people stay away.

'The Roman Catholics are much more devout, and so are the non-conformists. Then, about a week ago, Blackwell simply vanished. We searched his house, and all his belongings were gone, but there was no note, and we have not heard anything.'

'Knox told me that there was a church service tomorrow at

Gulgong. Will Knox take the service?'

Rouse laughed. 'No, that will not happen. We often have men of the cloth passing through these days on the way to Bathurst or going inland. I would love them to stay, but gold rush towns have their own problems, and most priests desire the quiet, easy life. Most have a particular sentiment. We have had so much trouble procuring one from the bishop. Priests prefer the luxuries of Sydney, not the country squalor.

'But on Wednesday last, I met a man by the name of Lyons who was on his way to Sydney. He has kindly agreed to take the service for this Sunday and maybe one more Sunday before returning to Sydney. He seems a decent chap. Most of the priests are not, to be honest, good men, but they perform the rites well and usually give a rousing homily. Lyons has never been to Gulgong before, nor does he know anyone here. He is staying with me at Guntawang, but tonight he is dining with the Knox's at Tom and Henrietta's farm.'

'I am like my brother,' admitted Chambers. 'I do not have much time for God, as he has not had much time for me these last few years. I will attend if only to meet the solicitor and find out more about Knox's alleged sale of the property. I wish I had more to go on. I really do. The house is empty. I can find nothing of value to aid me in my search, and aside from a portrait of my mother, Eliza, I can find no personal effects.'

Rouse looked surprised. 'You did not find his journal?'

'What journal?' Chambers was stunned.

After Rouse left, Chambers searched for his brother's journal until dusk fell, without success. Rouse told him that Henry had alluded to the journal one day when they met in the town of Gulgong during a disturbance due to the discovery of gold in what became known as the Happy Valley Lead. The township was in an uproar of excitement, and as an aside, he heard Henry say that this event merited mention in his journal. Rouse inquired about it, and Henry told him that he kept a journal, including in it some interesting facts from time to time. He never mentioned it again.

Chambers stood in the doorway to the homestead looking out to the path towards the front of the estate. He had lit one small lamp in the front room, which was fast becoming the only light in the entire house, except for the smouldering fire in the stove, which burned slowly away in the twilight. He closed his eyes and felt the cool wind of the evening. A kookaburra called in a nearby tree, and he could hear the typical sounds of another night in the bush. In the distance, he could see the smoke rising from the chimney of John Knox's farm and he kept thinking back to the night of his brother's death.

Biddy had not come. Maybe Mary had not found her. Maybe Biddy had decided not to come. She had no reason to do so. She didn't work for Chambers. He sighed and remembered her touching his cheek that night he rode into Home Rule. It was a strange thing to do. She must have had some connection with Henry. He did not think she was his lover or anything like that, but she knew him, and certainly, they were friends of some sort. There was some connection between them, of that he was certain.

Chambers walked back to the outside kitchen and prepared some small loaves of bread and boiled some tea. As he kneaded the dough, he wondered where his brother might have kept a journal. If it were to be hidden, where did he put it? How often did he write in it? What records did this journal contain?

That night, as he drank some tea on the back veranda of the homestead, a noise in the paddock startled him, and a mob of kangaroos burst out of the bush and into the clearing. Chambers remembered the surprise he felt the first time he saw a kangaroo when he arrived in Sydney, all those years ago, as a young man, in 1854. That first kangaroo seemed as surprised to see Chambers, as he was to meet him, on a field on the edges of the growing colonial town. It looked like a cross between a dog and a hare.

When he was a boy, he had read about the strange and wonderful creatures of this land, but he never expected to see one face to face. On that day, the kangaroo was solitary and seemed calm, so Chambers approached it. When it moved menacingly towards him, he quickly turned, got back on his horse, and rode away. He learned his lesson. He saw kangaroos again in 1861 when he visited again at the height of the gold rush. They were on the margins there as well, being pushed back, shot, and culled by the prospectors. But on his brother's farm, the kangaroos were wild, and they hopped across the paddock. They must have numbered in their hundreds as they leapt across the creek at the back of the property, up the small hill, and across the field. This was their land, and they did not need to ask permission to cross.

After the stragglers had passed the homestead, the wind picked up. Chambers walked back to the kitchen and poured himself some more tea, returning to his seat on the veranda step. He had resigned himself to the fact that the journal his brother had kept, was long gone. He would not have hidden it, as he did not expect to die that night, the night he came out onto the paddock only to be shot. It was possible that Blackwell had found the journal, but it was just as likely that it had been burned along with the other papers when the solicitor Johnson had come to make an audit of his brother's personal effects. It really depended, thought Chambers, on what the journal contained. It was entirely possible that his brother discontinued the record and burned it himself when he was preparing to marry Mary. It may have contained entries that he did not wish her to read.

All these possibilities were likely, thought Chambers. The journal was gone. Like the locket, the journal was a tantalizing hope for some resolution to the mystery of his brother's death, but it led to nothing. There was only darkness, conjecture, speculation, and nothing could be proved. Knox's wife died of a snake bite, the servant girl Millie went missing, and his brother Henry shot himself in the barn. A terrible night. Chambers knew the deaths were connected and he knew that Knox was at the centre, but he could not prove a thing.

The wind, which had begun as a slight breeze through the trees, had picked up force. The branches in the trees began to sway and creak. Chambers could hear them in the river at the end of the paddock. There was in the dark, an awful crack, like a deep groan, and a branch snapped off a tall gum tree, landing with some confusion into the scrub. It was a hideous sound, quite unlike anything Chambers had heard before. He was glad that there were no trees close to the homestead, otherwise in a wind like this, one might easily fall onto the roof. The wind was so powerful that Chambers had to retreat to the kitchen, but he soon retired to bed, not that he could sleep much. He tossed and turned as the wind raged outside.

The next morning, Chambers woke up on the hard bed in his brother's house. It had been uncomfortable. He went to the creek to wash. He took off his shirt and stood looking at the water. He felt tired. He did not sleep well the night before. He had the same nightmare, he had awoken several times and found it difficult to get back to sleep. Chambers cupped the water and splashed his face a few times.

The previous night he had spent the evening with a woman, the first time he had been so close to someone in years. He could hear her breathing as he lay on the veranda, and it felt strangely comforting to have someone nearby. All he heard the previous night was the raging wind outside. He rubbed his eyes and doused them with water, and then stared at the water once more. He must have given Mary quite a shock turning up like that in the hotel. Biddy was right. It was like someone coming back from the dead.

12.   THE WRATH OF GOD

Church of England building and surrounds, Gulgong

It was with some difficulty that Chambers found the Church of England building in Gulgong. No one he asked knew where it was or even that there was a Church of England building. Some tried to direct him to the newly built wooden Catholic Church, or the Methodist Chapel. Few it seemed, went to the Church of England. Fewer were invited. Most of the miners were poor, former labourers from Sydney, or other towns in Australia. They were not religious folk, nor regular churchgoers. Virtually no one he met qualified as members of the landed establishment like Rouse, Knox, and the small handful of pastoralists who lived in the district. By the time Chambers arrived in Gulgong, most of the churchgoers were already on their way to other houses of worship.

What surprised Chambers wasn't the hundreds of mining claims complete with tents, red flags, and shafts, nor was it the chaotic construction of temporary dwellings. It just seemed too quiet to be a gold rush town, even for a Sunday. It was about ten in the morning when he rode into town, and everyone he met looked exhausted as if they had only just risen for the day. It was a far cry from the great goldrushes of the past. This was but an echo. He knew he reached Gulgong by a few stone buildings surrounded by dozens of wooden structures, some posing as restaurants, hotels, drugstores, stores, and places of ill-repute. The main street seemed to be Herbert Street which stretched down the hill for at least two kilometres. In the distance, through the morning mist, Chambers could see market gardens.

Whenever he asked someone, they would have the same response. They would look up at him quite surprised and say: 'You would not be welcome there, dressed like that,' or 'a bit above your station wouldn't you think?' or 'I think you have been misinformed, that is the church for the gentry, you might want to try the chapel,' or words to that effect.

Chambers would look down at the men and around at the town, and think to himself, even in this squalid filthy backwater, there are those with airs and graces, thumbing their noses at all and sundry. When he persisted, they would frown and reluctantly provide some basic directions. He found the Catholic Church, the Wesleyan Chapel, and eventually the Church of England, on top of what was, not surprisingly, Church Hill, far from the mining leads and away from the centre of town. The land looked scorched. It was bereft of trees, shrubs, and the sounds of birds. It was a desolate sight, more of a mausoleum than a church.

It was, in Chambers' mind, the shabbiest church building he had ever laid eyes upon. If there was a God he thought, then he would be angry with the tardy, pathetic attempt at construction, especially in a town drowning in gold. Gulgong high society certainly gave God the crumbs under the table reserved only for dogs. It was a long building, made entirely of wood. Most of the beams were unevenly cut, with large gaps in the wall. The roof had shingles, sitting precariously on the structure, though they too, looked flimsy and fragile. Not a few lay on the ground tossed off during the previous night's strong winds. The grounds around the church were bare and lifeless, except for the horses corralled nearby and what seemed to be two large tables. He knew he was in the right place because he saw Jed Barton next to one of the horses. He waved and Jed waved back. Chambers rode over and dismounted.

'Morning,' he said to Jed, who tipped his hat.

'Morning Chambers,' he replied. 'The service already began a while back. I think Mr. Lyons is giving his sermon now.'

'Best to stay outside then,' replied Chambers.

'If you want,' said Jed. 'Do what you like.' He turned to one of Knox's men and introduced him as Rogers. He was short, with a bald head, fat cheeks, and small eyes that scrutinized Chambers with suspicion. Chambers recognized him. They had met the day before when Knox went to Henry's farm. Rogers said nothing.

'Is Johnson here?' asked Chambers. 'I only came to see him.'

Jed looked surprised. 'Nope, haven't seen him today. Knox wanted to see him too, so we can clear up the misunderstanding about your brother's place, but he isn't here.'

'What is your opinion on Henry's place?' asked Chambers.

'Well, I know you are his brother and all, and I don't wish to offend, but it is a fact that just prior to his death he sold the land to Mr. Knox. Knox was very generous. Money was exchanged.'

Chambers took off his hat. 'Thank you, Jed,' he said. 'I appreciate the honesty. It seems very straightforward. I don't know why Johnson sent word to me in China about the Will if the land had already been sold.'

'I was thinking about that too, ever since you mentioned it,' replied Jed, scratching his chin.

'That night and the next morning were terrible for the district. On one night we had the tragedy of Mrs. Knox's death and Henry's suicide. It was the night poor Millie vanished. Shamus was killed by Lee Peng the next day. Mr. Knox was quite distraught following the death of his wife, and so kept away from everyone for a few months, except for the wake which was held at Eliza. Maybe Johnson did not know about the sale.'

'It is possible,' said Chambers. 'How is Knox now? He must still feel her loss acutely.'

Jed nodded. 'He's not the same man. It would be a terrible thing to lose a wife.'

Chambers nodded. 'It is something we have in common,' he said quietly.

Jed looked surprised. 'I thought you were married.'

'I was,' replied Chambers. 'My wife is still in China. She is buried there.'

Jed's eyes widened. 'You didn't tell Mary, did you?'

'No, Mary doesn't know. You are the only one who does I think. It has nothing to do with her. I am just here for a few days and then I hope to return to China.' He looked at Jed, who seemed confused.

'Listen, Jed,' said Chambers. 'I know the way you looked at her the other night. I know that look. You love her.'

'I don't know what you are talking about,' protested Jed. 'Anyway, she went to see you the other night, and spent the night with you, so it doesn't matter.'

'She came to apologize to me for the way she spoke to me in the Hotel. She obviously loved my brother and probably still does.'

'But that's the thing, Chambers,' said Jed. 'I don't think she ever did love him.'

At that moment, singing could be heard coming from inside the church. It was plain to Chambers that they could neither sing nor hold a tune. Some of the horses began to get restless. It was an awful cacophony. It sounded like cats stuck in a well trying to escape.

'I will get something for the horses,' said Chambers and excused himself.

He walked over to the two large tables that had been placed near the church building. On them, were an assortment of cakes, scones, and sandwiches. A few men were tending to a campfire nearby, and he could smell the tea.

'What's all the celebration?' inquired Chambers, curiously.

'The visiting priest,' said another man, standing up. 'Mr. John Knox, the parish warden thought it might be nice to welcome him. We hope to persuade him to change his mind and stay.'

Chambers looked around and then down towards the goldfields. Most of the trees had been cut down, the roads were dusty, there were only one or two permanent structures in sight, and there was a strange smell in the air. It was like the putrid aroma of an open latrine.

'I'm sure you will have no problem convincing him to stay here,' said Chambers sarcastically. 'How many in your congregation?'

'About a dozen people if you include me,' he replied. 'We don't have any children yet, but the building is used for classes for one of the private schools.'

'A dozen in a town of ten thousand hardly seems like an appealing place,' said Chambers, 'maybe you need a new approach. Plant some flowers in the front, maybe a more solid building, like the Catholic one down the hill.'

'It is a disgrace they were allowed to build that,' said the man angrily. 'We tried to stop it we did, Mr. Knox, and the parish.'

'Why is that?' asked Chambers.

'They're all Romanists,' said the man. 'They are Catholics, filthy papist scum.'

'There were a lot of people going to Mass this morning. I saw at least one hundred people milling at the entrance,' replied Chambers. 'They must be doing something right.'

He extended his hand to the man. 'I'm Chambers.'

'You look like him, Henry that is. I'm Bob Maxwell. I work for Mr. Tom and Henrietta Knox.'

He was a short, ugly man, with black hair, a red face, and small beady eyes that seemed to protrude from a small head creased with many wrinkles. He could not look Chambers in the eye but kept surveying the scene as if he were looking for something. He had crumbs still dangling precariously on his stubbled chin. He didn't look well. He seemed off-colour and kept belching violently.

'Good to meet you,' said Chambers. 'What are you eating?'

The man lifted a half-eaten scone. 'I love these,' he exclaimed, still eating. 'They're really sweet and addictive. Mrs. Knox made a whole batch last night for our special occasion. We were pleased to host Rev. Lyons at the homestead. She made all of this lovely food for our luncheon today.'

Chambers surveyed the tables. There were lots of sandwiches, scones, cakes, and fruit, but he didn't see any apples.

'Do you have any apples?' asked Chambers. Maxwell shook his head.

Chambers was about to leave when he saw the visiting priest emerge from the entrance of the church, wearing a black cassock that extended from his head to his toe. He was a tall man, with thick black hair, a very narrow nose, slightly tanned skin, and a thick black beard. Glasses sat on his nose. He looked like quite a strong man.

Maxwell groaned audibly and loudly.

Chambers turned around to face him again. His skin was white as a sheet, drained of blood.

'Sorry,' he said, clutching his abdomen. 'I think I ate one too many of Mrs. Knox's scones. I should've left them alone. Please don't tell her that I ate so many.' Maxwell looked like he was about to vomit. He held his mouth.

'Excuse me,' he said and ran quickly behind the church. Chambers could hear him vomiting loudly, in deep, unnatural groans.

Chambers looked at the food. It had been sitting out in the sun for several hours. It was probably inedible. It always surprised him how the English were so careless with food. He was always careful and rarely drank cold water, unless it flowed from a stream, and even then, not in a time of war. Chambers had an iron constitution, but that was because he had conditioned himself through strict discipline over many years and a good diet. He had adapted to a Chinese diet, one that he missed in the colony of New South Wales where all they seemed to eat was bread, mutton, and a few potatoes. Chambers longed for some long, green, leafy vegetables, a nice clear soup, and a cleansing tea.

'Where's Maxwell?' asked Jed, looking around for him.

'He is just relieving himself,' said Chambers. 'I am sure he will be back soon.'

Jed looked disappointed. 'He has been eating the scones ever since the service began,' complained Jed. 'Those cakes will be the death of him.'

'Let's hope not,' replied Chambers.

'Mr. Knox wants to introduce you to everyone,' said Jed, asking him to come over to a small group of huddled parishioners gathered around the new priest. As soon as Knox saw him, he got everyone's attention.

'Here is Henry's brother, Nathaniel Chambers, all the way from China.' Chambers bowed slightly to everyone and smiled politely.

'Let me introduce you around,' said Knox, beaming, his face smiling from ear to ear. 'Ever since the unfortunate death of my wife, this little gathering has been my rock and my strength.'

Chambers found he could not say anything. He was astounded at the change that had come over Knox. The snarling, hideous bigot had been transformed into a kindly, gentle, polite man, being praised like a saint by all around him. They hung on his every word, and Chambers observed that Knox had them all mesmerized by his new persona, which he obviously kept in the church sacristy, and hung back on the wall when he left. He had become a Christian, suddenly, for a few hours on Sunday morning, enacting a weekly ritual, playing the part of the godly church leader, for all to see, and then, when everyone left, his heart would beat again, and he would stoop over once more, and spit at the world and everyone in it.

Knox was a hypocrite and a good actor. Surely everyone knew that, or maybe they just chose to see what they wanted to see. Jesus would have called him one, but Chambers saw little of Jesus in the Church. It was one of the reasons he never went. Chambers had read the New Testament as a boy and saw quickly that what it said in there and what the Church said and did were completely different. It was not a question of styles or rituals. The church hated God and everything Jesus taught. The church was about power, and the abuse of power, and it was a place where men like Knox thrived. Chambers knew that if Jesus turned up one Sunday morning, the church would crucify him before he had a chance to open his mouth and say: 'Father forgive them.'

The first person he met was Henrietta Knox, the sister-in-law. She was a short, but large woman, in an oversized white dress, whom

Chambers could barely see because of her wide-brimmed hat that obscured her face. She was quite young, in her forties, vivacious, and friendly. She probably already knew that Mary had stayed overnight at Eliza. No doubt behind that smile was the excitement at spreading malicious gossip about Henry's brother and his former fiancé.

Her husband, Thomas Knox stood quietly behind her, with a grey face of sincere resignation, sombre and dour, thin frame, and unusually large eyes that hung from their sockets underneath very thick eyebrows. His hands were those of a farmer, worn and rough and his shoulders were hunched over. Chambers knew a man of hard, solid work when he saw one. If John Knox was the heart, then Thomas was the backbone of the family, and Henrietta the voice.

Knox introduced him to Dr. Smythe, who said that he was the local medical doctor, who said several times that he had trained in Sydney at the Medical School, but he emphasized that he was born in London. Chambers didn't think he looked like much of a doctor, as he was nervous, his hands shook and twitched a lot, but this was the man who attended to Henry after he was allegedly found in the barn. Smythe kept grimacing when he spoke, but he was saying nothing funny, and his eyebrows kept rising as if had something lodged in his eye. He spoke as one trying to keep up an accent, rather than speak naturally and Chambers could not place it. He kept lamenting about the lack of civilized society in Gulgong and how most of his time was spent treating the ailments of the working poor, and prospectors, whom he seemed to hold in disdain, preferring the company of men of his own class.

The good doctor was standing next to another man whom Knox introduced simply as Constable Cooper from the Gulgong Police Force. He mumbled a greeting but kept looking intensely at Chambers, before telling him that he looked a lot like his brother. His handshake almost broke Chamber's fingers. He was wearing a black cloak which made him almost like a priest himself. Knox told Chambers that Cooper was always a busy man having to deal with the Irish Catholics who plagued the town like cockroaches. Cooper didn't say anything. He smiled at Knox and told him that all that mattered to him was the law, regardless of the religion of the man he encountered on the street.

Knox introduced him to a few others, such as Mr. and Mrs. Hall, the Clarkes, the Petersons, and the Phillips, all of whom were farmers. At the end of the many introductions, the priest called out to Knox and asked if he could aid him in the sacristy for the consumption of the elements of the Eucharist, but Rouse stepped in and went in his stead.

Chambers always thought it rather hypocritical of the Church of England to insist upon the prohibition of alcohol on Sundays and yet allow the Eucharist for those who attended the services. He wondered if the priest filled the cup to the brim to partake of as much of the blood of Christ as he was humanly able. He knew, as did everyone, that out of the big towns, few abided by the rules of the church, and that even on a Sunday, the goldfields stopped for nothing, even a day of rest. Even as they spoke, the town of Gulgong was coming alive, and Chambers could even see some children playing near a tent in the distance. The hotels were opening for the day and large crowds were all gathering.

Chambers was polite to all the church folk and after the barrage of questions, and introductions, Henrietta led everyone to the tables laden with food and some tea, leaving him alone with Knox, who was still in a playful mood.

'I want to apologize dear boy about yesterday, 'he began. 'It was rude of me to chastise you with the woman, it really was. Why don't you go and stay with Henrietta and Tom for the remainder of your stay here? I am afraid I do not cook much these days now that my wife is gone and when I do eat, it is usually with my relatives anyway. We would be happy to have you.'

Chambers looked at him. He was playacting but there might have been some truth in what he said. 'I would be happy to,' replied Chambers, 'if it is all right with them.'

'That is settled then,' said Knox happily. 'I know you don't go to church my boy, that much I worked out before when I knew your late brother. I guess it must run in the family, but I am not the one to judge. Our Lord ordered us not to judge, and I am the last to do that.'

He looked around clearly irritated.

'I thought that Johnson might dignify us with his presence to settle this matter of the homestead. I did buy it from Henry a few days before his death for quite a sum of money, which he received. I assumed, quite naturally, that it all went to Mary Kelly. I was astonished when Johnson told me later that the entire estate went to you, but by that stage, he had already written the letter. It was all rather unfortunate. I was still grieving you see, for my beautiful and faithful wife. Johnson would attest to that. I ignored all my personal affairs for several weeks. The question of Eliza was far from my main priority.'

Chambers looked at him carefully, trying to work out if he was lying or not.

Suddenly Rouse called out to Knox and Smythe telling them to come quickly. Chambers went with them into the church. It was a gloomy place, more like a tomb than a church, with thick, rough beams for seats, a dirt floor, tiny windows that rattled in the breeze, and a pulpit and altar made of packing cases. At the front of the church, lying curled up, clutching his stomach, was the visiting priest. He was moaning in agony. The floor was already wet with vomit. The doctor reached him first.

'He was consuming the leftover wine in the chalice when he just fell over in agony,' blurted out Rouse, holding up the empty cup. The doctor took the cup and sniffed it and placed it back on the altar.

'I felt sick this morning,' confessed Knox. 'Quite ill, in fact.'

'Did it involve vomiting?' asked the doctor hastily, leaning down to the priest.

'It involved everything,' said Knox quite embarrassed. 'Fortunately, it was in the early hours of the morning before others were awake. I was staying at Tom and Henrietta's.'

'Who else was there?' asked Rouse. Knox looked at him.

'Well, let me see, Tom and Henrietta, myself, Maxwell, Mr. Lyons, and the Clarkes.'

At this moment, Jed arrived at the church, his face white. He could see the priest lying on the ground, lurching around, crying out in pain, and holding his stomach.

'Maxwell is out the back,' he said to Chambers. 'He is vomiting his heart out. I am concerned for him.'

Chambers ran outside of the church and around the back, where the body of poor Maxwell lay still. Chambers knelt at the side of the dead man and felt his pulse. He saw the look of absolute terror on Maxwell's face, lying in a pool of blood and vomit. He had seen that face before. Maxwell had been poisoned. Chambers assumed naturally that the poison must have been in the scones. He wasn't sure of the type of poison and Maxwell had eaten a lot of scones. This was murder, plain and simple, cunning, but brutal.

By this stage, Jed had arrived. Chambers looked up at him.

'It is in the food Jed, don't let anyone touch anything.'

'Is he dead?'

'Yes, died a few moments ago, his body is still warm.'

'Dead God,' muttered Jed, staggering back, one hand over his mouth and the other taking off his hat. 'He was calling out for his sister. I didn't help him. Dead God, forgive me!'

Jed told him that Smythe had said that it was probably something they ate the night before. He was at the Knox estate looking after the property while his boss was at his brother's. Chambers knew that Smythe was a fool. He should have checked the chalice himself. Smythe did not even know what to look for. Chambers pushed passed him and ran back to the church and bumped into Rouse who had emerged from inside the church with Knox.

'Better not tell anyone that it was Henrietta's cooking last night that did it,' said Knox. 'I am sure the priest is in good hands with the good doctor.'

Rouse nodded. 'It is still quite unpleasant, 'he said. 'He has only been in the town a few days. I doubt very much that he would like to stay on as our priest after today. I am afraid that we must make do with whomever the bishop eventually sends us.'

'I know we don't see eye to eye on many things, Rouse,' said Knox, 'but I hope that the new priest will be better than Blackwell. Wherever that man ended up, I am sure that God was displeased with him.'

'I do not disagree with you,' said Rouse. 'I just would like to know what happened to him.'

Chambers stood in their path. 'Where is the wine in the chalice?' he asked.

'I threw it out,' said Rouse.

Chambers felt and looked disappointed. 'Maxwell is dead,' he said seriously. 'I will stake my reputation on it, but he was poisoned, and it was not last night's dinner, it was administered this morning. It is in the scones.'

Rouse believed him at once, pushing past him. 'Where is he?' he demanded, and Jed took him to where Maxwell lay dead. From the manner of his expression, Knox also believed Chambers was right. Maxwell *had* been poisoned. His face changed and became one of horror and fear. The playful churchman was gone, replaced by the man Chambers had met that morning he stood next to Mary.

'Henrietta, Tom, I must warn them,' he said to himself. Chambers turned and saw everyone milling around the tables eating the food.

Knox ran quickly over to his brother and his sister-in-law who were devouring sandwiches.

'These are simply delicious!' she boasted. 'Simply the best I have made.'

'Stop eating them!' demanded Knox trying to take the food from her mouth. He looked desperate.

'What's the matter, John?' she asked playfully.

'I don't think you should eat them,' he said. 'Maxwell has just died.'

She looked at him and laughed out loud. 'John, you are such a rascal, trying to turn people off my scones and cakes. Maxwell dead? A raging stampede of elephants couldn't stop that man!'

She struck him gently on the shoulder and shoved the rest of the sandwich into her mouth, her long tongue licking her lips, and eating with her mouth open, breathing heavily. She reached for another sandwich and pushed it in her mouth. Knox seemed helpless. He looked at Chambers with a fearful glare. He, the great John Knox, could not budge his sister-in-law. He was terrified of her.

Suddenly, Henrietta stopped eating, her hands fell to her sides, and her mouth opened, food dribbling out to the ground. She made a strange gurgling sound that seemed to echo in his stomach. She vomited up the rest of the sandwich, which splattered all over Knox's face and suit. She turned to her husband, Tom, and tried to speak, reaching out to him. Her eyes rolled back, convulsing violently, and fell to the ground, dead.

Chambers stormed past them all, reaching the first table, still laden with food, and with all his strength, turned it over. Plates smashed and glasses shattered everywhere. As he stepped back, he saw that Rouse had done the same with the second table. The men looked at each other. They both knew what the other was thinking. There was a killer in their midst.

13.   AN UNFORTUNATE ACCIDENT

More was made of the actions of Rouse and Chambers in turning the tables than the fact that Henrietta Knox had dropped dead in front of them. No one shared Chamber's opinion that poison was involved. Bob Maxwell's untimely demise was regarded as the natural consequence of a life of gluttony and alcoholism. Apparently, Henrietta and Tom had indulged his excesses for years, and while Tom were sad that he was dead, no one was surprised. The convulsive death of Mr. Maxwell was put down to drunkenness and a possible heart attack. Maxwell had complained the night before of shortness of breath, a condition he said, he had been plagued with for years. Tom Knox later that day buried Maxwell in an unmarked grave on his estate that afternoon by himself. There was no service, and only Tom mumbled a few words of remembrance.

What upset the tiny church congregation was that all the food was spoilt, and Rouse dared to allege that someone might deign to cause harm to a woman of such high social standing as Mrs. Henrietta Knox. John Knox's supporters all expressed the view that Rouse and this new man Chambers were consumed with jealousy. Rouse behaved badly. It was a scandal, and they would write to the bishop, as they often did anyway, with another complaint.

Mr. and Mrs. Clarke were the first to say that Henrietta had not been well for some time and that they had heard that she was taking medicine. They said that Mrs. Knox was always complaining of a weak heart due to the stressful life she lived in Gulgong, having to deal with all the unseemly poor, and irritable Chinese in the town, as well as the burdens that John Knox brought after the death of his wife. The local doctor, Mr. Smythe concurred. He had been treating Mrs. Knox for a weak heart condition and general ill health. for months, and he was not surprised that she died.

When Chambers challenged the diagnosis, Smythe, whom everyone held in the highest regard, gave him a stern rebuke, and told him that he was a gossip monger to even suggest that someone wanted to kill Mrs. Knox. He told Chambers of the many real health problems of the goldfields of Gulgong, and how he had buried two dozen children over the last twelve months, mostly due to scarlet fever. Influenza and pneumonia took their toll as well, among an assortment of other horrible diseases, most were too difficult to diagnose. Many died from spider or snake bites, and often from untreated wounds. When Chambers protested that it might have been poison, John Knox and Jed Barton seemed interested in his hypothesis, but kept quiet.

Mr. Lyons, the unfortunate priest who volunteered to help the parish for a week or two while on his way back to Sydney, was still inside the church, experiencing intense abdominal pain. Rouse wanted to take him back to Guntawang, but simply moving the priest to a sulky brought about such intense spasms of agony, that the doctor decided to move him down the street to the now vacant church rectory, where Blackwell used to live. Jed Barton, and Mr. and Mrs. Clarke helped the priest into the sulky and took him to the rectory, and Mrs. Clarke made sure he was tucked up in bed before they all returned to the church. When they returned, both Mr. and Mrs. Clarke were showing signs of nausea and Mr. Clarke started vomiting uncontrollably even before the sulky stopped in front of the church. The stench was wretched, and Mr. Clarke could hardly stand. Chambers saw Mr. Clarke vomit up blood.

Rouse and Smyth asked Tom Knox about the meal the night before at the homestead. Tom said it had been a simple meal of mutton, and damper, with some vegetables from the garden. Tom Knox went to his grave distraught that his wife cooked a meal that led to her death. For most of the day the old, hardened Tom Knox nestled his wife's head in his lap, on the ground next to the church, stroking her hair and talking with her, while no one said anything. No one else at the luncheon and service experienced any symptoms of illness due to the luncheon, which caused Smyth to conclude that the evening meal the night before must have been to blame.

Mr. Lyons lay at the rectory for two more days, visited by Dr. Smythe several times who had not the slightest idea what to do, nor could he ascertain the cause. He was more trouble to the priest than anything else. Rouse would visit late on Monday to apologize profusely for the turn of events. He could not convince Lyons to stay longer. He didn't blame him. He said that he wanted to leave the district as soon as he was able. Smythe also visited Mr. and Mrs. Clarke regularly. Their illness grew more serious. Neither could keep any food down and both experienced bouts of frenzied agony. Their son tended to their needs, but Smythe feared the worst. He still clung to his view that this was some stomach ailment brought on by a bad bout of food poisoning, but in reality, he had no idea what was going on.

When he left the Clarkes on Tuesday around noon, he was planning to go to Mudgee to get further advice from other doctors, as he was out of ideas. He was called out to the Happy Valley lead later that afternoon to help a miner who had suffered severe injuries from a collapsed mine shaft the day before. Exhausted, and feeling the onset of nausea himself, he returned by horse to his homestead early that evening on the edge of Gulgong, near the bush, where he lived alone. It had been a hot day. As soon as he dismounted, he was bitten several times by a snake. He managed to reach his medicinal cabinet in his house, but he died in agony on the floor. His twisted body was found a few days later, his face contorted in a horrible grimace.

After the church members of the Gulgong parish tidied up, everyone left, no one offering any comfort to Tom Knox who was still holding his wife. When he saw his brother leave, he got to his feet and yelled at him. The silent, morose pastoralist shed his sombre timidity and burst into anger.

'Our family is cursed, John. First, father, then your wife, and now mine. Why is God punishing us for what father did? We should never have come to this cursed land. I know our father left us with his debts, but all we have found in this land has been misery. Leave here brother, go back to Ireland, while God still gives you breath.'

He looked into his brother's eyes, turned, knelt, and scooped up his dead wife, taking her slowly to his carriage. John Knox said nothing, and he stopped Jed from helping his brother. They watched him leave alone, then they rode off to Crooked River.

Chambers and Rouse were the last to leave the church grounds.

'Knox is here to pay off his father's debts in Ireland?' asked Chambers.

'It seems so,' replied Rouse stroking his beard. 'I have long suspected that.'

Chambers kicked the dirt. 'It could have been the church that killed them,' he proposed. Rouse looked at him disapprovingly.

'You probably need a new church building Rouse. I mean, what an ugly building this is, especially in a gold-rush town. You all have enough money, and how little attention you pay to the house of God. Maybe Henrietta and Maxwell suffered God's wrath?'

'God doesn't work that way,' disagreed Rouse. 'The Lord gives, and the Lord takes away, blessed be the name of the Lord, but he is not out for revenge.'

'Are you sure?' retorted Chambers. 'Two dead today, and three more unwell. That's almost half your congregation. You might not have anyone left by the end of the week.'

Rouse glared at him. 'I cannot believe that someone would callously murder Mrs. Knox. She was a malicious gossip Chambers, but that is hardly deserving of death. Every church has an insatiable gossip. Gulgong had Mrs. Knox. It is why Mrs. Rouse is not here today. We have both been on the receiving end of Henrietta's forked tongue these last few months, ever since I lost my grandfather's title deed for the paddock at Home Rule.'

'What do you mean?' asked Chambers.

'They discovered gold on my property, near Home Rule, and the court demanded I produce the original title deed for the land, which, unfortunately, I could not do immediately, as it had been mislaid. Before the end of the day, hundreds of men had arrived on the paddock and made claims until we found the necessary legal paperwork. But it caused quite a stir, and Mrs. Knox said some unflattering things about Mrs. Rouse.'

'I'm glad it was all resolved by the courts,' said Chambers. 'You are lucky to have them here. But I tell you this, people will kill for anything, given the right motive and opportunity. You see the goodness in people, and their potential to do good. I see the reality, that given the right setting, the best person is capable of the worst things imaginable. In this world, reputation is everything, and if someone is out there trying to besmirch reputation, or destroy public standing, then that person should watch his back. Some words cannot be taken back, and some utterances will always lead to blood.'

'This is not China,' said Rouse. 'This is Australia, and we have the law.'

'But how often is it broken in this town?' asked Chambers. 'Why do you have Joe Mitchell in town, a retired police officer, as well as detectives, constables, and magistrates, if a crime is not expected to occur? I can imagine the magistrate spends most of his time settling petty disputes over mining claims and shafts and red flags, but out there, in the bush, there is no law, no one to see what you do. Out there lurks death, waiting to tempt anyone bold enough to take a life. Take it they will. As for Mrs. Knox, I don't think she was the target. I believe it was John Knox. If she was disliked, he is despised, even by you Mr. Rouse.'

'And you Chambers,' retorted Rouse, clearly irritated, not used to someone with the tone of voice Chambers was using.

'Then we are all suspects,' replied Chambers. He mounted his horse and looked down at Rouse.

'Where are you off to?' inquired Rouse.

'Gulgong,' replied Chambers. 'I need a drink.

14.   EUREKA

Royal Hotel, Gulgong

Chambers rode down Church Hill towards the township of Gulgong. The further he went from the church, the safer he felt. He didn't like churches, even decrepit, shabby ones like the one in Gulgong. For him, they always represented the abuse of power hiding behind the beauty of divine mysteries. Chambers spent most of his nights under the stars, staring up into the vastness of space. Alone, he felt the presence of a divine being more closely than he ever did squashed like sardines next to angry, sweating people, listening to strange ritualistic chants, and talking about a stern, angry God who hated everyone. From time to time, he had joined little gatherings of people who met under trees talking about life and faith, but he felt trapped in the rigid rules of the established church. It reeked of everything his father stood for, the old regime.

The Church of England was a symbol of British power, a reminder that there was only one correct way to worship God and he was a God made in the image of England. It was only when he was fighting and killing the Chinese in the 1840s that he discovered that England had finally begun to reluctantly peel back centuries of laws against the Roman Catholics and Protestants who had refused to bow to the national church. He had met dozens of men like Knox, good 'Christians' on Sunday, but men of the world the rest of the week. Maybe there was something magical about the earth around a church building that would change a man from a sinner into a saint, if only for a few hours, so he might commune with a god angrier than he. If there was a God, Chambers thought, then all this subterfuge would be known to him, so it would be far better to approach God without hiding anything. He wasn't joking when he suggested to Rouse that maybe God was having his revenge on the congregation of Gulgong. The people who had gathered to worship God seemed unconcerned that Mrs. Knox had died, and no one seemed to be bothered that Mr. Maxwell had breathed his last. It was like their lives had no value. Nobody offered their support. No one comforted Tom Knox. They just left him alone, as they were all so busy. What important business were they all rushing off to? It made no sense to him. There was money in this town, a lot of it. He heard that the men who found Adams Lead and Black Lead were pulling out gold by the bucket load in 1871. Yet, the Church of England parish building looked like it was built by paupers and almost no one was welcome. Surely there would be a reckoning for all of this. If there was a God, then surely, he would take notice.

When Chambers arrived in the town of Gulgong, the main action was along Herbert Street which stretched down from the uppermost parts of the town landscape towards the bush, like a long river, meandering down the hill. There were beginnings of other streets, competing for attention, and something resembling a theatre hall, though it looked crude and poorly made. Herbert Street was alive with people. It felt like a busy street in the town of Sydney, not the backwater of Gulgong. There were many hotels, boarding houses, and restaurants to choose from, and not a few brothels located furthest away from the Leads. There was only one shabby Church of England, but more than a dozen Hotels, all full to the brim with patrons on an early Sunday afternoon.

Chambers could see men arguing, men fighting, men gambling, and men drinking. There was a strange-looking man carrying a camera on a tripod, followed by an equally odd-looking woman carrying large, heavy bags. He was leading her like he was on some expedition to the darkest corners of the world. The road was full of horses, men riding, men walking with their horses, horses standing still in front of hotels, and horses laden with goods. A stagecoach raced past, overflowing with people. It pulled up suddenly and everyone poured out. There was talk of a narrow escape from bushrangers. Dust was everywhere. Chambers could see further out to the edge of the town. There were many mining tents where prospectors had set up camp, and beyond that, he could see small mines in operation, as far as the eye could see.

But Chambers had come for a specific purpose. He lied to Rouse about wanting a drink because he did not want anyone to know what he was up to, though he suspected that this ruse would not last more than a day or two before the secret was out. He had indeed received a letter from the Gulgong town solicitor called Mr. Johnson, who had written to him that his brother had bequeathed to him a small farm and its contents. He was surprised that his brother left him anything considering they had been estranged since they were boys, but maybe Henry had no other choice. Maybe time had its own healing quality. What was more surprising was that his brother died so young. He remembered standing in the trading office of his old friend Ross Duncan, in Shanghai, surrounded by papers and books, reading the letter from Johnson, while Ross smoked his large pipe. He remembered Ross' question: 'what was the cause of death?' Johnson's letter only said that Henry died as the result of an unfortunate accident.

That Sunday afternoon, Chambers was full of trepidation. He had come to see a man, a dangerous man, a leader of men, whose charisma resulted in the deaths of many who should never have died. This Chambers found unforgivable, even now all these years later. He had known some of those young men, good men, who threw their lives away for bits of gold and scraps of paper. As for this man Chambers was going to meet in this town in the middle of nowhere, they had been good friends once. Gold had thrown them together and gold tore them apart.

In the end, it was a woman who separated them. Chambers prevailed, and he won that contest, but life has a way of overturning the best-laid plans. He had not seen either the woman he lost or the man he fought with, for almost twenty years. He did not expect to ever hear from him again. He wondered if he would ever recognize him. He doubted that they could ever be friends again, but he came because he needed information, nothing more. Their friendship was dead.

Chambers saw the Royal Hotel and tied up his horse nearby. He walked up the steps and through the front door. It was like a hotel one might find in the town of Sydney or Melbourne, but with more dirt and dust from the road, and a rougher clientele, full of smellier, dirtier, men who had not washed for days, if not weeks. Chambers could sense the eyes of a few men looking in his direction, slightly puzzled, and he knew that he must have reminded them of his late brother. They did not pay attention for long, returning to their liquor and their conversations. In the corner of his eye, he could see a bartender rush quickly through the back door, so he had probably gone to find Chamber's old friend. Chambers sauntered over to the bar, and lent on it, surveying the alcohol on offer, most of it spirits, rum, and alcohol as tough as the men who drank it. There was a time when he drank like a fish, certainly in the days when he knew his old friend who now ran the Royal Hotel.

He also recalled the day he stopped drinking. He was with Frederick Townsend Ward. They had fought hand-to-hand with the fanatical religious troops of the Taiping rebels in early '62. That day, in a village north of Shanghai, stuck behind the wall of a ruined house, Chambers huddled with another foreigner, from Ireland, a little man whose name he had long forgotten. He, like Chambers, loved to drink, and there, in the middle of a fight, took out his flask of whiskey to have a sip. His guard was only down for a moment, enacting a repeated daily ritual, a little sip from the flask. From nowhere, at that very moment, one of the disciples of the false Messiah emerged from the scrub and took aim. The Irishman's blood splattered all over the wall and he fell over, quite dead into Chamber's arms. Maybe it was the death of his friend, or the smell of blood mixed with whiskey, or just the fear that it might happen to him, but Chambers never drank again.

'As I live and breathe!' proclaimed a deep Irish voice behind him.

Chambers turned around surprised.

'My dearest friend!' shouted the man, his arms outstretched, laughing heartily, his eyes full of tears.

Chambers turned to see his old comrade Richard Noble standing there, with a grey beard hanging below a wrinkled face, a bulge hanging over his belt, and red cheeks, most likely the sign of many years of hard liquor. His face was pudgy, and his eyes were red. He embraced Chambers and began to sob. Chambers did not know what to do, so did nothing and let his old friend squeeze him tightly. Richard pulled himself away, tears running down his red cheeks.

'It has been far too long,' he said genuinely, looking him in the eyes. He wiped his right hand on his apron and held it out for Chambers to shake it. Chambers shook Richard's hand firmly. He could feel the roughness of his palm and fingers. He also felt overwhelmed with irrational emotions he could not understand. He pulled the man back and hugged him.

'It is good to see you too Richard,' said Chambers.

He let go of his friend and looked at him. He was now having mixed thoughts about the meeting. Maybe it was not going to be as bad as he thought. Maybe Richard had forgotten all the ill will. Maybe Richard had forgotten about Emma. Chambers looked at Richard. He had not aged well. He was in his late forties but looked like he was well over sixty. He had the appearance of a bitter lifelong bachelor.

'Can I have everyone's attention?' he shouted to the other patrons in the hotel.

'You probably look at this man and wonder if Henry has come back to you. Well, he hasn't. He shot himself at his farm, God rest his poor soul. This is Nate Chambers, his brother, and you should know about him. He is my good friend from the old days, a comrade, a real comrade of all miners everywhere, and all who love freedom from the tyranny of government, a comrade from the barricade, and a friend of Peter Lalor's, a veteran of Eureka.'

There it was. The moment he was dreading. Eureka. The day his life changed forever. He was aghast and horrified that Richard brought it up. It was ancient history. It was all in the past. He had spent two decades trying to forget his role in the whole affair.

'Drinks are on the house!' shouted Richard.

Everyone cheered. A few men came up to Chambers and shook his hand. Richard pulled him away from them and led him to a room behind the bar, closing the door. The room had a table and a few cupboards. He poured two glasses of whiskey. Chambers politely refused.

'I don't drink anymore,' he said.

Richard was astonished. 'What happened to the old Chambers eh?' he mused, pouring the contents of Chamber's glass into his own. He sat down at the table and Chambers sat opposite him. His smile quickly disappeared.

'You are here about the letter. Did you receive it?' he asked. Chambers nodded. He explained how he received the letter from Johnson the solicitor bearing the news of his brother's death, but he also received a second letter with the first from Richard Noble. He had not mentioned this second letter to anyone. It was this letter, or rather short cryptic note, which brought Chambers back to the colony of New South Wales. He was not really concerned about the house, or the horses. That was just a ruse. Richard's note was short:

'Nate, your brother Henry is dead. They say it is suicide, but I doubt it. It was murder. I'm at the Royal Hotel in Gulgong. Do not trust anyone in the colony. This is a bad business, just like in the old days, you never know whom you can trust. Your old friend and comrade, Richard Noble.'

Richard sipped his whiskey.

'I am sorry about Henry,' he began. 'I really thought it was you when he walked into the Royal a few years ago. As soon as he discovered I knew you, he left and never came back. I found out little bits and pieces about him while he was here, but we know Mary Kelly quite well. She's a good Irish woman, God knows we need them here. Her late husband, Thomas, was a strong republican, a good man, but he died in Bathurst, God rest his soul. Mary ran the Shamrock and Thistle with her brother Shamus. It collapsed a while back; badly built I suppose. I heard you had a run-in with her a few days ago.'

'You know about that?' asked Chambers.

'This is a country town, everyone knows everything,' laughed Richard. 'You cannot keep a secret in Gulgong.'

'Except if it is murder,' added Chambers. Richard's smile vanished.

'Indeed,' he said. 'Except murder, which occurs here all the time. Unless someone is shot in full view of a dozen people, it is almost impossible to find the culprit. It is not like Sydney town. There are more police and government agents there than sulkies. It is a different world here. Like the old country. The farmers have the law in their pocket.'

'Men like Knox,' said Chambers. Richard nodded slowly and cautiously.

'And Rouse,' added Richard. 'Though Rouse, to his credit, is more of an aristocrat, and spends most of his time in his kingdom, up at Guntawang. He rarely condescends to the world of mortals, like us.'

'What can you tell me about the death of my brother?' interrupted Chambers, who had come all the way from China to have this conversation.

'Well, that's just it, I don't know much at all. It's what I've been trying to tell you. Unless you see it with your own eyes, it's almost impossible to prove. There has been a lot of gossip about his death though.'

'What do they say?'

'Well, most of it concerns Mary. Some say she was after his money, and the pressure of marriage got too much for him. I traced that story back to the priest, Mr. Blackwell. He said that Mary was always going on about money. I don't believe it though. Blackwell was a pathological liar, among other things. Mary never talked about money to us. Others say that he was killed by the aborigines, or that he had a run-in with one of the Chinese traders.'

'Nothing has changed since Eureka then,' reflected Chambers. 'It is not long before Australians blame everything on the aborigines or the Chinese.'

'The Celestials and the aborigines have their fair share of suffering now. We all do,' replied Richard.

'What about Knox? Did he kill Henry?' asked Chambers.

'Knox is Irish, like me, unlike you, but he is the bastard-kind of Irish, a protestant, his ancestors 'took the soup' probably, converting to Protestantism after the famine. I suspect they left Rome at the first chance of making a bit of money.

'Rouse is your man. He is English, an aristocrat, as I said, much like you, like your brother pretended to be. Knox's father went bankrupt in Ireland. His sons John and Tom have spent most of their life paying off family debts. That is what drives John, a desire to restore his family honour, and their place in high society. I respect that. The English do not like to see the Irish succeed. You know that. My heart tells me that Knox did not kill your brother. I don't believe he wanted to kill your brother. They were, as far as I know, good friends. Knox is Irish. You know what the English are like. They blame everything on the Irish out here.'

'What about Jed Barton?' asked Chambers quickly.

'Well, mused Richard sipping the whiskey. 'That is a different matter entirely. The local gossip is that he killed a man over a bet a few years ago. I don't know if it's true. As I said, you can do anything out here in the country. He works for Knox. He has a good reputation. He likes to drink a lot. His brother works on a large claim with some friends at Happy Valley. Why do you think he is involved?'

'The same night that Henry was shot, Mrs. Knox died, and Millie their maid, vanished,' insisted Chambers.

'I am not sure about that,' replied Richard. 'From what I hear, Millie has gone back to Sydney town to find work, and the local doctor said that poor Mrs. Knox died of a snake bite. I think it is just a coincidence.'

'Nothing in life is a coincidence,' said Chambers seriously.

Richard said nothing and sipped his whiskey. He wanted to change the subject. 'You have somewhere to stay? Why don't you come and stay with us tonight? My wife is out today with her friends in Home Rule, but she will be back this evening.'

Chambers looked at his old friend. He was surprised that he got married, as he swore that he would never marry anyone except his old flame Emma.

'I know what you are thinking Chambers,' said Richard. 'You are surprised that I married after our competition over Emma, all those years ago.' Chambers nodded.

'I was young Nate,' replied Richard. 'I was foolish, selfish, greedy. I think we all were in those days. In fact, I have been married twice. The first lady died of pneumonia in '61 and then out of the blue another woman came into my life the very next year and saved me, if truth be told, literally saved my life. We ran a Hotel in Sydney for a few years before coming up to Gulgong in '70 when they found gold.'

'I am happy for you Richard,' said Chambers.

'How about you?' asked his old friend. 'I heard you married a Celestial.'

Chambers smiled politely. The tone in Richard's voice told him that his old friend had not changed in his prejudice towards the Chinese. It was the same at the Barricade. Chambers knew that those brave foolish men on the barricade fought for freedom, but they also wanted it all for themselves. It was only skin-deep. It never made much sense to Chambers. Surely if freedom is freedom, it was for everyone. He decided to tell Richard the truth.

"I was married to a local girl in a small village deep in the mountains in China, but she died last year.'

'I am truly sorry my old friend,' said Richard sincerely. 'I truly am sorry. Was it from illness?'

'No, she was murdered by a local warlord during an attack on our village. We fought on the same side during the Taiping war, and at one point we were even friends, but he decided to go and make a name for himself, which he certainly did.'

'Which war?' asked Richard. 'We don't get much news here about China.'

'The war against the Taiping,' replied Chambers.

'I thought that was over years ago,' shot back Richard.

'Some wars are never over,' said Chambers, more to himself. 'And some should never have been fought.'

Richard knew he was talking about the Eureka Stockade. Chambers had always believed that it was a tragic mistake, but over twenty years, reality had become a myth and a legend, catapulting some of its heroes into fame and fortune, while the names of the dead were long forgotten. The reality was always more painful than sentiment, no painting or poem captures the fear of the first volley or the sound of shells, or the mumbled prayers of a man facing certain death. Chambers had not forgotten them. He added their names to all the others who died next to him. He lived, while they died. His great cloud of witnesses. He owed them his life.

Richard had gone to pour himself another whiskey when the door opened. A strange man stood there, with long wavy blonde hair and a bleached face, wearing a black cape, and looking like a cross between a priest, an undertaker, and a magician. A young, vivacious, and fresh-faced girl was behind him, with wide, smiling eyes.

'Ah, there you are, hidden away in here,' said the man. Turning to the woman next to him, he blurted out 'I told you he would be in here drinking, didn't I?'

The woman nodded furiously with a smile. 'With whiskey no less,' she added.

'We have just been in Home Rule,' said the man cheerfully. 'What a delightful little place.'

'Elsbeth and I need to work on the photo plates,' he said with a devious smile. 'Emma's invited us to dinner tonight at this divine establishment. It was kind of her. Maybe we will take a photo of you both.'

He left as dramatically as he arrived. 'Come, my beauty!' he announced to the woman next to him.

He bowed, and they both went into the hotel.

Emma.

Chambers looked at his old friend Richard Noble who turned his eyes away nervously and poured himself another drink. His old friend had married Emma and that explained everything.

15.   EMMA

Chambers had climbed aboard the British navy juggernaut, the Nemesis in 1841 and fought the Chinese navy. He had served under the British flag in what became known as the First and Second Opium Wars. He had fought alongside Frederick Townsend Ward until he was mortally wounded, and then General Charles Gordon as part of the Ever-Victorious Army, a foreign militia that supported the Chinese government against the false Messiah who had set himself up as the brother of Jesus. Chambers had bled and killed in countless battles, fought in four wars, and seen unspeakable horror and death. He was one of the most experienced and decorated foreign soldiers in China, with no small amount of reputation and fame. But sitting at that small table in the back of the Royal Hotel in Gulgong, he felt trepidation like he had never felt before. He looked up at Richard.

His old friend nodded. 'We found each other quite by accident in Sydney. My wife had died, and her husband had also died.'

He sat down at the table. 'We both had children at that time. It made sense to us that we got married. After all, I still loved her, even though I married someone else soon after the barricade was stormed. You see, I thought that she had married you.'

'There is no need to apologize,' said Chambers reluctantly. 'It was a reasonable assumption given what was said, and what was done.' He looked away up to the ceiling and surveyed the room. It was bare and worn. Thick beams ran up and down the walls, hewed from gum trees.

'There is no need to apologize,' he repeated. 'Though I have every reason to.'

'Would you like that drink now?' asked Richard. Chambers still refused.

'You've changed a lot since 1854,' concluded Richard. 'The old Chambers would never turn aside a whiskey, nor even a nasty one made in a home distillery. The last time I saw you was when you helped Peter Lalor escape from the police.'

Chambers nodded and thought back to those days, those painful, awful days, when he left the woman he loved, to return to China.

'After the stockade, I laid low for a while and returned to Melbourne where I met up again with Emma. It was there I received word from China that my father was desperately ill and near death. Emma would not go with me to China, so I went home to help my father, with every intention of returning as soon as possible. I didn't expect to be long. From the tone of the letter, I assumed my father would have died before I arrived in Shanghai, but when I did, I discovered he was still alive, so I stayed. I wrote to Emma explaining the situation and never heard from her again. I wrote a few more times, but I heard nothing. That was, if I remember, early 1855. We were soon at war with China again, and so I made the decision to stay. I hadn't heard from you until you sent me word that Henry was dead.'

'Richard was responsible for the letter, not me,' said a tall, sophisticated woman who walked into the back room. She was wearing a long grey dress and boots.

It was Emma.

'I told him not to write it. Imagine our shock when your brother turned up in Gulgong. We thought it was you, then we were grateful it was not.'

'I asked him to stay for dinner,' said Richard. His wife looked at him disapprovingly. She did not look at Chambers at all, preferring to stay standing behind her husband.

'How did you know where to look?' asked Chambers.

Richard told him that Henry had mentioned that his brother was living in Shanghai and that he was famous.

'Famous?' scoffed Emma. 'The word of Henry Chambers was hardly worth much, and you only have Richard's opinion that he was murdered. It all seemed quite straightforward to me. He was going to do what men in your family always do, and that is to leave without a word, and his guilt made him do what he should have done a long time ago.'

'Are you saying that he was going to leave Mary?' asked Chambers, disbelievingly. 'But they were just about to marry.'

'So were we,' retorted Emma sharply, glaring at him. 'You managed to escape all the way to China, and then you blamed it on your father's illness when you should have been in Melbourne with me.'

'I am not going to argue with you, or Richard about the past,' said

Chambers. 'I am here to find my brother's killers and bring them to justice.'

'So, you are not here to kill them?' asked Richard, quite surprised, looking up at his wife. 'I assumed you wanted revenge. The old Chambers would not have hesitated.'

'You are right, I was a lot angrier when I was younger. Everything was straightforward, but war has a way of changing the way you see the world. But even in the old days, I held to the law. You have never understood me,' replied Chambers. 'I believe in the law, even in China. I don't even carry a gun anymore. I believe in true justice, not murder.'

Emma looked at him intently. 'You are telling us the truth aren't you,' she observed, quite surprised.

'Of course, I am telling you the truth. I abhor needless violence and I want to see justice done.'

'Then you will not see it served in the case of Henry,' said Richard. 'I told you how it works out here. There is no law, except if you are part of the aristocracy. They own the police and the courts. There is no justice for the ordinary man.'

'Surely you don't believe that?' retorted Chambers. 'What happened to all that talk of freedom and equality, and building a better world?'

'Freedom doesn't provide food for dinner,' said Emma. 'There are only so many fine speeches that Richard could give. Not all of us are like the great Peter Lalor.'

'Aha!' shouted a voice in the doorway. 'Did I hear someone mention Peter Lalor?' proclaimed the strangely dressed man who let slip Emma's name. He looked quite dishevelled and was out of breath.

'I was just looking for a bottle of whiskey,' he said to Richard eagerly, but when he realized the person speaking was Emma Noble, he became very polite and reserved again.

'Elsbeth and I are busy processing those photo plates,' said the man quite seriously to Emma.

'I will get you a bottle,' she said and left with the man.

'Who is that?' asked Chambers.

'Merlin,' replied Richard pouring himself a long whiskey.

'Merlin?' asked Chambers incredulously. 'Like Merlin the magician? You must be joking?'

Richard laughed. 'He is a photographer. He has been in Gulgong for a while taking photos of life on the goldfields. He has quite the reputation.'

'I am sure he does,' mused Chambers, thinking of the woman.

'Oh no, she is just one of his assistants. She is a local girl. She helps with the plates, and she is a fine girl,' said Richard. Chambers nodded.

'I am sure she is a fine girl,' replied Chambers politely.

'His full name is Henry Beaufoy Merlin, and he is a bit eccentric, I grant you that.'

'Is he joining us for dinner as well?' asked Chambers. Richard said that he and Elsbeth were staying at rooms in the Hotel and would be at dinner with Emma, her oldest son, David, and Richard's eldest, Gregory, both of whom worked on claims at Home Rule, if they returned in time.

Richard showed him to his room at the back of the Hotel, a tiny, modest affair with a bed, a bedside table, and a mirror. There was a small window. Chambers collapsed onto the bed as soon as Richard left, leaving his boots on, dangling over the edge. He closed his eyes and drifted off to sleep.

He woke with a start, his mouth dry. He rubbed his eyes and breathed deeply. His head was thumping, with a pain across the forehead. He had the nightmare again, the recurring dream, which prevented him from sleeping well. He stood up and saw that someone had placed a wash basin, a jug, and a towel on the bedside table. He washed his face. After he dried it with a towel, he looked at himself in the mirror. How did he come to be here?

When he first arrived, there was such clarity. He knew what he needed to do, and then when he found the locket, he assumed it would be easy to find Millie buried somewhere on the property, and the answer to the riddles of the night his brother died. But there was more to this story than he originally thought. There was Mary, Henry's fiancé, who lived in fear of violent men in her life, including possibly Henry, who was bitter and full of regret. The Chambers were known to be men of drink, lovers of hard liquor, which was another reason Chambers gave up drinking. He did not want to become like his father or end up like his brother. He remembered the whites of Mary's knuckles on the veranda, a woman standing in absolute fear. How many times did that fear find a home in Mary's heart when she was being courted by Henry?

There was Biddy, the young, strong aboriginal woman, who was not ruffled by the sandstorm and yet whose life had been marked by pain. All her people had been massacred and poisoned by the descendants of those living in Home Rule, Gulgong, Mudgee, and Bathurst. The men who did the killing were probably still alive. Why did she touch his cheek the way she did? What did that mean? Were Henry and Biddy close? How could she live in a town where people had murdered her family? Did vengeance mean nothing to her?

Chambers chuckled to himself. It would not be the case in China. Vengeance was commonplace. It was the lifeblood of the people. He had seen entire villages wiped out by the vengeful Taiping, and entire villages destroyed by the government. Surely, such a reality was true here as well, or the land would be forever cursed. Justice needed to be served. Here, the squatters and landed aristocracy stole the land, and murdered its people, and then went to their churches on Sunday to thank God for his many blessings. But blood is blood. It needs atoning. It cannot be simply forgiven. Someone needs to die.

Then there was Knox. Chambers knew there was something dark about the man the moment he heard his name. Knox, the hypocrite. Chambers had met so many of them in China, and it taught him that religion was simply a shirt someone wore on Sunday morning, only to be taken off as soon as the service was over. He knew all about the rituals and rules of the church, but far more about the dark recesses of the heart. Almost everyone felt comfortable gossiping about Jed, but no one dared raise an objection against John Knox. He was beyond criticism. It was the same everywhere. Membership in the Church of England gave people a strange immunity.

Chambers then thought about what Richard had said: nothing is really hidden out here in the country. It is almost impossible to keep a secret. If that were true, then the identity of his brother's killer was not beyond his grasp. Someone knew something, and he needed to get to that truth, even if he had to rip it from their clenched fist. Chambers took out the locket again and looked at it carefully in front of the mirror. He held in his hand the only clue he had, something real and tangible. It had been torn off the wearer, for the chain was broken. Henry was outside that night. He would not have shot himself. After all, he was going to be married.

If nothing else had happened, then Chambers would settle for some resolution to his brother's death. But at the Church of England service, he saw something he did not expect to see at work in the staid, boring, uneventful colony of New South Wales. Someone had put poison in the food at the luncheon and as a result, two people died, and others became ill. They even managed to poison the visiting priest who didn't even live in Gulgong. He saw the surprised faces of Rouse and Knox. They knew it was poison. But who was the target – Knox or Rouse?

Chambers knew he had a problem. If it was poison, then there were few options. The killer lacked expertise because those affected had nothing in common except their presence at the church service. Henrietta and Maxwell were not the intended target. Why would they be? A wife and a servant, a priest, and a few other unimportant people in the town of Gulgong?

Chambers stopped himself and put the locket back in his pocket. He changed his mind. He was wrong, he had to be. If the killer lacked expertise, then something else would have been evident, and that would have been a taste of poison. Good poisons rarely came without a taste, and they needed to be hidden by some other taste to camouflage the flavour. No one mentioned that the food tasted strange or that something was wrong. Everyone was eating the food quite happily and then Henrietta suddenly keeled over and died. Maxwell had a stomach-ache and died in his vomit. If poison was used then it was good poison, well made, even bottled, perhaps brought to Gulgong, rather than created in someone's kitchen, though that was still quite possible. Maybe a store like William Fung stocked various kinds of poisons or even the elements that constituted poisons.

He decided that he would go to Home Rule the next day and ask William. If the poison was bottled, then anyone could have administered it and the variable effects of the poison could be attributed to this.

"Still vain, I see,' said Emma, who was standing in the doorway, seeing Chambers staring at himself in the mirror.

'No,' replied Chambers, 'I was just thinking about today.'

'Shocked at seeing me again?' she asked seriously. 'All that guilt coming back, is it?'

'No, I mean that was a surprise, I grant you that, but no, I was reflecting on the deaths of Henrietta Knox and the station manager Maxwell this morning at the Gulgong church service.'

'Yes,' Emma replied sombrely. 'It is sad that God took that woman far too soon.'

'God had nothing to do with it,' shot back Chambers.

'Don't tell me you think she was poisoned or something?' laughed Emma, 'Richard says that you have changed, but you haven't. You are always looking for trouble and trouble finds you. Why can't you just let things go? They're not your responsibility. Just sell your brother's farm and go back to China!'

'Henry sold the farm,' retorted Chambers. 'A few days before his death. The money is gone, so where is it and who took it? And where is Blackwell, the one who was the last to see him alive? Where is Millie? What happened to her? What happened to Biddy's brother? Where is he? All these missing people, and all these convenient excuses to cover up all the unanswered questions, questions that people in this town refuse to answer.

'No, I've changed Emma. I'm not the same man who left you for China all those years ago. I am sorry I never came back for you, but I had my duty, duty to my father, duty to my country, and duty to the Crown. You care for no one except yourself and maybe you can afford to do that, but I cannot. I appreciate your husband's offer, but I will now leave for Home Rule.'

'You want to see Mary again?' taunted Emma.

'What?' asked Chambers, surprised.

'Don't play games with me. She spent the night with you at Henry's place. We all know about that. Jed told Henrietta. It didn't take you both long. A fine pair you are, both of you. The whole town knows about you spending the night together. It was the last thing the poor woman said to me. You have not been here a week, and already you are the centre of gossip.'

'You care about appearances in this cesspool?' exclaimed Chambers, 'This backwater, this stagnant pool? When the gold dries up, it will be just a small town if that, and all that will remain will be memories. But it will be famous for nothing and nobody, but it will not stop you. You will simply make it up, and the real history will fade into the air because when the time came to help Mary and help me, you did nothing. I know you hate me, and you always will, but do not hate Mary. If you have anything left of the goodness of the woman I once knew and loved, then help her, if you refuse to help me.'

Chambers pushed past her, walked down the wooden corridor, and then out into the hotel, which was full of miners coming in from their diggings. He wanted to get as far from Gulgong as possible.

16.   MERLIN

Herbert Street, Gulgong

Chambers was walking so fast out of the Royal, he ran into a young woman as she was walking up the stairs into the hotel. They collided at the entrance, their bodies intertwining, and their faces almost touching. Chambers quickly apologized to her, but she was quite elated about the experience and refused to stand aside, trying to engage him in conversation.

'I see that you have met my Elsbeth,' said Merlin, who was a few steps behind her, walking across the dusty road of the main street of Gulgong.

'I'm honoured to meet you,' said the girl, politely curtsying, with a beaming smile. Chambers bowed in return.

'Pleased to meet you too,' he said quickly and pushed past her. He wanted to get to Henry's farm before dusk fell. Already the sun was hurrying toward the horizon, and he had no intention of staying in Gulgong overnight.

'I thought you were staying with us this evening,' said Merlin, following Chambers who had reached his horse. 'I was so looking forward to your conversation, and so was Elsbeth, whom you have met so unceremoniously in the doorway.'

'I'm sorry to disappoint you,' said Chambers, untying the rope. Merlin reached forward and held onto the rope so that he could not finish untying the knot.

'I know you think little of me, most do,' said Merlin. 'But allow me the opportunity of proving you wrong.'

Chambers looked up at him. Merlin released his hand.

'I do not think little of you,' said Chambers, turning to Merlin, who looked like the ancient magician of Arthurian lore. He had a thin, tightly trimmed moustache, small, beady eyes, a gaunt face, and neat hair. He had painted his face and wore faint lipstick, from what

Chambers could discern and he wore the suit with disdain as if he preferred the cloak and magician's hat. But there was something about this Merlin, that Chambers found familiar, and yet something he did not expect to see in Gulgong of all places.

Merlin tightened his hold on Chambers and whispered into his ear.

'She is not mine you see. She is quite free to choose anyone she desires, and she certainly has her eye on you. I know what attracts her to you. I feel the attraction too. It is obvious to me. We are not lovers, Elsbeth and I, though most people think that we are, it serves our purposes, and people let us do what we need to do, they think we are strange and eccentric, but I have captured them at their most intimate and most vulnerable, and they did not bat an eyelid.

'The things people do and say when they do not see you at all. The things you can do when people are not looking. The mischief you can make. We all wear masks Chambers. We all hide from each other. I see this in you too, you are Emma's long-lost lover, Henry's brother, the bearer of the face of a dead man, but they do not know who or what you are. I do. I see you in my dreams, when I lie back and contemplate the vast eternity of space, men like you, who hide in the shadows of the legends of others, long forgotten, but key players in history. Elsbeth shuddered when I mentioned your name. Maybe she saw you in one of her dreams, or nightmares, of fire, and death.'

'Who am I then? asked Chambers, his curiosity piqued.

'Well, if you don't know dear boy,' said Merlin. 'Then we're all in a lot of trouble.'

He grinned broadly.

Chambers knew Merlin was not himself.

The magician called Elsbeth.

'Elsbeth, the tripod and camera, and a bottle of whiskey!' he turned and danced on the spot, waving his hands up in the air. He was about to put his arm in Chamber's so he could swirl him around as well but stopped and apologized.

'It would be so delightful to hear more of your exploits in the Orient dear boy,' he said. 'And yes, it is indeed opium that you smell on me. We have a little den by the river where we smoke, or I am sure it is the river, or somewhere near here. Elsbeth knows how to get the stuff. It comes and goes, and now, I must bid you farewell!'

Merlin bowed deeply and took the tripod Elsbeth was carrying. She kept a tight rein over the liquor. She looked Chambers up and down and smiled.

'I very much enjoyed bumping into you just now,' she said. 'We should do it again sometime.'

He smiled and bowed slightly. The magician and his assistant left. Chambers sighed. He was in some kind of purgatory, with magicians and sirens, ghosts and memories, enemies and friends, all dancing around him. Chambers caught a familiar face in the corner of his eye. It was Jed walking past. He called out to him. The man walked over, and Chambers realized immediately that it was not Jed, but someone who looked like him.

'I'm Pete Barton,' said the man. 'I'm Jed. I do look like him a bit I suppose, but you certainly look a lot like Henry.'

'Did you know him?'

Pete laughed. 'I sure did. We were good mates.'

'Did he shoot himself?' asked Chambers.

'That's what they say,' replied Peter.

'But you don't believe it,' inquired Chambers. Peter shrugged his shoulders. He said that the doctor pronounced him dead from suicide and so did Blackwell, who was now missing, though he didn't trust the priest because he worked for the squatters and had nothing to do with the miners or the town of Gulgong. Chambers produced the locket he found at his brother's place and asked Peter about it. The miner looked at it closely and told Chambers that he thought it was a beautiful thing to behold, but he did not remember Henry having it in his possession. Peter scratched his head and then saw someone walking across the road behind them.

He called out to him, and the man waved, walking over. He was well dressed in a suit and hat, quite out of place in a town like Gulgong. Pete introduced him as Mr. Robinson, the town jeweller. His eyes lit up when Chambers produced the locket and let him examine it. Robinson took off his glasses and put the locket up to his eyes.

'It sure is beautiful,' he said. 'A little tarnished from exposure to the elements, sadly, judging by the scratches here, but quite beautiful.' He opened it and seeing nothing, closed it shut. He looked at Chambers.

'This is not the kind of possession a woman leaves lying around. This is a precious thing, something a woman is likely to have near her or on her constantly, and not something she would be likely to forget.' He kept examining it.

'Chambers found it at Henry's place,' said Pete. Robinson looked up.

'You're the brother no doubt, from your appearance,' said Robinson. 'Well, it is not Mary Kelly's.'

'Why would you say that?' asked Chambers. 'Did you know her?'

Both men laughed.

'I do know her, but she doesn't wear jewellery of any sort, though I have tried to sell her necklaces and lockets over the years.'

'Why is that?'

'I don't know,' said Robinson, adjusting his hat. 'Everyone is different. Maybe it gets in the way when she is working, maybe she just doesn't like them. I don't know.'

'Have you seen the locket before?' asked Chambers. Robinson turned it over and looked intently at it.

'I don't believe so,' he said. 'Though it is familiar. I have sold all kinds the last two years to various people.'

Chambers resigned himself to reality. If anyone knew about the locket in Gulgong, it would be this fellow Robinson. He was back where he started, a series of speculative assumptions about the night his brother died. He had the locket and assumed it was Millie's and that could place her on Henry's farm that night, but now it seemed it was just a lost piece of jewellery tossed aside and could have belonged to anyone. The priest, Mr. Blackwell was missing, and so Chambers could not speak with him, and his brother's journal was gone. Tomorrow, he would meet Johnson and Knox and probably discover that the sale of the property was made, but if so, where was the money? That too was probably long gone. As Richard had said a few hours before, it was almost impossible to prove a crime unless one saw it occurring. Henry's death was ruled accidental and at some point, he would have to accept that. In a way, he was relieved.

Robinson could see Chambers was disappointed. He looked at Pete.

'Henry was a good man wasn't he Pete?' Pete nodded. 'We all have our crosses to bear. I know he struggled with life; we all did. But he was a good man and Mary would have seen him right.' He looked at Chambers.

'Listen, Mister,' said Robinson. 'I tell you what I will do. I will check with my assistant if he's seen the locket. He does a lot of the work when I am in Home Rule and Mudgee. We have a detailed inventory. If this locket has passed through any of our offices, then we will be able to check it. Do you mind if I take the locket and ask? He is at

Home Rule today visiting his brother.'

Chambers was reluctant to let him have it, but he didn't have anything else to go on, so he agreed to let him take it. Robinson said his goodbye and scurried off across the busy street, passing two stagecoaches.

'Do you want a drink' asked Pete. 'You look like you need one,' Chambers said that it would be good to talk to someone who knew his brother and that Pete could do the drinking. He agreed and said that was a good deal so long as Chambers was paying. Pete suggested the Royal.

Pete Barton was quite a different man from his brother. They shared the same name, and the same looks, but Pete was a miner and had been for some time. Chambers could tell that from his hands, and his face. It had seen a lot of knocks, and he carried lots of wrinkles from long exposure to the sun. His skin was like leather. He had a hardened appearance, but it wasn't one of character, but lifestyle. Pete's eyes shone brightly, and his whole demeanour was one of expectation. He would not stop talking about gold, the diggings, prospecting, and Happy Valley, the latest gold lead on the Gulgong goldfields. He arrived soon after Tom Saunders discovered gold near the Rouse estate at Red Hill in 1870. He had been working in Mudgee for many years in various trades.

Chambers could see that Pete lived for gold, and he had come into some recently. He lived on the outskirts of town with his wife and young son. In this, he was different from most of the men who had come to mine in Gulgong. He was putting down roots. He was doing well. He was trying to play a role in what was Gulgong society, even though he knew that he was on the margins. He fully admitted to Chambers that he had been a violent man in his younger days. He told Chambers that a good woman changed his life, and she convinced him to settle down and start a business. He was only working at Happy Valley to make enough money to open a store in Gulgong, probably trading timber or something like that.

Chambers asked about Jed, but his brother looked at him warily and was reluctant to say much about him, except that Jed took a job at the Knox estate as the station manager against his advice. Knox had a bad reputation. There were stories about how he made his money, none of them good. Knox's wife was a good woman though, and Pete was saddened to hear of her death from the snake bite, though he was suspicious about that as Mrs. Knox was a cautious and careful woman and it seemed unlikely that she would have been bitten by a snake. But Peter admitted that snake bites had taken quite a few prospectors in the country and Gulgong and that it was not uncommon to be caught unawares.

Jed had told him that Millie Thorpe had returned to Sydney after Mrs. Knox died and that he heard the shot at Henry's farm the night he died. He was with the cattle on the Knox estate. Pete said that Jed went to Henry's farm early the next morning to have a look because he was suspicious. He found Henry dead with a bullet in his head, lying under a blanket in the barn, and the priest, Mr. Blackwell, getting ready to leave. Blackwell told him that he had been discussing the wedding with Henry and that he began to spiral into one of his depressive episodes, from which he found it difficult to escape. The two men wrestled with the doubts and the despair and Blackwell thought that Henry had overcome the darkness. But, sadly, he had not. He went out to his barn and killed himself.

Chambers asked about Mary's brother Shamus and how he was murdered the next day in Gulgong. Pete didn't know much about it. He heard from old Bert Palmer, the hobo drifter and prospector, that Shamus and Lee Peng had been arguing the day before about something and that it must have been the Celestial who murdered him. A few others in town witnessed the argument and that was enough to convince Cooper, the constable from Gulgong to arrest him. He heard that the Celestial tried to run, but he was accidentally struck down by a stagecoach that was racing through the town. Pete didn't care much for Lee Peng. He was a Celestial, and he was glad that there was one fewer in town. He waxed lyrically about how Australia was not the home of Celestials and that they were nothing but trouble.

Chambers had heard it all before. He heard it on the lips of Richard Noble and the others at Eureka, when they were pretending to talk about freedom, and he heard it in country Victoria in 1861 when the miners rose against the Chinese. It was the same old thing, the tired cliches, the weary diatribes against China, the sentimental proclamations about Australian identity, which was entirely white, with no room for shades of any kind, not even the first people who trod the land.

But Chambers knew that reality was never black or white. The world moved in the shades but more often in the shadows. It was in the dark when the true business of life was done, the darkness of night, but also the dark recesses of the human heart. It didn't take long for Pete to stop talking rationally, and he began to spit out the old phrases he had heard thousands of times before, of prejudice, then loathing, and then bitter hatred. By then, Pete had already drunk himself catatonic, and Chambers was quite weary of the conversation.

It was then he felt the hands of a woman around his waist, trying to tickle him. He held her hands and pulled her around. It was Elsbeth, with Merlin behind her.

'Have you been drinking all day?' asked Elsbeth. 'I like a man who can take his liquor and still stand up straight, not like Pete here, who is teetering and tottering and slobbering!'

'Come here, my good man,' said Merlin to Pete Barton, taking him to a nearby table. 'I am sure Mrs. Barton will be here to collect you at some stage.' He looked back at Chambers.

'The night is young my dear Chambers,' he proclaimed. 'The stars tonight are beautiful, have you seen them? Elsbeth and I have been out on the town, looking up into the sky and drinking something, what was it dear, whiskey, rum?'

'It was whiskey Merlin,' said Elsbeth smiling. Merlin was still holding his tripod and was burdened down by several bags.

'I will put these in my room and be back to join all these delightful people,' he said, stumbling out the back door. Chambers turned to Elsbeth, who sat down next to him and smiled.

'What is your story Elsbeth?' he asked.

She laughed. 'My story?'

'Are you and Merlin together?' he asked.

'Are you interested if we were not?' she asked.

'I'm curious,' said Chambers. 'Everyone assumes you are together, and you seem quite happy to play along, but I suspect that you are very much in charge of your life and of Merlin.'

She laughed and looked at him.

'I am discovered,' she said quietly. 'I do play the game, yes, and they all think that we have something together, but you see Chambers, Henry Beaufoy Merlin is a brilliant man. He is intelligent, and he is very much a success, and I want to learn from him as much as I can, and that isn't much these days, as a woman. As you know, we have our well-defined roles to play in life, dutiful wife, happy wife, and docile wife. Take Pete here. He comes to drink every night, and then goes home drunk, beats his wife, terrifies his children, and then goes to Happy Valley in the morning, a pillar of the community. Pete is a picture of the life all women face these days.'

'And my brother?'

Elsbeth's smile disappeared, and she became serious. 'Sometimes we don't need to know everything about our family,' she said quietly and respectfully.

'Did my brother Henry raise a hand against Mary?' asked Chambers.

Elsbeth placed her hand on Chamber's hand which was resting on the bar and looked into his eyes.

'I came here after your brother died, but I have spoken with Mary, and I must be honest with you, there are some women out here, in this violent place, who want protection, at whatever cost. Mary wanted that protection, and yes, it came at a cost. I have seen that look in the eyes of so many women out here Chambers. Yes, your brother beat her, I am sure it was when he was drunk, but yes, violence was part of her life, even with Henry.'

Chambers looked over to Richard, who had been serving drinks at the bar. He had overheard the whole conversation with Pete Barton.

'Is this true' he asked Richard.

His old friend frowned. He nodded several times and went to serve a customer.

'I assumed as much,' admitted Chambers. Elsbeth released her grip. 'It is more common out here than you would think. But being here with Merlin is worth the risk,' she said.

'And if you get in trouble, who is there to protect you?' asked Chambers.

She looked at him and smiled.

'Knife or gun?' he asked.

Elsbeth laughed. 'Why not both?' she replied.

'Why not indeed,' said Chambers smiling for the first time that night.

'I heard you don't drink,' she said. 'I have not seen a weapon of any kind. It is kind of strange for a former soldier not to carry a gun.'

Chambers smiled. 'There are many ways to kill a man that does not require a weapon,' he said cryptically.

'Maybe you can give me some hints later,' she said, smiling. 'Here comes Merlin, right on cue.'

'Here are my two darlings,' he said loudly, calling out to Richard.

'Some whiskey and a table my good man for this veteran of the stockade, I would love to hear your stories you know. I have heard a lot from Richard, but he wasn't at the stockade that day, so he would not know what really happened – the smoke, the volley fire from the troopers, the cries of the dead and dying, the calls for freedom, and the triumph of the human spirit.'

Elsbeth could see that memories of Eureka were painful for Chambers and that he had no intention of talking about it, so she turned the conversation away from the topic of photography. They all sat at a table near the back of the Hotel. They were joined by Richard from time to time serving drinks and eventually Emma, who sat furthest from Chambers and avoided eye contact. Elsbeth could sense the tension, but Merlin was oblivious to everything, lost in his world of shutters, tripods, photographs, exhibitions, and fame. Richard wanted to simply keep the peace and hoped that Chambers would leave as soon as possible so life could go back to normal.

Chambers, however, kept thinking of the locket and whether Robinson would find out something about the owner, the wearer, and how it ended up in the paddock at his brother's farm. At some point during the evening, Pete Barton stood up and stumbled out of the Hotel into the night.

17.   GHOSTS OF THE PAST

Royal Hotel, Gulgong

'Tell me about China,' said Emma. 'What is it like, and why is it better than Australia?'

The question brought the pleasantries of the evening to an end. For at least an hour, everyone had been enraptured by Merlin's discussions about his photographic exhibitions around Australia, and Elsbeth's reflections on the latest fashions and customs of people in Sydney, but the conversation had neatly avoided the two topics Chambers did not want to discuss – Eureka and China. He felt the eyes of everyone looking at him.

'It is a beautiful country,' he said finally. 'It is quite unlike anything on God's earth. It is not more beautiful than the landscape here. It is different. There are more mountains, more rivers, more water, and greener forests. There are monkeys, and other wild animals, little villages deep in the mountains, covered in mist, hardly visible, and often forgotten.'

'Is that where you went to hide with your Chinese wife?' asked Emma abruptly. Chambers did not show any sign of offense, but he answered her question calmly.

'I lived in one such village for a short while yes, with my wife, Mei, a young woman whose husband had been killed in the war.'

'What war?' asked Emma, laughing. 'We didn't hear of any war in China.'

Merlin leaned over the table and looked in her direction.

'I assume Chambers is speaking of the Taiping Rebellion, Mrs. Noble,' he replied.

Emma looked dismissively at him. 'That was over years ago,' she scoffed. 'The only thing I remember about that was General Charles Gordon, teaching those Celestials how to fight, after all, what do they know?'

Chambers sighed audibly. 'You are right Emma,' he replied. 'The war against the Taiping was over years ago, but it has taken many years to finally quell the rebellion in most of the provinces. The Christian rebellion, such as it was, was only one of many threats to the Chinese. There have been rebellions in the West from some of the followers of Mohammad as well. It has been a nation in a constant state of war for almost two decades. There is not a family in all of China that has not been affected, who has not lost someone they loved.'

'Such a barbaric people!' exclaimed Emma. 'It hardly surprises me at all that they have been killing each other. We tried to give them civilization, but they have no interest in it. We gave them proper clothes to wear and a proper religion, and all the marks of civilized people, but look what they do, they don't even look like us. I mean, look at Mr. Fung walking around Home Rule like the proper gentleman, he looks ridiculous.'

Richard and Emma roared with laughter.

'The Chinese people have an ancient civilization,' countered Merlin, 'many thousands of years longer than our own. They had cities, poetry, art, and culture when our ancestors were running around naked in England and Ireland.'

'Maybe so,' retorted Richard. 'But look where it got them. They were no match for us or our civilization. Britain, for all its faults, is the empire of the world and is the supreme power. The Chinese are languishing in opium, ancient traditions, and ineffectual leadership.'

'I am sure that Chambers would agree with much of what you say,' said Merlin. 'But surely the advantage came with more powerful weapons, rather than any other claim to superior culture.'

'Nonsense,' replied Emma laughing. 'The Chinese will never amount to much. We are the civilized people of the world, as Charles Darwin told us in his writings, we are closer to God.'

'I don't think God has anything to do with it,' said Elsbeth. 'I spoke with William Fung several times, and I don't agree with you Emma. He's a fine gentleman, regardless of what clothes he wears, and Sarah is a fine woman, and I love their children, they are so delightful. William's brother I think or uncle or one of his relatives served in the Chinese navy during the first terrible wars over opium, and he was killed by a British ship called the Nemesis. William always says that they won because they had the larger cannons, nothing more.'

'That is ridiculous!' exploded Emma. 'Mr. Fung, not William, his fake English name, has no idea what he is talking about. The Europeans have a destiny, and the Chinese don't. It is as simple as that. We are blessed by God, and they are not. We have a Christian civilization, and all they have ignorance and superstition.'

Richard noticed that Chambers had gone quiet and had reached for his whiskey flask. He gave him a glass. He watched as his old friend poured what seemed to be dark liquor into the cup slowly and steadily.

'The Spirit searches all things, even the mind of God, which sometimes is hidden from our gaze,' said Chambers quietly and softly.

'I thought you were an atheist,' said Richard. Chambers grimaced as he pretended to drink his whiskey.

'Charles Gordon used to say that to me when we were about to go into battle. He used to say a lot of things. The were often quite profound.'

'Charles Gordon?' asked Elsbeth very interested. 'Do you know Gordon?'

'I served with him. I consider him a friend, and the closest person to Jesus I have ever met, if I believed in God that is.' He looked at everyone at the table.

'William Fung is right. We had the bigger cannons. In 1841 we had the Nemesis. She was a big ship, at the time the biggest naval vessel ever constructed, like a leviathan from the book of Jonah. The Chinese navy never had a chance. I didn't know the names of any of our victims. I guess I do now.'

'Were you on the Nemesis?' asked Richard cautiously.

Chambers nodded. 'When I was a boy, young, naïve, and eager to prove myself. I am not the same man. That man died one day on a battle I would love to forget but each day remember. As for the day the Nemesis rose out of the sea, the Chinese navy was wiped out. It wasn't a battle; it was a slaughter.'

'Have you spoken to William about it?' asked Elsbeth. Chambers said it was the first time he heard of William's story.

'Despite all that has happened,' said Chambers, 'that war still casts its bitter shadow. The consequences of that war, the ignominy for China, the humiliation, and the shame, will last for centuries. It will not go unpunished. Too much blood was shed. How long will we remember it?'

'It was the beginning, wasn't it?' asked Merlin rhetorically. 'It was the beginning of the takeover of China, and the slow decay of the

Manchu Dynasty.'

'It is not yet dead,' replied Chambers. 'If it falls, we don't know what will take its place. The government has tried to make itself in the image of the West, but it is probably too late, I must admit.'

He sipped from his glass of water as his mouth was dry.

'Yes,' he admitted. 'I served with Gordon, and Ward, two good men, two good soldiers, but the Chinese were not without warriors, and I fought alongside them as well. The Taiping were demons, demons straight from hell, and every inch was won with blood.'

'I remember that their leader thought that he was God or something like that,' said Merlin.

'He thought he was the brother of Jesus,' replied Chambers. 'He was another Son of God, or so he proclaimed. He killed anyone who didn't convert to his version of Christianity. He slaughtered entire towns, villages, and anyone who opposed him. They all died; men, women, and children, there was nothing like it in all Chinese history, engineered violence driven by one man's insane visions of himself. His madness drove us all mad, and we have spent years trying to find peace.'

Chambers looked up from his glass. Everyone had fallen silent. Merlin and Elsbeth looked stunned, while Richard and Emma just stared at him.

'So yes, Emma, I went to a tiny mountain village to find peace, after the land had been soaked in blood. But, as providence would have it, the war found me, an old friend who had fallen in love with glory and who cast all friendship aside, a man who saw an opportunity to make a name for himself. This man killed all the civilians in our little village, after luring all the soldiers away on a wild goose chase. He crucified them all, including my wife. I tell you, there is nothing quite like a crucifixion. No wonder they crucified Jesus. There is nothing like it in all the world.'

Chambers sipped from his cup. 'We had no time to grieve. We gathered the men who were left and pursued him. He had destroyed a few other villages as well, so by the time we caught up with his army, we had quite a number, maybe one hundred against his thousand. But we had lost everything, and they were just chasing glory.

'What did you do?' asked Elsbeth quietly.

'We used his own tactics against him, we attacked him at night using the darkness, or fire, or fog. Finally, after several weeks, we trapped them and destroyed them in a ravine. Only a few dozen escaped, including their leader and I was tracking him with a few other government agents until I received Richard's letter that my brother's death was not suicide.'

Everyone turned and stared at Richard. There was a long silence. No one felt able to say anything.

'Do you think Henry Chambers was murdered?' asked Merlin eventually.

'I just think it was suspicious, and Nathaniel had the right to know,' he replied with a deep sigh. At this time, Mr. Robinson came in and saw Chambers sitting at the table. Everyone gave their greetings.

'Can I get you a drink?' asked Richard getting up from his seat, 'Whiskey?'

Robinson nodded.

He dragged another chair to where Chambers was seated and sat down next to him.

'I am afraid I have bad news,' he said quietly. 'I have bad news about the locket you gave me.' He spoke with hushed tones for he did not want other people to hear him.

Chambers sighed. So, there was no definitive answer on the locket. He was back to the beginning of his search. Robinson graciously accepted the whiskey and drank it all in one gulp, placing the glass back on the table.

'Tell me what you know,' insisted Chambers.

'The locket belonged to Millie Thorpe, there is no doubt about it. It was hers. My assistant repaired the chain only a month ago. It was her most prized possession, Mr. Chambers, you do realize that she would not have parted with it. It was the only thing she had that belonged to her late mother. Where was it found?'

'In the paddock at Henry's place,' replied Chambers.

'Then,' said Mr. Robinson, with his face sombre, 'I am very much inclined to suspect that poor Millie Thorpe is no more.'

Chambers stared at him, and Robinson returned the locket which he put in his pocket and then turned to the others at the table. They had heard what Robinson had said and they were all shocked, except Richard who was staring expectantly at Chambers. Nathaniel nodded to him, and Richard grinned slightly.

Chambers stood up and turned to those who were left in the hotel. There were still a few miners standing around. 'Listen, everyone,' he shouted, 'I want your attention.'

The Hotel fell silent. Chambers waited until he heard nothing.

'As Richard Noble has probably told you, my name is Nathaniel Chambers. He is right, I was at the stockade at Eureka in 1854 with the great Peter Lalor. I was there when the troopers stormed the barricade, and I saw my friends and comrades cut down by the government on that foul and awful day. I can tell you this. There has not been a day like it in this country, nor will there be a day like it again. It was a day that democracy was born in this great nation of Australia, where freedom was conceived, not in America, nor Britain nor Europe, but here, in this land.

'Now, the spark that was lit in Australia has started burning across the world. The stockade was many things to many people, but for me, it was about standing with your friends, and not letting them down when they needed you. Friendship is the greatest thing in the world and the greatest thing a friend can do is stand by you in your darkest hour. Richard Noble, the man who sells you whiskey and listens to your stories is one I am proud to call my friend, for he stood with us that day against tyranny. I was there. I know what he did.

'Richard was not on the stockade, and I know that many of you dismiss him and his stories as fanciful make-believe. You Australians love to tell a good yarn and spin a good tale, but I want to tell you the truth, perhaps something that Richard himself never told you, but now is the time. I see it in the way you look at him, the way even his wife looks at him, that he was someone of no importance, someone who could have made a difference, but didn't, because all that matters to you was the stockade. But that is not true. Not everyone can man the stockade. It takes a certain kind of courage. Not everyone can face a full volley and stand firm, but we all have our roles to play. It is not cowardice to avoid war, it is not the act of a coward to shy away from the battle. I know there are a lot of pretenders out there claiming this and that about the Eureka Stockade, and they are trying to make a name for themselves. Eureka was about what was right, and what was wrong, and that was why we made our stand, fighting for simple justice. It was flawed justice, and we did it as men bringing our own weaknesses and our own failings, but we knew we had to do something because something needed to be done. Sometimes we need to make a stand, no matter the cost. Richard knew that.

'There is something that is opposite to that of a friend and that is a traitor, a Judas, someone who spreads malicious lies about you, someone who stabs you in the back, someone whom you know who is out to destroy you. What few people know about Eureka was that there was a traitor in our midst, a turncoat, a spy for the troopers and the police. This man was our friend, and he was with us from the beginning, but all the time he was feeding information to the police. As you know, some of the police were corrupt and some of the soldiers were too keen to kill. They were in the pockets of the squatters and wealthy landowners.

'What you might not know is that Richard found the traitor and prevented him from getting to Peter Lalor. He took a bullet for Peter Lalor, and for that reason, he was not there when the troops stormed the barricade. But he was there with us in spirit, and he stood with us, even though he was not there, and even today he stands with all of you, all of you who love freedom and want to see justice. That is why you came here to this town to dig for gold, to make a new life for yourselves and for your families.

'I am also the brother of the late Henry Chambers of Gulgong, whose body was found by the missing priest Mr. Blackwell a year ago in the barn at his farm. Doctor Smythe said that he took his own life. I do not believe that. He was about to be married to Mrs. Mary Kelly whom he loved very much. He had just sold his property 'Eliza' to Mr. John Knox of Crooked River.

'Let me tell you what I do know. I know that the brother of Biddy is missing. I know that the priest Mr. Blackwell has disappeared. I know that little Millie Thorpe who worked as a maid for John Knox never made it to Sydney. In fact, she never left Gulgong. She was murdered. My brother was murdered. He was murdered the night Mrs. Knox died of a snake bite at Crooked River. This was the same night Millie Thorpe was last seen.

'Today, at the Church of England service in Gulgong, Mrs. Henrietta Knox was poisoned, and so was Mr. Lyons, the visiting parish priest. Mr. Maxwell, the station manager of Tom and Henrietta's farm, was also poisoned. He is dead. I believe John Knox of Crooked River was the intended target, but they did not get him. I know what poison looks like. I was trained in London as a medical doctor and have treated hundreds of patients around the world. I can tell you with absolute certainty. Someone went to that church service to kill John Knox.

'This is a country town. There are many secrets and many bad things that have happened here over the years. I am not interested in that. But Millie Thorpe was a young girl, not an adult, not a miner, or a squatter, just a young woman with her whole life ahead of her. Now, she is dead. Help me find the killers and bring them to justice. I believe that this whole sorry mess hinges on where the body of Millie Thorpe is right now. Someone knows what happened to her. Someone here knows where she is. God is watching all of you now to do the right thing. It might cost you everything, but you must do the right thing. It is never too late to make the right decision. You dig each day in your mines, looking for gold. You go deep into the earth, and you know the silence. In fact, the whole world is silent, and all you hear is the beating of your heart. I pray that the voice you hear from this day forth, in the silence of that empty mine is my voice calling in the wilderness of this land, 'who killed my brother? Who killed Millie Thorpe?' Not all of you were with me on the stockade with Peter Lalor, but if any of you love freedom and see any future for this nation, speak now, and come forward.'

Chambers looked at the door to the hotel and saw Jed Barton standing there, staring at him with a look of horror on his face. When he saw that Chambers had spotted him, he turned around and left.

Chambers sat back down at the table.

'Bravo!' shouted Merlin, 'My dear fellow, what a splendid speech you gave. I must take your photograph tomorrow for my collection. What an addition it will make.'

Elsbeth stared at Chambers.

'You do realize that you've made yourself a target now,' she said. 'If there is someone out there who did kill the girl, they will come after you. I hope you have a guardian angel protecting you.'

Chambers laughed.

'It is funny you should mention that. I have over the years been most fortunate and often pondered whether that was true, whether God was watching out for me or whether some guardian angel was there to make sure I survived. Sometimes one never knows the identity of true friends who for whatever reason never reveal themselves directly. There were many times in China, especially after the fall of the Taiping, that I felt I was followed by something, or someone, who had their eye on me. I had not thought about it until now Elsbeth. Maybe you are right.'

'Maybe it is God,' she said gently. 'God moves in mysterious ways, his wonders to perform,' she said with a smile and rested her hand on his. 'But God doesn't want you to throw away your life carelessly. Be careful and watch your back.'

Emma turned to her husband. 'You never told me about the attempt on Peter's life Richard, was that because you killed the assassin? Is that why you didn't tell me? I am your wife. I have borne you three children. There is no need to keep such secrets from me.'

Richard said nothing.

'Why my love, why the hell did you write to him? He will have the whole town whipped up into a frenzy by tomorrow. Do you want that? He is charismatic, just like Peter. He is more genuine than Peter ever was. But he is not just anyone. He is still grieving the death of his wife and his brother, and he has survived years of war in China. His wife was crucified my darling, no man should ever witness that, and he talks about it as if it is nothing. He is in pain, Richard, terrible pain. Can't you see it in his eyes. He is so angry he doesn't see anything clearly. He will see Gulgong burnt to the ground to find his brother's killer.'

'I knew exactly what I was doing, my dear,' replied Richard. 'We would not have had Eureka without this man, though no one will ever know it. I didn't kill the man who attempted to take Peter's life, though he most certainly wanted to kill Pete. As for Henry Chambers my dear, it is not just him, it is Biddy's brother George, Mr. Blackwell, Millie, and all the others these last twelve months, all of those who died violently or vanished mysteriously. This town has gone to hell. It is rotten to the core. Not even Rouse can do anything. You see it in his eyes. It is all getting out of hand. It is too much for him. He is not his grandfather. Even John Knox is in danger and if half of what Chambers said about the poisoning is true, then no one is safe. This town needs to be cleansed by a good dose of justice. If anyone is to cleanse it, then it is Chambers.'

He stood up to get Mr. Robinson another whiskey.

'But at what cost?' asked Emma to herself quietly, silently trembling. 'But at what cost?'

18.   THE PROBLEM WITH JOHNSON

Herbert Street, Gulgong

Chambers, Merlin, and Elsbeth talked long into the night, with frequent interruptions from miners who came to talk to him about the Eureka Stockade and ask questions about the allegations that he had made in his speech. The miners loved him because of his connections with the Eureka Stockade and they kept asking him to visit their claims and spend time with them. Some of them sang ballads, and others recited poems, and Chambers laughed heartily for the first time in months.

Merlin and Elsbeth told him they were going to visit the gold lead known as Happy Valley the next day to take a photograph and so Chambers decided to go with them. Merlin said that Happy Valley saved Gulgong after a long dry spell which almost convinced the town that the finds in Black and Adams Lead had run out, hence the name.

Chambers needed to settle the matter of Henry's house. He also knew that his speech would have unsettled Rouse and Knox, and he was awaiting their response to his challenge. He had the locket, but he needed more than that to get to the truth of his brother's death. He needed some information about the whereabouts of the former priest, Mr. Blackwell, or whether anyone had seen Millie Thorpe. He suspected that neither would be forthcoming, as most people probably didn't know anything. He also knew that after tomorrow he would have little reason to stay in Gulgong or Home Rule. Knox owned Henry's farm and he had little firm evidence of criminal activity aside from his instincts.

He also did not want to get involved in any vendetta against the Knox family. Everyone blamed Knox for something. But the poisoning at church was a bad business. It was not simply revenge. Whoever was responsible didn't care who they hurt, as they poisoned people who had nothing to do with Knox, such as the hapless and ineffectual priest, and poor Maxwell, who was just a farmhand. Chambers knew full well the power of vengeance and how families often warred against each other for generations over some real or imagined crime of the past. Knox was a squatter and had no doubt made enemies over the years. Chambers suspected that it all had to do with someone who had been wronged in the past, some old unresolved grievance. It could have been anyone, anyone with a grudge and with access to poisons, even medicinal ones. They were not hard to obtain. But Elsbeth was right. He had to watch his back.

It was dawn when the three wrapped up their conversation. Merlin had fallen asleep at the table, holding a bottle of whiskey, and Elsbeth was by Chambers' side playing with a glass. Richard and Emma had long retired to bed, and most of the miners had left for their tents, boarding houses, or brothels.

'Do you sleep well these days?' Elsbeth asked.

Chambers looked at her and smiled. 'Why do you ask?'

'Well,' she replied. 'We have been talking all night and well into the morning. I enjoy your company, but I get the feeling you are avoiding going to bed entirely.'

Chambers laughed and smiled. 'I have not slept well since my wife died. I have a recurring nightmare of arriving too late and not being able to save her. When I do sleep, it is because my body has collapsed and needs to stop.'

'I hope when this is all over,' she said genuinely, 'that you go somewhere to find peace and rest. You are a soldier. You have it in your blood. I am not entirely sure if you could ever just settle down. There will always be a war to fight, but there needs to be a time of peace, otherwise, why fight in the first place?'

Chambers nodded appreciatively. 'And what will you do?' he asked.

'Merlin is going to Sydney soon and I will go with him. He has big plans for his photographic exhibition. I believe he has great potential if he stays healthy. He is quite anxious about the photographs. He is always expecting perfection.'

'He is a remarkable man,' said Chambers. 'He is a bit eccentric, but he is a good man, and they are hard to find these days.'

'I better get him to bed,' said Elsbeth. 'Goodnight, Nathaniel Chambers, or good morning!' she said with a smile. Chambers put his hand on hers and squeezed it.

'Thank you for your friendship,' he said. He sat for a while at the table in the empty Hotel until the first rays of the sun came through the door and windows. He was thinking of resting his head on the table when he saw Richard emerge from the back room.

'Are you still here?' he asked, rubbing his eyes. 'I am about to fix some breakfast. Would you like some?'

Chambers nodded sleepily and asked if he could have some coffee. Richard smiled and said there was still whiskey if Chambers changed his mind.

'It was quite a speech you gave last night,' said Richard, leaning across the bar. 'You do realize that by today, everyone will know about it, and the allegations you made.'

'Absolutely,' replied Chambers. 'As you said, nothing is a secret in this town, unless of course, it involves murder. I knew what I was doing. I don't expect anything to come of it though unless someone feels terribly guilty that they have committed murder, which is highly unlikely, wouldn't you agree?'

Richard laughed. 'I would agree. I don't expect anyone to come forward unless they met God and felt the need for confession. I need to be honest with you. I slept on it. I think the problems of this town are too great, the corruption is too far gone for anything to change. Gold is their idol here, and money buys and pays for everything. Maybe you might see justice in Sydney or Melbourne, or even in China, but not out here. Here, there is no justice.'

'Why don't you leave and go back to Sydney?' asked Chambers.

Richard sighed. 'I think we probably will if I can be perfectly honest,' he replied, 'Emma's family are in Sydney.'

After breakfast, Chambers washed his face and body in his room and went to meet Rouse and Knox at Johnson's office to settle the matter of Henry's estate. He wondered what it would take for Rouse and Knox to become allies and it was certainly the speech he had given the night before. Both men were standing in front of Johnson's office glaring at him as he walked up the dusty and dirty street toward them.

'Do you have the locket?' asked Knox gruffly. Chambers said that he did and produced it. Knox looked at it seriously and handed it to Rouse.

'It belonged to the girl,' Knox told him, ignoring Chambers. 'She must have dropped it when she was leaving town, or misplaced it, or someone stole it.'

Rouse nodded in agreement. 'It hardly merits the allegations you made last night Chambers,' said Rouse sternly. 'You do not have one shred of evidence that the girl is dead, except for this locket, and it is just a trinket.'

'I found it in Henry's paddock Knox,' replied Chambers. 'Why would it be there?'

'She probably dropped it,' said Jed, who joined them in front of the office. 'She was always over there visiting Henry, they were friends, and she saw him as a kind of uncle.'

'Let me tell you what I think happened that night Jed,' replied Chambers, staring at Knox, 'the night Mrs. Knox died from the snake bite.'

'I don't want you to talk about my late wife!' bellowed Knox. 'How dare you even bring up her name you pompous bastard!'

He turned on Chambers and raised his right fist to strike him, but Chambers brushed his flying fist aside and used his bulk against him to throw Knox forward onto the dirt in the middle of the street. Knox cried out in pain, as he sprawled in the dust.

'Shoot him Jed!' he shouted, 'Shoot him!'

Rouse and Chambers turned to see Jed with his revolver raised.

Chambers looked into Jed's eyes. They were quivering.

'Shoot me, like you shot Millie,' insisted Chambers. 'I am not afraid to die. Maybe it is my time. Then I can join my wife Mei who was crucified on the hill along with her friends. Shoot me now, Jed, you shot a child, why not shoot a man, do what you are told by your master John Knox, you obviously do his dirty work, so he can keep his hands clean.'

Jed looked at Chambers and then at Knox. He seemed like a man in turmoil, not knowing what to do. Rouse moved towards Jed slowly, hoping to snatch the pistol from his hand, but Jed noticed this and turned the gun on him.

'Stay where you are Mr. Rouse, I don't want to shoot you as well.'

'You don't have to shoot anyone,' replied Rouse. 'You are your own man; you are free to make your own choices. Put the gun down!'

'Shoot the bastard!' yelled Knox, lying on the ground trying to get up. 'Shoot Chambers like the dog he is!'

'This isn't Ireland, old fool!' shouted Rouse. 'This is Australia, and you must obey the law.'

There was a loud shotgun blast. It came from further down Herbert Street. It echoed across the streets of Gulgong in that early morning, waking up the entire town. Everyone turned to see Emma Noble standing there, holding a shotgun in the air. Behind her was Richard, also armed with a pistol and several miners were with him. Richard was calling others to join them who had heard the shot and were emerging, half asleep from their tents and half-dressed from their hotels.

'Stand away Jed Barton, if you value your life, and put down the gun,' urged Emma, pointing it at him and walking up the street.

'I am a mother and a wife Jed Barton, and I have shot animals before, and so help me God, if you shoot Chambers or Mr. Rouse, I will empty the contents of your brains all over this street.'

Jed turned to leave and came face to face with Merlin and Elsbeth. Merlin was holding a pistol and it was pointed at his chest.

'It is a fine day for a bit of shooting dear boy,' he said, breathing heavily. 'The first bullet will go through your heart, as surely as there is a God in heaven. The second, well, that's entirely up to me.'

Richard was yelling for more miners to come and come they did, racing up the street, most wondering what all the commotion was about. What they saw shocked them. The great Mr. Knox was sprawled on the ground, unable to get up unaided, Emma Noble was holding a shotgun, and Jed Barton had his gun unholstered and was waving it around. Among the miners was Pete Barton, who had come into Gulgong on his way to his claim.

'Jed!' he called out, 'what is going on?'

'Nothing to see here!' shouted Rouse, taking the gun from Jed and tossing it to Elsbeth. She took it and Merlin lowered his pistol. Rouse went over and lifted Knox to his feet. He had great difficulty in standing, confirming what Chambers had assumed when they had first met at his brother's farm. Knox's spine was damaged. He must have been in constant pain.

'Nothing to see?' blurted out Knox, tearing himself away from Rouse. 'Nothing to see?'

He tried to regain his breath. 'You are a treacherous dog Rouse!' he screamed angrily, pointing at him, and shaking his fists.

'You always take the side opposite to me, all these interlopers on my land. They are nothing but trouble, mark my words.'

Jed went over to Knox, apologetic, and made his master lean on his shoulder.

'You saw what happened at the church Jed, they tried to poison me, and they killed poor Henrietta instead, and poor Maxwell. Even that dreadful priest of yours Rouse, who gave the worst homily I have ever heard was poisoned. They want me dead. They tried to poison me!'

'Who?' demanded Rouse. 'Who wants you dead? If you want our help, then out with it, man, tell us plainly, tell us the truth!'

Knox took a step back. 'It could have been anyone!' he admitted angrily, looking at all the miners gathering around them on the street.

'It could have been anyone, you are all out to get me, you want Crooked River for yourselves, you always have. I am not part of your little Gulgong society, I am not part of the chosen group of people who gather here, I am an outsider and what I have built I did it myself, without your help, without your care.'

'Control yourself, Knox,' urged Rouse. 'You are upset and not thinking straight. Stop talking before you say something you will regret.'

'You hypocrite!' he bellowed. 'You and your kind here, and all your secret meetings, and your traditions and customs. After all your family has done here, all the killing your family has done, and you lecture me, you dare to lecture me!'

'I will not have you slander my family name Knox,' retorted Rouse. 'You are a coward and a liar, but you are still grieving for the loss of your wife and now your sister-in-law and I grant you leave for that, you are not in your right mind.'

Knox stood still and looked at Rouse, then at Chambers, and then at Emma and Richard.

'Oh, I am in my right mind,' said Knox slowly and methodically. He then looked at Jed in horror. 'What have you told them?' he demanded, pushing Jed away angrily. 'Whose side are you on? Are you also against me?'

'I haven't told them anything Mr. Knox!' defended Jed.

'What is there to tell Jed?' asked Emma.

Jed looked at Knox, his face full of fear.

'The night Mrs. Knox died from the snake bite Millie was upset,' said Jed. 'She saw her mistress die, as did I. It was an awful thing. Millie left the farm in a state. She rode out in the night towards Henry's farm, and I tried to stop her, but she was too fast for me. I guess that is why the locket ended up at Chambers farm, but what happened afterward I do not know, I still believe that she went to Sydney. Maybe Henry gave her some money to help her on her way. I don't know, but what I do know is that the last time I saw her at Crooked River, she was alive.'

'You and your bloody trinket,' said Knox. 'All for nothing, all those wretched lies you told last night.'

Rouse and Chambers looked at each other. They both knew Jed was lying. Why didn't he say this right from the beginning? If he was so concerned about her, why didn't he follow her to see to her well-being? Did Millie leave before or after the shot that apparently killed Henry Chambers?

Rouse looked at Knox, fuming and cursing, then at Emma and Richard, and finally at Chambers. He understood what had just happened. Chambers had brought everyone together, he had set the wheels in motion, and that train would only stop when it reached the end of the line. This was the Chambers Fung warned him about. Chambers brought people together, people who had nothing in common and he gave them a voice and a purpose. He was a true leader. For the first time, Rouse knew that Chambers had uncovered something sinister and awful, something he had long suspected, but could never prove. Rouse was reluctantly but resolutely resolved to see it through, even if it meant turning Gulgong upside down.

'Let me tell you what happened that night Jed,' said Chambers. 'Just to refresh your memory.' He walked onto the road and up to Knox, 'and you too Knox,' he said.

'Millie rode to Henry's farm that night. I believe several shots were fired. One compelled Henry to end his conversation with Mr. Blackwell the priest and go out to his back paddock. He saw Millie coming towards him, fleeing from Crooked River. I believe that shot wounded Millie. The two met in the paddock where another shot rang out which killed my brother outright. The same person who was trying to kill Millie accidentally shot Henry. I believe that Millie died of her wounds somewhere and that she has been buried. I believe that it was all a tragic accident, that none of it was meant to happen, that the people responsible wish it never did, and have felt guilt for over a year, and they are yearning to be set free from the lies they have been telling.'

Rouse kept his eyes on Jed Barton. The more Chambers spoke, the more Rouse realized that Jed knew far more about that terrible night than he was telling. Knox said nothing and let him speak until he had finished. There was silence. Chambers looked at Emma who was still holding her gun. He nodded in her direction. She smiled at him for the first time. He looked over to Elsbeth and Merlin, who was leaning against the solicitor's office. Merlin looked exhausted and drained. He was holding his chest and coughing. Chambers nodded to Elsbeth and then turned to Rouse.

'The only one not here today is Johnson,' said Chambers. 'He wasn't at church yesterday, so, where is he?'

'That is the first normal thing you have said all day!' shouted Knox. 'I want this matter of the farm settled, and you out of Gulgong as soon as possible.'

Chambers was about to say something, but in the distance, he saw Joe Mitchell and constable Cooper riding down towards them. Both men seemed upset and angry.

'Something terrible has happened,' said Chambers. 'I know the look of death when I see it.'

'What has been going on here?' demanded Mitchell, getting off his horse quickly, 'why all the guns?'

'A simple misunderstanding Joe, nothing more,' said Rouse trying to defuse the tension. Mitchell walked over to Rouse and Chambers, ignoring Jed and Knox.

'Johnson is dead,' said Mitchell. 'It appears a large branch fell on him in the storm the other night. A few other branches had fallen on and around his homestead as well.'

'What was he doing out in the storm?' asked Rouse.

'I have no idea,' said Joe. 'I need to go and find Powell and Hannan, we need their expertise here. Two days and four suspicious deaths. I am out of my depth.'

'Four?' asked Chambers. 'Mrs. Knox, Maxwell, and now Johnson, so who is the fourth?'

Joe was about to speak when everyone heard a growl from Mr. Knox, a deep, guttural cry of pain. They all turned to see Knox on the ground again, crying and weeping and cursing God.

'What is going on?' Rouse asked Joe.

'It is Tom Knox,' sighed Joe. 'Cooper and I went to see him today, to find out how he was, after the death of his wife. I'm sorry Rouse, but it appears that he shot himself in the head.'

19.   JOE MITCHELL RIDES FOR MUDGEE

The Road Between Home Rule and Mudgee

In 1872, the people of Home Rule and Gulgong saw Joe Mitchell as an old man who said little, and always seemed to be in the pub. He was known as a friend of the Rouse family and had a career as a police officer when he was a younger man. But there was much more to Joe than first appearances. Joe Mitchell had spent his life as a police officer in the colony of New South Wales. He was born in the growing town of Sydney in 1811 and became a 'trap' or mounted trooper in 1833. In those days, the frontier wars were being fought across the new nation between the indigenous peoples and the settlers who stole their land, raped their women, and poisoned their drinking water.

Mitchell was a committed colonist. He drank from the well of inculcated prejudice and saw a hatred of the indigenous people as natural as putting on his leather boots every morning. He took the side of the settlers and wanted to exterminate aborigines from the face of God's earth or compel them to adopt 'civilization.' He believed all the stories of the alleged brutality of the aborigines during the Bathurst wars of 1824 and saw them as pestilence.

His first post was at a place called Singleton, and he served under Sargent Temple, who on the first of June 1836 led his troopers and some pastoralists on a killing spree in a place called Barraba that lasted several months. It involved the premeditated murder of over eighty aboriginal men, and dozens of women and their children. The goal was to 'cleanse' the land of indigenous people to allow the pastoralists safe access. Mitchell went into Barraba with all the typical prejudice of a man born in his time. He had no qualms about shooting dead an unarmed aboriginal man. He hesitated only for a moment before he hunted down and shot the women. But shoot he did. So did the others. It was murder, plain and simple, a genocide. They went back to their homes, cleaned their rifles, and got on with their lives. Joe didn't see them as human. He saw them as less valuable than cattle, beyond the grace of God.

He started drinking after Barraba, and he was posted in 1840 to the sprawling and pretentious town of Bathurst, ever hopeful of replacing Sydney as the central metropolis of the colony. He never slept well after Barraba, the spirits of the dead oppressing him while he slept, their cries echoing in his ears. He hoped that the daily nightmares he experienced would remain in Singleton, but they followed him to Bathurst. Marriage and children made no difference to the nightmares, and the daily drink could not extinguish a deep self-disgust that throbbed in his heart.

He spent most of his career in Bathurst hunting bushrangers and criminals. He had been involved in a few of the big, unsolved cases such as the Mudgee Mail Robbery of 1863 when thousands of pounds of gold were stolen. Most of it was never recovered. He also took part in the search for the infamous Chinese bushranger Sam Poo in 1865. He was a close friend of John Ward, the constable who was mortally wounded by Sam Poo in February of that year. Joe and his wife knew the Wards well. His death was tragic.

That event helped Mrs. Mitchell convince her husband to leave the police force and retire to a small farm on the outskirts of Mudgee. She always knew that her husband was haunted by the past, but she didn't know what to do except pray for him. Little did she know that he had betrayed her almost from the beginning of their marriage.

Joe had a secret, a secret known to only a few men. He had fathered a child out of wedlock, to an aboriginal woman. He had met her when he travelled to Mudgee on one of his assignments. Despite murdering many aborigines in the past, his infidelity was the only guilt he truly admitted to himself. He was a man of contradictions and inconsistencies, and since he could not resolve any of them, he chose to forget the child. He was too ashamed to have anything to do with mother or child, and so ignored them for years.

But his friend, who knew him best, refused to let the matter rest and insisted that Joe be involved in the life of the girl, even from a distance. Rouse had, therefore, asked Joe to come up to Guntawang to help him clean up the town of Gulgong, a town that had discovered gold in 1870 by one of his employees, a man by the man of Tom Saunders who was looking after sheep. It was a ruse. The local police constables were, of course, on the whole, good men except for Constable Cooper, as far as Rouse could tell. Cooper was a thug, took the occasional bribes, often turned the other way, arrested the wrong people deliberately for a fee, harassed the local women and their husbands, drank heavily, and was not well-liked. But, when he needed to work, he did his job well, by and large, and helped to keep Gulgong safe, as safe as a gold rush town could be. Most of the police work was done by the other constables and two detectives, but Rouse knew that like a rotten apple, or one weevil in a sack of wheat it would not be long before corruption sank in. The yeast for this corruption was the friendship between Cooper and John Knox.

Cooper, Knox, Henry Chambers, and Blackwell started riding out together in 1870 into the Bush, with their rifles. They never returned with game. Rouse suspected what they were up to. They were out hunting aborigines for sport. When Henry arrived in Gulgong, Rouse knew that he would find in Knox and the others a kindred spirit for Rouse saw in him a wickedness that others do not perceive easily, a sadistic side that didn't need drink to bring it out, the kind of brutality that no education can erase. Rouse knew that Henry was a blackbirder in Queensland. Rouse was opposed to his presence in Gulgong. Many men who arrived in Gulgong and Home Rule in search of gold saw aboriginal women as fair game, and Rouse often thought about the safety of the many aboriginal people who lived near or around Guntawang, which was supposed to be a place of peace.

Rouse, like his father before him, was a man who wanted others to live up to the standards he lived by. He tried to live by the strict teachings of Moses in the Book of Common Prayer in the Church of England, the strict adherence to the Ten Commandments, a God who demanded regular confession of sin, and the highly ritualistic ceremony of the so-called Eucharist. Rouse appreciated stability, order, and regularity. He respected men who, like him, lived a well-ordered life. He was strict and a disciplinarian and Guntawang was a mirror image of the man he was and the father he inspired to emulate.

Guntawang rose out of the rough terrain of the Australian bush like an oasis in the desert, a beautiful, English-style homestead, amongst the chaotic and dry Australian landscape. Rouse's grandfather, Richard, was the man who built Guntawang, against the harsh terrain and constant hostility of the local aboriginal people. His grandson had grown up with the stories. He knew that there had been trouble, but he had a job to do, a reputation to uphold, and a family to provide for. He did not believe the land belonged to anyone other than himself, but he did not go out of his way to antagonize anyone.

But Rouse was no fool. He knew what went on in the world around him, and one of the things he noticed was that many of the important pastoralists would entertain liaisons and relationships with aboriginal women. He did not think it was appropriate, not because they were aboriginal, but because they had no intention of marrying them. Most of these liaisons were between married pastoralists and young aboriginal girls. Many were raped. He knew that Joe Mitchell had fathered the girl who came to be known as Biddy and his hope was that his old friend would at some point, acknowledge that the child was his, and provide support. She and her half-brother George had done well. George worked for John Knox and Biddy had a small farm of a few goats and vegetables. She was taught to read and write by missionaries who lived in Wellington.

There was a time when Rouse saw Biddy and Henry together. Despite his hatred of the aborigines, Henry was drawn to her, perhaps because of her spirit and attitude to life. Rouse had seen the two of them talking together a few times in Gulgong, and he noticed a slow softening in the heart of the angry Mr. Chambers, who had come to Gulgong to live alone, away from society. Rouse didn't know how close the two became, but when Chambers began courting the widowed Mary Kelly, he knew that whatever relationship he had with Biddy was probably over. Rouse would from time to time, greet Biddy with sincere politeness, and had helped her mother over the years. But with the arrival of Joe Mitchell, Rouse hoped and prayed that the old police officer would finally admit to himself and to Biddy personally, that he was her father.

That Monday morning, after Cooper and Mitchell found Tom Knox dead, and Johnson killed by the widow maker, Rouse agreed that the retired policeman should go to Mudgee and bring back the two detectives Charles Powell and Robert Hannan. Rouse feared for the town of Home Rule and Gulgong.

Bodies were starting to pile up and he was looking at a major scandal that could rip the town apart. Knox was the magnet for chaos and death. His wife, brother, sister-in-law, neighbour, and wife's friend in Gulgong had all died in the span of a year. Now, Johnson, Knox's family solicitor, was dead. Something had to be done. Rouse was worried that Chambers might take matters into his own hands if he found out what was going on. William Fung feared the same. Rouse could see the loathing that Chambers had for Knox. He was desperate to find the reasons behind the death of his brother. He watched how Chambers incited the confrontation between himself and Knox through the provocative speech the night before at the Royal, a confrontation that almost ended in a shoot-out on the streets of Gulgong if Emma Noble had not arrived with her rifle.

Fung had only to mention the name of Gordon for Rouse to become concerned. General Charles Gordon was the most charismatic military leader in the British Empire, a man who was said to enter battle with only a walking stick, a man of a fanatical Christian disposition, who believed in the existence of Jesus Christ, and saw everyone as his brother. Gordon's reputation was legendary, and so if anyone associated with that man turned up in Gulgong, he might incite a revolution. Rouse's suspicions were confirmed when he discovered that Chambers had also been at the Eureka Stockade and was possibly a secret republican. Rouse was already having trouble with Richard Noble, the self-appointed leader of the Irish miners. The sooner the 'Knox problem' was resolved the better.

Mitchell rode towards Home Rule after leaving Gulgong late that morning. He agreed with Rouse. Detectives were needed. The other constables were still housebound, and the magistrate was up to his neck in mining disputes. Knox was adamant someone was out to kill him, despite the official statements from the local doctor, who said that the two deaths were simply coincidental. Joe had seen what was left of the skull of Mr. Johnson, the solicitor, and there was no doubt that the poor man was killed when the tree branch stuck him during the terrible storm on Saturday night. What brought him out of the house on that night was another matter, but there was no question in his mind, that his death was an unfortunate accident. Nevertheless, he needed Powell and Hannan. They were proper detectives.

Joe reached the outskirts of Home Rule and rode through it. It had certainly come a long way in the last six months, rising out of nowhere to become a town. The terrain around Home Rule had been farmland and many small mines had been built to dig and carve out the gold from the various leads that crisscrossed the landscape. A lot of work was also being done along Cooyal Creek. If one took a fork in the road at the junction where Home Rule merged into Canadian Lead and followed it through the scrub, one would arrive at a dirt track that meandered through the bush until it came to a small farm. That was where Biddy lived.

Joe expected that one day he would take that path to see her. He knew why Rouse had asked him back. Rouse wanted him to meet the daughter he had never acknowledged, but he could never bring himself to go beyond a simple hello. After all, she had no reason to talk with him. He stopped at the crossroads and pondered what his life might have been if he accepted Biddy into his world. He resolved to meet her when he returned from his trip to Mudgee and this nasty business with Constable Cooper was settled. There was no need to rush things. He had plenty of time.

It was then that he saw her. In the distance, Biddy emerged out of the scrub, possibly heading into Home Rule or Mudgee. She waved to him. He raised his right hand and tipped his hat in her direction. She smiled. Mitchell smiled to himself. That decided it. He would visit her when he returned. He turned his attention to the road ahead and set out for Mudgee.

Joe had not gone far up the road when he heard a horse galloping towards him from the direction of Home Rule. As the horse grew closer, he realized that it was Cooper. Joe knew that Cooper was corrupt, but as far as he could tell, not a violent criminal. Cooper was good at his job and was relatively respected in the town, though he was close to Knox and his faction. This was not uncommon in country life, and Rouse also had a good relationship with officers of the law. Joe knew that Rouse did not understand the life of a policeman, its difficulties, and problems, and how the police officer had challenges that few understood. There were many temptations. He did not envy Cooper, stuck out in Gulgong, a tiny backwater with pretentious aspirations. It was only there because of Rouse and Guntawang and the growth of the gold town was just another little town in the outback of Australia.

"Afternoon,' he said to Cooper, who rode up to him, exhausted from his ride.

'I'm glad I caught you,' panted Cooper, struggling for breath. 'I thought I would miss you.'

'What is the matter?' asked Mitchell.

'I was hoping to ride with you,' panted Cooper. 'I saw you leave Home Rule, and I'm surprised how far you have got already.'

'Sure,' replied Mitchell. 'I would be happy with the company.'

The two men rode side by side along the bush path. They chatted a little about the day's events in Gulgong, and the awful death of Tom Knox, John's brother, as well as the tragic events of the Sunday luncheon at the church.

Mitchell thought he heard a sound in the scrub further back down the track. He turned around to see what it was. It might have been another rider along the path, or perhaps a mob of kangaroos. He found it hard to focus his eyes because of the hot, glaring sun. He decided that must have made a mistake. He turned back on his horse to see Cooper pointing a pistol at his chest.

'What are you doing?' he asked fearfully.

'I'm sorry Joe,' replied Cooper coldly. 'I won't allow you to get Powell and Hannan. I am trying to tie up all the loose ends with this Knox business. I owe John too much. Someone's out to get him. I suspect Henry's brother. I will deal with him later today. I just need a day or two to work it out, but you see, I don't want you messing it all up. You don't understand what is going on here, you never did.'

Joe could see that he was about to be murdered and he could do nothing about it. His rifle was out of reach, and his mouth was dry. This was it. His last thoughts were about Biddy.

One shot rang out in the valley. Joe was struck in the chest, the bullet going straight through his heart. He coughed up blood and was thrown backward off his horse to the ground. He was dead before he hit the dirt.

The sounds of the shots startled what Joe had seen further back along the track. It was someone on a horse, a woman. Her horse tossed her rider to the ground and cantered away. Cooper tried to see who it might have been. She had called out as she fell, and then scrambled into the scrub. By the time Cooper had reached the horse, he knew who it was. It was Biddy. Cooper smiled to himself. He was going to have some fun before returning to Gulgong.

Biddy was horrified by what she saw. She could not believe it. Joe was innocent, just a nice old man who was friends with everyone. Poor Joe Mitchell had been shot dead, in cold blood, like some animal. Biddy picked herself up and disappeared into the undergrowth. She sat still, hidden in the scrub, and a feeling of rage began to rise in her chest, a rage she had never felt before. She could hear Cooper coming closer on his horse, or she could smell him, a combination of booze and the stench of sweat. There was also the smell of blood, the blood of the man he murdered. Cooper's shirt was drenched in Joe's blood.

'Biddy!' called out Cooper, slowly. 'Biddy! Where are you, little girl? I am not going to hurt you!'

He kept walking slowly through the bush. He was coming towards the trees she was hiding behind. He could not see her at that moment, but it could all change if he came too close.

'Actually, I am lying. Of course, I am going to hurt you. I am going to kill you!' yelled Cooper, 'I am going to enjoy it. I will hunt you down and kill you, like all the others, all the little aborigines we hunted over the last few years, the good old days, with my mates Knox, Blackwell, and your lover Henry Chambers.

'He never told you, did he, what he got up to before you turned his head and became his lover. Good old Henry was the best shot, and he could hit a man from across the valley. Oh, and when you came along, we knew all about it because he told us every single, intimate detail. Biddy darling, he certainly chose poorly when he decided to marry that crazy Irish woman. I feel sorry for you Biddy, I really do.'

Cooper paused and surveyed the bush around him, trying desperately to find the woman. He was getting restless.

'All this hiding is pointless Biddy!' he yelled. 'You are alone here. No one is coming to your rescue. I can promise you that.'

Every word Cooper spoke had one purpose, to force her into the clearing. He had no idea where she was hiding. That was good. Every word he was uttering was keeping her alive. She stared at him and watched his every move. He had holstered his pistol and was now holding his rifle in both hands. He was an ugly man, always unshaven, with stubble on his face, a greasy and slimy face, with wandering eyes that undressed every woman he looked at.

'Have you found your brother?' he yelled out. 'I wonder what happened to him?'

He laughed out loud, putting the gun up against a tree and stretching. 'Poor George, here one day, gone the next. No loss though. After all, he was just another aborigine. Have you found him, Biddy? I bet you haven't. He was buried deep, where no one will find him.'

Cooper laughed. 'Your poor, stupid brother, he wanted to betray us, and tell everyone what we were up to, you see he found out the big secret Biddy, the big secret, what this is all about, and he wanted to run, he wanted to run all the way to Henry and tell him. John tried to shoot him, but he got away and ran to the creek. Jed caught up with him and shot him dead.

'But do you want to know the funniest thing? No one cares about George. No one. No one looked for him. No one searched for him. Only you mourned for him. The others, your so-called friends, don't care. He is just another aborigine. He is of no value to them whatsoever. Even your friend Mary, who stole your lover. She didn't care about George. She never looked for George. It is the same with Rouse, the great hypocrite. Where do you think his wealth comes from? How do you think he was able to carve his little English village in the middle of the Bush? How many of your people did his family murder to make that happen? Have you ever thought about that?'

Biddy was trying to force herself to stay still. Her heart was in turmoil. George was dead. She felt his passing the moment he was shot a year ago. But searched for him she did. She looked almost everywhere for him, but she could not find him. Poor George. She knew that he had been killed, but to hear that John tried killed him, horrified her.

George idolized John Knox. He looked up at him. He worked for the Knox's because they gave him a chance, and he loved the work. No one else in town took George on because he was an aborigine. Why did Jed shoot him? What terrible thing happened to bring that about? What did George do? What did he see? Biddy couldn't understand. There was so much she couldn't understand but did she really have to? Cooper had told her what she needed to know. Jed Barton killed her brother. He would pay. He would pay with his life. She would kill him and John Knox. She would kill them after she dealt with Cooper.

'Have you found your father yet?' yelled Cooper. 'I am surprised your mother let you live, I really am. So many were just killed, bringing all that shame on the family. All the farmers had their aboriginal women, you do know that they all drank from that well. Maybe you should've asked Joe about it. He was in Mudgee years ago and took up with a local aboriginal girl. I heard she had a child. I heard lots of rumours about that man. I always wondered why Joe kept coming back here. Maybe it was to see you.'

Cooper changed direction. A noise startled him. There might have been a wallaby or a wombat or something in the scrub further down the path away from where she was. Biddy picked up a small stone and threw it into the bush as far away from her as possible.

'Ah, there you are,' he snarled and started to run towards where he heard the stone fall. Biddy saw her chance, stood up, turned, and ran deeper into the bush. She kept running until she heard a shot and felt the sound of a bullet pass her head, striking a tree a few inches away. Cooper was not nearly the idiot she had hoped him to be.

He reloaded the rifle. Biddy took a sharp left in the scrub leaping across some rocks and scampering through some thicker bushes. The branches scratched her and tore her clothes, but she needed to put some distance between herself and Cooper and make it difficult for him to follow her. She took an unusual turn in the path, towards some boulders, and jumped over them. These rocks would slow him down. Then she looked further down the path. It curled to the right and went up a steep incline.

She knew the place. She had been a little confused for a moment, but she was now more confident that she could lead Cooper to a place of great danger, and if she were fortunate enough, she might be able to escape alive. She knew the spot. She and George had been there many years before as children. She could hear Cooper rampaging through the undergrowth, cursing as he got stuck repeatedly in the sharp bushes, making him use his rifle as a machete to cut his way through. Biddy meanwhile had reached the top of the small hill for which she was aiming. She had run into the brightness of the sun. It burned her eyes and blinded her and that is what she wanted Cooper to experience. She looked around frantically and found what she wanted and waited.

A few moments later, Cooper emerged from the scrub, exhausted. He had run uphill and lost his breath somewhere in the scrub that he had forced his way through. He had reloaded his rifle, but he only had one bullet left. It was the middle of the day and he had not drunk any water since leaving Gulgong a few hours before. His water was at the horse which was somewhere further back along the trail. He began to realize that he had probably made himself too vulnerable by venturing into the Bush.

This was Biddy's world. She had the high ground. The sun broke through the tree branches and shone directly into his eyes, and he was blinded. He closed his eyes for a moment, to shield himself from the glare, and at that moment, Biddy attacked with ferocity and anger. She struck Cooper across the face with a thick branch of dry wood. He immediately dropped his rifle and was knocked to the ground. Biddy picked up the rifle. Cooper was dazed and climbed slowly to his feet, dazed, holding his head with both hands.

'Any last words?' she asked.

'Are you going to shoot me?' scoffed Cooper, surprised, and horrified seeing the gun. His eyes narrowed and he grimaced. 'You are nothing Biddy, just nothing.'

Biddy just stared at him, raising the rifle. 'You will never find rest, even in death,' she cursed and shot him between the eyes. He fell backward, down into the gully.

20.   HAPPY VALLEY

Happy Valley Lead, Gulgong

Earlier that morning, Chambers went with Merlin, Elsbeth, and Richard to Happy Valley to photograph some new mining claims. Pete Barton had sunk a shaft there on a claim he held with some friends, and he was eager for Merlin to take their photo. Merlin was ecstatic and he and Elsbeth went to prepare the tripods so they could take some photos for his collection.

Knox had stormed off with Jed Barton and Cooper, fuming and cursing. Rouse rode off with Joe Mitchell. Given that the solicitor had been killed by the falling tree branch, the matter of the house could not be decided until Johnson's firm, based in Bathurst, was notified of his death, and another solicitor was sent out to resolve the matter. This might take weeks, even months. It seemed that Chambers was going to stay in the colony of New South Wales for a while yet.

It was not the news Chambers wanted to hear. Chambers had hoped that Johnson would confirm what Knox had told him and that he might know at least where the money might have ended up, resolve the matter of his brother's death, and return to China. He was desperate to continue the hunt for the man who murdered his wife. Whatever happened to Henry was nothing compared to the betrayal he experienced at the hands of a man he trusted, a man he held as a friend. He knew that government forces were also hunting the man, and he wanted to be there when he was captured. Every day he stayed in New South Wales, the more distant the prospect of fulfilling that goal became, and this discouraged him. Chambers also wanted the matter of his brother's death to be resolved in a few days, as it would greatly ease the mind of Mary Kelly and others, as well as shine a light on the corrupt business dealings of John Knox and his cronies.

Merlin came up to him with his tripod over his shoulder, and several bags under his arm. He was beaming. 'I would love to visit China one day and take some photos there!' he exclaimed. 'It must be a beautiful place, and the people would be fascinating, with all those different customs. I know a little of India, but China would be an incredible place.'

Hearing Merlin talk of China made Chambers homesick. He longed for the food again, the chaos of the street markets, the smell of the vegetables, and the peace and quiet of the mountains. He was English, and a patriot, but had not spent much time in England. His sister lived in London with her wealthy and influential husband, and he had visited England a few times, and Australia three times, but most of his life he had spent in China.

He knew that Merlin meant well, but it would not take him long to loathe the new experiences of a foreign land, the different language, the many different customs, and the distrust of foreigners. It was the same in Gulgong and Home Rule. Chambers was an outsider, a foreigner, not one of them. Nor could he be. He was an oddity, a specimen of admiration. His value was known only by his association with others – Peter Lalor and Charles Gordon. They didn't want to know him for who he was, only his past.

Pete turned up in front of the Royal Hotel with his horse and open carriage. A little boy of about ten years of age sat in the back, his face wrinkled in tiredness and his eyes bleary, but they widened when he saw Merlin, and he jumped down to meet him.

'What a fine boy you have Pete Barton,' exclaimed Merlin, messing up his hair. 'I see a future politician here!'

'I would just be happy if he did not become a miner, like his father,' replied Pete. 'This is Ralph, my boy. He wanted to see the camera you have.'

'And you shall, my boy,' said Merlin, lifting him back onto the carriage. 'The world of photographic splendour awaits. My trusty assistant Elsbeth will show you all you need to know, and if you are a good lad, then you can hold the tripod while I take the photo, how would you like that?'

Ralph said that he would be happy to help Merlin in any way he could. Elsbeth, Chambers, Merlin, and Richard climbed into the wagon, and Pete set off for Happy Valley.

'It is such a pleasant name,' said Elsbeth.

'We had a bit of a rough patch for a while,' replied Barton. 'We had success at Adams Lead, and then Black Lead, last year, and then it all kind of dried up. It was looking for a few months that the gold had run out. Then we found gold at Happy Valley. We should have called it 'Salvation' Lead. It saved the town.'

As the wagon continued along the road, Elsbeth continued to talk with Chambers about China. 'I don't think I would do well in China,' she mused. 'I think there would be too many people, and I wonder what I would do there.'

'There would not be many opportunities for you if you did not know the language or be willing to accept their customs,' said Chambers. 'The foreign towns are entirely different, like Shanghai and Hong Kong. There are basically like copies of London or Sydney with a Chinese flavour.'

'How deliciously fascinating,' said Merlin. 'It is a terrible shame it is such a violent place though.'

'It was also a shame that we had to invade China,' said Elsbeth. 'But they only have themselves to blame because they denied to us trading rights.'

'It was all about opium,' replied Chambers. 'It had nothing to do with trade. It was about money and wealth, not principles.'

'Don't tell me you are taking the Chinese side?' asked Elsbeth sarcastically. 'That sounds very unpatriotic.'

'It is the truth, Elsbeth,' replied Chambers. 'My father and I, in those days never hid from those basic truths. The Chinese exported tea to Britain in huge quantities. The terms of trade were in their favour and so the British government tried to force the Chinese to accept opium in equally massive quantities. This the Chinese opposed because while opium might be fun for you and Merlin to play with, is a destructive drug that destroys civilization. The Chinese refused to trade in opium and so we used that as an excuse to start a war. What we did was calculating, cruel and vindictive.'

'To force the Chinese to adopt opium?' asked Merlin.

'Precisely,' replied Chambers. 'Britain wanted access to the raw materials and resources of China to fuel their factories. If it were not for opium, we would have found another reason to invade. You see, it is all about money.'

'But as Emma said last night, we are blessed by God and have the destiny to rule the world,' insisted Merlin sarcastically.

'God doesn't bless nations, Mr. Merlin,' said Chambers. 'The only nation he chose were the Jews, and we have no right to expect God to take sides in our petty national squabbles. The Chinese have a civilization that goes back thousands of years. The Manchu, who run China, are not Chinese. They are foreigners, but there have been so many dynasties in China it is difficult to remember them all. You cannot reduce China to one thing or England for that matter.

'But it is different here. Gulgong exists for gold. Australia was built simply as a place to dump convicts after the American colonies were lost. All Australians do is export their goods to England. This nation is just a factory for the British Empire. If George Washington didn't become a tyrant and start a war with England, then none of us would be here today. Australia was only chosen because England lost the American colonies.'

'Surely you jest,' said Merlin, realizing what Chambers was saying. 'You cannot compare China with England; it is simply not possible.'

'It is perfectly possible,' replied Chambers. 'This town, this is not civilization. Civilization needs more than simply money to bring about meaning. If it is just about money, then you have nothing. I would say that when a society exists for one reason, it is not a civilization. I have learned over the years since Eureka that civilization is not just about one single idea or one single philosophy. If it is just about democracy, it is not civilization. It needs to be more than that. There needs to be a multiplicity of voices, opposite voices, different voices, and different experiences. One of the great strengths of England is its diversity. There are different voices, different histories, and different stories, all coexisting together. That is civilization. That is also China, or at least the China I knew growing up. Civilization is about ideas, history, poetry, music, the freedom of different voices to express themselves, poverty, wealth, opportunities, happiness, and despair all in the same house. That is civilization.'

Elsbeth and Merlin were just staring at him. He could tell that they did not understand. He was speaking a foreign language to them.

'I think you have been in China for too long,' insisted Merlin. 'The British Empire is the greatest Empire the world has ever seen, and nothing will ever change that,' he boasted confidently. 'It will continue for centuries to come.'

'I am afraid everything changes,' replied Chambers. 'Often sooner than you think. Who knows what will happen next year?'

'I am confident I shall be continuing with my photographic collection wherever Elsbeth and I decide to go,' he said with pride.

Chambers smiled. 'I heard that Gulgong has a theatre or Opera House. That is the beginning of civilization. Last night, rough men with grit and grime sang ballads and read poems, while drinking malt whiskey, and here, Pete Barton's little boy Ralph wants to learn about photography. This is civilization. Gold is just a pretty metal.'

'But there is a town here,' said Elsbeth, a chemist, a drapery, a dozen hotels, restaurants, tea houses, boarding houses, there is talk of a school being built, a post office, and even churches. This is civilization!'

Chambers asked what the towns would do when the gold ran out. Merlin and Elsbeth only laughed and said that it was unlikely to occur any time soon and when it did, the towns would still survive because people would have built up a sense of community.

'They are here for themselves,' insisted Chambers. 'They are not for the community. It is the gold that brings them, a little shiny metal, of disreputable value. Now, in Gulgong, there is the Opera House, built last year. That is a bold move. It might bring a little bit of culture to the place, but you also need to admit that the town is filthy, there is rampant disease and a lack of civic duties here. I see no evidence that people are working together, they are simply working for themselves. Smythe said that he spends almost every week burying a young child in the graveyard, and dozens of diseases afflict the adults. It is hardly a safe and happy place to live.'

'If you don't like Australia,' said Elsbeth, 'why not return to China?'

Chambers thought it was a rude thing to say. He ignored her. 'I am here to find out who murdered my brother, and when I do, I will hold all of those people responsible and see that they face the full justice of the law.'

'You have really changed a lot, Chambers,' said Richard who up to that point had been listening quietly. 'When did you develop a sense of the law?'

'When Lalor and others decided to take on the colonial troops at Eureka, inciting all those impressionable young men with talk of victory, liberty, and freedom. None of those men were soldiers, none had faced a volley from hardened troops, and none had seen war. They were all boys, fresh-faced and naïve, with no idea about what was going to happen. They had their heads full of romantic notions of freedom and liberty, but if they knew what really was in store for them, then they would've run for the hills.

'You know I tried to warn them what was going to happen, but I was shouted down. Now Lalor struts around talking about democracy and freedom, and all those men are still dead, and all those women are still widowed. If you take up arms against your government, you have forfeited your life, but Lalor said nothing about that. He just lost his arm. Australia lost part of its soul.

'I have seen much worse on the field of battle in China, but I never saw evil like I saw that day at Eureka. The rebels wanted blood. They wanted their revolution. Thank God for the colonial government and its many mercies. Thank God for the amnesty. When did Australia become a nation? It wasn't at Eureka, no that was a terrible mistake, it was when the government showed mercy and people went back to their ordinary lives.'

'But you have been a soldier all your life,' argued Richard. 'It's a bit rich judging Peter Lalor and the men at the stockade. They are heroes. They are the heroes of Australia.'

'I always served under authority, under the leadership of others, and when the wars were over, I put down my rifle,' replied Chambers.

'But you want revenge for your wife and family,' said Elsbeth. 'I don't see how your actions are any different.'

This cut Chambers to the heart. At the thought of his late wife, he saw her face looking at him from the burning cross, her body in flames, crying out to him, and blaming him for not protecting her. He turned his face away and shut his eyes.

'Do you see my gun Elsbeth?' he asked angrily. 'Do you see me carrying one? My sword is in my heart, and it is always unsheathed. I am always ready to fight, but I choose not to. If I pick up a sword again, then I will kill as I did before, but like a soldier, I know that those who live by the sword die by the sword, and I counted that cost a long time ago.'

Elsbeth said nothing. She saw that the mention of his wife upset him deeply. Merlin had tired of the conversation and began coughing again as he was readying his equipment.

'Welcome to Happy Valley,' interrupted Pete Barton who quickly got off the wagon, and helped everyone down.

'I think we should take advantage of the weather gentlemen,' said Merlin, 'it might change at any moment, and I would like to get at least one photograph of all of you in front of the poppet. Merlin arranged for the men to take advantage of the light. There were clouds approaching in the distance, and Merlin seemed worried about them, but Richard told him that he was not concerned and would evacuate the mine if it rained. Shafts often collapsed under heavy rain and filled up quickly and he was not going to be responsible for putting men in harm's way.

Richard called a few other miners over to be in the photograph. They were excited to join. Merlin had become quite a celebrity in the area, taking photos all over the gold fields, and he promised them that he would come back in a few years to take more and see how the town had grown. All in all, there were seven men, Chambers, Noble, Pete Barton, and four others. Merlin insisted that Elsbeth join them, and she stood next to Chambers, who had his hands on his hips. Pete Barton was leaning on a pick and Richard Noble was slouched over, with his hands in his pockets. The other men were huddled together under the poppet.

'History in the making!' exclaimed Merlin, 'in the greatest town in the world!'

After the photo was taken, Chambers rolled his eyes and turned to Richard. 'I wish Eureka never happened,' he said, 'but there are a lot of things I cannot change, and we just must live with what cards we have been dealt. I do not criticize you or Emma, Richard. You have done well here, and it has all the makings of a town, a pleasant place to live, but there needs to be something more than gold to keep people together. You and I both know that.'

Richard smiled reluctantly and nodded.

'I am greatly blessed with Emma,' he replied, 'and I agree with you about Gulgong. We do need more than gold to keep it going. We need a sense of community, and we need people to feel that they belong here. That is why John's outburst this morning is so distressing to all of us. He has just brought all the old enmities here from Ireland. I love the old country. I love her streams and her rivers, her hills, and valleys but my home is here, my love is here, and this is where I am proud to call home. But there is not a day where my soul does not linger over the fields of Ireland. God bless her, but God bless here, and God bless us. This is Australia, why don't they leave their disputes at the wharf when they arrive, and be like us?'

'Because you don't know who you are yet,' replied Chambers. 'You can't fight for something if there is nothing to fight for. Home Rule, what a silly name. This is not Ireland. If you want to fight for Irish independence, then do it, go home and fight for it. John Knox keeps his old identity intact because he doesn't feel confident that there was anything in this land comparable to replace it. He is right. If you do anything, Richard, ensure people like John Knox and others feel part of the community, and people like Biddy and William Fung. It is their home as well. Why are they not welcome here? If you do not, then what is the point?'

'I would love to go into the mine,' insisted Elsbeth, looking at the wooden poppet.

'A mine is no place for a woman,' insisted Pete Barton. She glared at him.

'Chambers would let me, wouldn't you?' she asked, sidling up to him.

'I don't need to give you permission to do anything,' said Chambers. 'You are free to do what you like, but I think Pete and Richard are in charge here and we have to do what we are told.'

She frowned and walked back to help Merlin. Chambers turned to Pete. 'Why is she not allowed to go down the mine? Surely it is not because she is a woman?'

'She has no experience. She is wearing the wrong clothes. It's because of the last few accidents we have had down there,' said Richard. 'Peter and his mates have complained that they dug too far in this mine shaft. In many of the leads, there have been cave-ins and not a few deaths. It takes a certain kind of person to be able to go down the mine. It is not for everyone. I believe we need less enthusiasm and a more sensible approach to mining. Pete agrees with me, but most miners do not. They are just too eager to get as much gold as they can, whatever the risk.'

Pete nodded to everyone and went down the shaft via the poppet pulley which was a small platform lowered by a rope. Chambers went over to the poppet and stared into the abyss. It was dark, but he could hear Pete Barton.

'Where does it go?' he asked the foreman.

'It is not far down, and it leads to a small tunnel. It is not proving to be productive, but Pete will dig out some rock, put it in the bucket and I will raise it to the surface.'

'Doesn't he need a lamp?' asked Chambers.

'There is already one down there,' replied the foreman, 'with Simon, who protects the claim from being jumped.'

'That doesn't still happen out here, does it?' asked Chambers.

'It is one of the biggest problems of the mining claims,' said Richard. 'There is always someone from each claim on the sites, and there are so many disputes these days over boundaries, finds, and claims. Home Rule is divided over the granting of frontage or block claims and the Commissioner is spending all his time up there trying to resolve it.'

'Surely you have more than one gold commissioner? Does he have agents working on his behalf?'

'Only one man for over a dozen Leads and hundreds of claims,' said the foreman, exasperatedly. 'It is a crazy situation. He is always exhausted and overworked, and he takes forever to resolve the disputes.'

'What about Rouse and the other pastoralists? How do they manage?' asked Chambers.

'Rouse is a cunning fox,' said Richard. 'He leases out his paddocks to claims as long as he gets a percentage, about a fifth, equal to the fifth man on a claim, so he has done well.'

'He is also chairman of the Guntawang gold company,' added the foreman. 'The problem on the goldfields are not the claims on farmland, but on crown land, the goldfields proper.'

'I am amazed,' exclaimed Chambers. 'After twenty years, the same problems are still here. At least you have rights now, and some protections, but the situation is hardly ideal.'

The foreman and Richard agreed. 'Why don't you stay here, marry a good woman, and help the miners?' asked Richard abruptly. Chambers looked at him and said nothing.

'Do you have any woman in mind for me Richard?' he asked.

'Well, Elsbeth here has eyes for you, and there is also Mary Kelly,' he replied with a smile. 'We also have Chinese restaurants and market gardens so you can keep up that good Celestial diet. I saw the way you looked at Emma's cooking last night, my old friend.'

Chambers laughed. He thought he had managed to disguise his horror about the evening meal.

Chambers looked down into the shaft. It was like a soup of darkness. He had been underground before. He didn't like it. The mind plays tricks. The smell is awful, and the air is stale. He turned back from the edge and walked over to Merlin who was preparing for another photo, this time looking out across the Lead looking towards

Home Rule.

Suddenly there was a loud noise that seemed to come from underground, and a cloud of dust spewed out of the shaft into the air. Elsbeth fell forward onto the tripod and both she and Merlin grappled with the camera to protect it as they tumbled to the ground.

Chambers and Richard knew exactly what had just happened. Ralph ran up to the edge of the shaft, but Richard pulled him away. He started calling for his father and tried to break free from Richard. He was crying. Elsbeth and Merlin took the child and tried to comfort him. Richard grabbed a shovel and was about to descend the rope when Chambers stopped him.

'You have Emma, Richard,' he said. 'She would never forgive me if I let you do this.'

He handed Chambers the spade. He undid his belt and slid the spade under the belt, tightening it again, and he stepped out into the void, holding the rope.

'Three jerks on the rope means I need help,' he said to the foreman. 'We will need it.'

Chambers took one last look at the world above ground, grabbed the rope, and made his way down the shaft. He pulled on the rope to steady himself and pushed back at the edge of the earth so that he slid slowly down the mine shaft. The further he fell, the darker it became until he could see nothing. It was hard for him to adjust his eyes, but when he did, it was hard to see anything at all clearly. The dust from the shaft was still thick.

He coughed violently, as the dust was getting into his lungs, and there was also something else, a foul smell in the air. The air was stale, and the rocks were giving off an odour. Reaching the ground, he pulled out a bandana and covered his nose and mouth and then pulled out the spade.

A voice groaned from the ground near him. It was Pete Barton.

'Is that you Chambers?' he gasped wearily.

Chambers stretched his hand into the dark. Pete was half buried by the rock and dirt. The entire roof of the cavity had fallen on him. Only his upper chest and shoulders were exposed.

'Simon was digging into the rock,' gasped Barton. 'We felt the earth move. He pushed me backward. I think he must be dead.' He coughed and gasped for breath.

'I will get you out. Ralph is waiting for you at the top.'

'You will not have time Chambers,' panted Pete, trying to move his arms. 'The roof will collapse again soon.'

'Nonsense!' rebuked Chambers. He tried to turn around in the shaft, but it was confined and restricted. He grabbed his spade and began to dig the dirt above Pete and shovelled it behind him. He tossed as much of the soil as he could behind him, and soon was able to move Barton slowly out from under the rock.

Barton screamed in agony as soon as he was moved and Chambers realized the man had both his legs broken, and probably not a few ribs as well. It became apparent that Barton must have been crouching down when the roof collapsed and fell backward, his legs being squashed under him. Chambers was finding it difficult to breathe and with each work of the spade, he became wearier and began to tire He reached back and tugged on the rope three times and continued to pull Barton out of the rubble.

The foreman reached the base of the shaft first, followed by another man Chambers could not see in the darkness.

'Barton has both legs broken,' coughed Chambers. 'He has breathed in a lot of this foul air.'

The foreman coughed loudly, 'You are right, the air is foul.' He pulled out a bandana, wrapping it around his face.

'I need rope,' said Chambers to the other man. 'I am going to tie Barton to my back and climb out of here. Simon is still behind this wall. I don't know if he is alive or dead.'

The other man grabbed the rope and returned to the surface.

The rope was tossed down quickly. As soon as the rope came, so did the rain. It was a relief in one way because it diluted the stench, but it posed another problem.

'That's the last thing we need,' confessed the foreman. 'This mine will fill up like a pond and drown us if the rain is heavy. We need to get Barton to the surface as soon as possible. We could get a tray and lower it down,' he suggested.

I don't think Barton has time,' said Chambers. 'He is almost out of breath, and he is in incredible pain. We need to move him immediately.'

The foreman nodded. The two men tried to get Barton up, but he screamed loudly in agony. With every movement, Chambers had a feeling he was back on one of the battlefields in China. Dirt, grime, sweat, rain, and death, they all came back to him and filled his mind with dark images of the past. He saw faces of men long dead, all crying out to him from the abyss below, their ghostly arms reaching for him to drag him to the depths. He could see the light of a lantern and this light extinguished the images and quietened his relentless guilt. The men above tried to reassure him that it was all going to be all right, but Barton kept repeating that he was going to die, and his wife and child would have to fend for themselves. Chambers angrily told him to be a man and set a good example for little Ralph whom he was going to see again. Chambers shook him but Barton had fallen unconscious.

The foreman lifted Barton up and put him on Chambers' back, with his arms over his shoulders, tying a rope around their waists and a second rope around his upper chest to hold Barton in place and prevent him from arching back. Barton was a heavy man, thought Chambers, and immediately regretted his decision, but he could not think of another alternative. The foreman called out to the men above to pull them up. He tugged on the rope a few times. Another miner descended and tried to find out what happened to Simon.

'I am right behind you,' said the foreman.

The rope began to move. Chambers pushed against the wall of the shaft as they rose. The ropes tied around him quickly made their presence felt, squashing the air from his lungs, and making it difficult for him to breathe. Barton was probably right. He was not going to make it. Both his legs were broken, and he had a lung full of dust. He was probably going to die. But little Ralph needed to see his father again. It could not end like this. Chambers kicked the wall with his feet trying to climb faster, but it was almost impossible to move. As he ascended, he heard shouts of joy from below. Simon had been found relatively unhurt. Barton had pushed him out of the way, and he bumped his head on the rocks, but he was alive.

Then the unimaginable happened. The man operating the wheel on the surface must have let go of the rope and Chambers and Barton fell a few feet, stopping violently. It could have been a mile. A few feet were enough to wind him. The ropes dug into his chest, and he almost lost his grip. Chambers tried to call out, but he had no breath. He crashed against the wall of the shaft. The rain was very heavy now and the walls of the mine shaft were soaking wet. Chambers felt the rope slipping as well. He sighed in relief as the pulley began to move again, but he was out of energy. The slip in the rope took away all his remaining strength and he was exhausted.

The foreman cursed loudly and said that he would break the neck of the man who allowed it to happen. They encouraged him as best they could, but Chambers knew that he was the only one who could change the situation. He cried out in pain as the rope tore into his arms and waist, but he stuck out his feet again to the wall and began to rise once more. When his head emerged above the hole, he could see that it was raining hard. There was quite a crowd now gathering at the poppet. Aside from the people he knew there were quite a few miners.

The last thing he saw was Jed Barton standing by the pulley. He was the one operating the rope. He was the man who let it fall. He did it deliberately. Did he know that his brother was in mortal danger? Did he not care about his own flesh and blood?

A group of men pulled Chambers and Pete Barton up to ground level and quickly untied them. Chambers managed to get to his feet, and he saw Merlin. First, he saw one Merlin, then two, then three. All three images of Merlin merged into one hazy picture and lights flashed before his eyes.

'How many of you are there?' he asked and fell to the ground unconscious.

21.   A HELPFUL DISTRACTION

Guntawang, the estate of Richard and Charlotte Rouse, near Gulgong

Chambers awoke to the warmth of the sun on his face streaming in from a window on the far end of the room. He opened his eyes slowly and looked up. He could see a spotless white ceiling. His eyes followed to the end of the ceiling and then down the wall to the window, which was open. A cool breeze was blowing, and the curtains were shimmering. He breathed in and could smell the scent of flowers. He tried to turn his neck and winced as it was painful, and he saw a small vase of flowers on a side table. Their fragrance was faint. On another cabinet with a mirror, was a wash basin, a jug, and a towel. Draped over a seat were a white shirt and a new suit of clothes. He checked himself and ran his hands over his chest. He was without a shirt and lying on the softest bed he had ever laid upon. The bed was too short for him, and his feet stuck out at the end under the blanket. When he was acquainted with his surroundings, the pain returned to him with a vengeance. His neck ached and he felt like he had ropes tied around his waist and hands.

Ropes.

He then remembered the pit, the caving-in of the mine, and the rescue. It all came back to him. He could not remember anything after pulling Pete Barton to the top of the shaft. He wondered whether Pete was still alive, but more importantly how he ended up in this room, and where he was. It was the prettiest room he had ever been in and reminded him of the house he lived in, when he was living in China with his mother, in the good days before she fell ill. This was a woman's house, and certainly a woman's room, he thought, as he tried to rise. He felt sharp pains all over his body where the ropes had been, but he persisted and managed to sit up, then slide out of the bed and stand up, even though it was quite painful. He sighed and walked slowly over to the basin, poured some water in it, and using the cloth he began to wipe his skin slowly but winced whenever he came to a bruise. He looked at himself in the mirror. His body looked like it had been whipped. He knew he was going to feel the pain of the rope burns for quite some time. Chambers walked over to the window and looked outside. There were horses, lots of them.

He was in Guntawang.

A few hours later, Chambers stood by the window, fully dressed in the clothes kindly prepared for him by the Rouse family. The shirt fitted nicely, but the trousers were a little baggy for his liking. His clothes were so filthy with dirt, grime, and mud, that they were being washed, scrubbed, and cleaned. He hurt all over, especially around the waist and upper back where the rope had made its mark, and his neck was stiff, so it was painful to move it even slightly. Rouse had prepared all the comforts so that he was able to shave and prepare himself for the morning, even polish for his boots, which had been scrubbed and cleaned. Chambers looked outside and could see the splendour of Guntawang for himself. The grounds were immaculate, like a manicured English garden. There was a long white fence cutting across the lawn, and Chambers could see a well-kept hedge and several buildings in the distance.

He thought that he could hear music being played on a piano in another room. The sounds echoed through the otherwise silent house. He thought to himself that a man might find peace in a place like this, sitting on the veranda and watching the sunset, and waking to the sounds of the kookaburra and parrots. He could tell why Rouse was here, but he also knew that where he was didn't just appear overnight. Nevertheless, it was beautiful and peaceful, and he could not remember the nightmares of the night before. He stretched and walked to the door. He found himself in a hallway. The walls were painted and covered with portraits.

He followed the music and came to a large room with some chairs, a small table with flowers in a vase, and in the corner, a woman was playing the piano. He could only see the top of her head as she played and did not appear to have noticed him enter the room. Chambers walked over to a portrait he saw on the wall. It was a man, much like Rouse, standing tall, dressed in riding clothes. The music stopped.

'Mr. Chambers,' said the woman. 'I am so sorry. I did not hear you. It is good to see you up and about after the events of yesterday.'

She was a small woman in a blue dress, with her hair pulled back.

She was younger than Rouse and Chambers was not sure if this was his daughter or his wife.

'Do not stop on my account,' he replied. 'It is beautiful to hear Schubert in the morning.'

'I love his music,' replied the woman cheerfully. 'So does Richard. He is outside attending to the affairs of the day.'

'Thank you for your kind hospitality,' said Chambers bowing to Mrs. Rouse.

'It is our absolute pleasure,' she replied. 'You saved poor Pete Barton's life. Constantine told us all about it.'

'Who is Constantine?' asked Chambers.

'The man who was with you in the mine shaft. He is one of the most famous miners in the area, quite prodigious in his efforts to find gold.'

'He knew what needed to be done and I am glad that he was there.'

'He is a good man too,' said Mrs. Rouse. 'There are lots of good miners in the various leads, we just hope they stay around after the gold runs out.'

'I am sure they will,' said Chambers. 'You have the Opera House near Gulgong now, so that is sure to bring some culture into the area.'

'It is sorely needed Mr. Chambers,' she exclaimed.

'How is Pete Barton, by the way?' asked Chambers.

'He is badly injured, but will probably live, thanks to you,' said Richard Rouse who entered the room. 'I see that you have met my wife, Charlotte,' he said.

'I was listening to her playing the piano. It was truly a refreshing surprise to hear out here in the outback.'

'Pete Barton shouldn't be in the mines, he has too much dust in his lungs. When the mine collapsed, he almost died. You saved his life,' said Richard, changing the subject.

'I did what needed to be done at the time. I was surprised that so few people were there at the time.'

Richard laughed out loud, his hands on his hips. 'Please explain darling why that was the case, while I get Chambers a drink. Brandy?' Chambers nodded, and Rouse went into the next room.

'In the outback Mr. Chambers,' said Mrs. Rouse, there are termites, and they build huge mounds of dirt in the middle of nowhere. On the surface, it appears there is nothing going on. When someone breaks the termite mound, you see what is really happening. There are thousands of these little ants, all scurrying and moving around, and there are these tiny tunnels, hundreds of them, all going in different directions, all with ants in them, all of them busy at one time, all working hard. That is Gulgong, Home Rule, and Canadian Lead. There are hundreds and hundreds of mine shafts and diggings in the area. Every day there are accidents and there have been many deaths. I suspect nobody even noticed about the mine collapse, as they were too busy digging their own claims.'

'Is it that significant?' asked Chambers.

'There are over a dozen gold leads Chambers,' said Rouse, who had reappeared, giving him a glass of brandy. 'There is Red Hill, and Black Lead, and Adams Lead that come from there, Perseverance, Happy Valley, Parramatta, Black Swan, Caledonian, Ford's Creek, Fraser, Rapp's Gully, Star of the South, Victorian, Three Mile, All Nationals, Star of the South, Royal George, Welcome Reef, and of course Old Gulgong.'

'How many people are here then?' asked Chambers.

'I think there must be at least ten thousand around Gulgong, twice as much in and around Home Rule,' said Mrs. Rouse. Chambers' eyes widened. He was genuinely surprised. He had no idea there were so many.

'Have you invested in the gold industry as well?'

'I am the principal shareholder of the Guntawang Freehold Gold Mining Company. We are doing well. To be honest with you Mr. Chambers this is nowhere near the amount of gold that was found in the gold rush of the 1850s, but it is not insignificant.'

'Let us not talk about gold Mr. Rouse,' said his wife. 'Poor Mr. Chambers has been through a terrible ordeal. I am sorry that it has taken us so long to invite you to Guntawang.'

'I am grateful to be here, and I appreciate borrowing some of your clothes. I will return them when mine have been cleaned.'

'There is no need Chambers,' replied Rouse, slightly embarrassed, 'We are not in want here. God has indeed been very gracious with his many mercies. You are also not without friends.'

'What do you mean?' asked Chambers.

'Mary Kelly was here most of this morning, to see how you were faring. She rode here yesterday as well when she discovered what had happened to you. You had quite the entourage, with Mr. Merlin, Ms. McEvoy, Constantine, and Richard Noble, as well as Emma. They all care deeply about you. I think Constantine and Richard have told everyone in Gulgong now what you did for Pete Barton.'

'Mary was here?' asked Chambers.

Mrs. Rouse looked at her husband again. 'She has been here a few times since you arrived,' she replied. 'Partly to allay the gossip that Jed Barton has been spreading about her, but also because she is afraid, terribly afraid.'

She looked at her husband. Rouse spoke reluctantly as if he was revealing a secret.

'She is terrified of John Knox, and his cronies Barton and Cooper,' replied Rouse sipping his brandy. 'Did you know he has lost a few of his men recently?'

Chambers said that he didn't.

'Including a man by the name of Rogers,' continued Rouse. 'He was a cattle rustler a while back, quite an unsavoury man by all accounts, and well known to Powell and Hannan, our detectives. Rogers has been acting as an informant for the police for the last few months. We have considerable evidence against Knox now, especially to do with cattle rustling, thievery, and petty crime. Rouse let Rogers go yesterday because he caught him snooping around and so we lost our man on the inside. The only lead left is Mrs. Kelly and what she might know.'

'Do you think she knows something?' asked Chambers.

Rouse sipped from his brandy slowly.

'Her fiancé died the night before the day her brother died in her arms. He would have said something, but she is adamant that he said nothing to her about who stabbed him. My instincts tell me that Knox and Barton were behind it all. They blamed it on William's assistant Lee Peng. He was a bit of a rascal, but I agree with William Fung, he was not a killer. I have long suspected that their deaths were connected but to date, we have no evidence to proceed with any arrests. So, I believe Mary Kelly has been living in a state of terror for almost twelve months.'

'Then you turned up out of the blue, she lost her temper and told you off, but I don't think it was anything personal,' said Mrs. Rouse.

'That is why she came to see me at my brother's farm, to apologize,' said Chambers. 'You are right. She is absolutely terrified of Knox and his men.'

The clock struck ten.

'We are having a few people over for a luncheon at noon today, Mr.

Chambers, said Mrs. Rouse. 'I hope you are able to stay.'

'I would be honoured Madam,' he replied. 'Thank you for the invitation.'

For the next two hours, Chambers ambled around Guntawang by himself. He visited the stables and saw the horses, as well as the sulkies and carriages that Rouse and his men were building and repairing. He chatted with some of the workmen for a while. They all knew who he was and what he had done the day before. He walked across the paddock. A few, large eucalypts stood tall, the last reminder that Guntawang had been hewn out of the Bush by Rouse's grandfather in the 1820s when Biddy's people were fighting for their survival.

He knew in his heart, that Knox, Barton, Cooper, or all three, had something to do with the death of his brother, and part of him wanted to find a gun and enact revenge regardless of the evidence, but he had been in this situation a dozen times before and he knew that action without evidence was perilous, especially in this land colony of New South Wales. He also knew that gold, as beautiful as it was, had the danger of pulling Guntawang into its maelstrom of death and destruction as it did everywhere it arose. The things people would do to each other for a piece of yellow metal were truly astonishing.

He thought of the debacle that was the massacre at Eureka, and the pointless, brutal, selfishness of the riots in Young over the presence of the Chinese. Even here, in Gulgong, at the tail end of this poisonous period, crime, theft, murder, all the handmaidens of the gold rush, were out dancing in the light. No doubt Hannan and Powell, the famous detectives, were hunting down a few criminals, but Chambers knew that the lust for gold brought out the darkest hues of the human heart.

He knew that Mary had lied to him about what her brother told her the day he died. Rouse knew this as well. Chambers suspected that Mary knew that the name of Shamus' killer was probably Jed Barton, Knox's lackey. He also knew in his heart Millie Thorpe was dead. Henry was dead and Blackwell was missing. There were too many coincidences. Now, Knox was claiming the house was sold. If so, what happened to the money? He also knew that someone was trying to poison John Knox, but they failed dismally on Sunday, killing the wrong people. From Knox's outburst in public, it seemed clear that the Irishman was convinced someone was out to get him, and that list was very long.

Most people hated Knox and many probably wanted him dead.

Most of the people he knew who hated Knox were not there at the service, and so he had to exclude them. Biddy, Mary, and William were not there. He ran through his mind the rest of the people at the service. Whoever tried to poison Knox managed to get to everyone except the man himself. They even poisoned the visiting priest, who had postponed his journey to help Mr. Rouse for a week or two.

Chambers then realized he must have been wrong. He had been deceived. There was no poisoning on Sunday. There couldn't have been. It was just a tragic event, in a tragic town, where death, dysentery, and disease were commonplace. Smythe had already told him this on the day that he spent most of his week burying young children. Poor Henrietta Knox, the town gossip, must have spent too much time spreading malicious gossip about everyone in the town than attending to the careful preparation of some food, and that was her undoing. If anything, her death, and the suicide of her husband, made Knox even more paranoid that someone was out to kill him.

Chambers realized he had fallen for Knox's ruse. It must have been all deflection away from Millie's locket. There had been no attempt on Knox's life. The locket belonged to Milly, and she would not have left it behind. Knox was using their tragic accident with Henrietta to conjure up a fictitious scheme that someone was out to ruin him. This would deflect all attention away from the locket and the detectives would be chasing ghosts. It was Knox. He took advantage of the Sunday chaos to make him the victim, not the villain.

Chambers looked back at Guntawang. He suddenly remembered the locket. He raced back to the house and the bedroom. He asked one of the maids about his clothes and she told him that nothing was found on him except a few papers, which they left in the room. No locket was found on him.

Someone had stolen the locket. Chambers realized suddenly who it was, and it all became clear. Jed caused the accident in the mine shaft to create confusion, not to kill him. In the aftermath of the accident, no one would have stopped him from trying to help his brother. Without anyone noticing, Barton relieved Chambers of the locket, the only physical evidence he had. Barton had the locket, but Chambers knew that this was the first real mistake Jed and Knox had made.

22. TWO WOODEN CROSSES

Richard and Charlotte Rouse invited Henry Beaufoy Merlin, Elsbeth McEvoy, Rev. Albert Lyons, and Nathaniel Chambers to dine with them that day for what Chambers would remember as a banquet. Everyone inquired about Chamber's health and were all keen to discuss his rescue of poor Pete Barton the day before. They sat in the main dining room of the Guntawang homestead, a grand room, more like a room one might have found in Sydney, or Melbourne, quite the opposite to the shack-like temporary dwellings in Home Rule and much of Gulgong.

Guntawang was much more to the liking of Ms. McEvoy, and Rev. Lyons, that much was obvious. The priest was much more talkative than he had been before, and he lamented the dreadful conditions of the manse in Gulgong and was appalled at the dilapidated state of the Church of England building. Merlin proposed to Rouse that the town invite the celebrated architect Edmund Blackett to design a new building in keeping with the expectation that the town might be grander in the future. Rouse was reluctant to adopt the proposal as a Blackett-inspired structure would be extraordinarily expensive, but Merlin admonished him gently, reminding him that the gold that was being dug out of the ground would be more than enough to provide sufficient funds.

'We have our own little chapel at Guntawang as well,' added Mrs. Rouse, it was built quite some time ago.'

'I would love to see it,' said the priest. 'I am always impressed by the dedication and faith of the pioneering families.'

'This is absolutely delicious,' added Elsbeth, grinning widely. 'It makes such a pleasant change from our peasant food at the hotel in Gulgong. There are only a certain number of potatoes one can eat in any lifetime.'

Merlin chuckled. Chambers agreed but said nothing. It was the first good meal of vegetables he had eaten since arriving in the town. It was haricot stew, with vegetables. There was also some fruit on the table, which he relished, but showed his usual restraint.

'In the old days, we had to contend with more basic meals,' said Mr. Rouse. 'I remember as a child, my father expecting us to endure such things as 'slippery bob' which sounded almost as bad as it tasted.'

Everyone laughed. Chambers had also tasted kangaroo brains when he arrived in Australia in the early 1850s. Once was enough. Sheep brains made a good, hearty meal, but slippery bob was true to its name.

'Tell me Mr. Rouse, how did your family come to be here at Guntawang?' asked Lyons.

Rouse put down a knife and fork, wiped his hands with a napkin, and looked at the priest.

'It is quite a story to be told,' he said. 'Don't let the beauty of Guntawang fool you. It was not always like this. My grandfather came to this area in the early 1820s to raise cattle, here and at Biraganbil, where my cousin is now, trying to run horses. In those days, the locals were very hostile toward us, and there was a lot of trouble. But my grandfather persisted and in time there was a little town here, a church, stores, a racecourse and school, an oasis of civilization in a rugged, harsh land. We even had a hotel for weary travellers.

'We started growing wheat in 1851, but we could not get the labour, so we brought in Chinese from the continent. One of them was William Fung, whom you have both met no doubt. I keep telling him to move to Sydney, but I think he stays out here out of respect for my grandfather. William is a fine addition to our community.

'Loyalty and respect, Lyons, are the things of greatest importance here, alongside family and the church. That is why you are most welcome here. I know that you have decided to continue your journey back to Sydney and I do not blame you after the debacle on Sunday with the food poisoning. It is just a shame, as it is so difficult to find reliable priests who want to stay out here in the bush. Most prefer the city lights with all the conveniences. Blackwell was not the best of men, everyone knew that, but it is as if God simply took him away.

'But I am diverting from the topic at hand. So, we had wheat, cattle, and sheep. I believe I can speak for my grandfather and father when I say that we were quite content in this land without the gold. Indeed, we were progressing nicely out here without it, but gold was discovered just near here in 1852 at Guntawang, and then in 1867 at Two Mile Flat, near the Cudgegong River, but it was Tom Saunders' find in April

1870 that started the current gold rush, and rush is not adequate to describe it. I think the word 'stampede' is more appropriate.'

'What problems do you face out here Rouse?' asked Chambers, 'Richard Noble was talking about a dispute over frontage and block claims. Is that becoming an issue?'

'Absolutely,' replied Rouse. 'One would think that mining was a simple thing, but miners and governments find all kinds of ways to make something simple complicated. There are two different types of claims, and they have to do with the depth of the shafts, the nature of the claim, and the number of people working it. The most common method on the goldfields has been the block claim, but Browne the Commissioner has introduced frontage claims out at Home Rule. Many miners believe that this new type of claim is just another excuse for the government to enact excessive legislation.'

'What do you think about it?' asked Merlin.

'I don't see anything wrong with two types of claims as long as there is a fair and impartial dispute process. The problem is that Browne is the only one here and he is exhausted. Last year, we had a fine man by the name of Arthur Hannibal Macarthur, who was the police commissioner and the magistrate. I remonstrated with Sydney to send other men, but they did not, and poor Mr. Macarthur dropped dead. He was only 41.'

'I heard about that,' said Elsbeth. 'That is truly awful. Poor man.'

'Almost immediately,' continued Rouse. 'The government responded by sending us Hannan and Powell, the detectives, and other constables. They all do the work now that Hannibal did last year. Sydney town has no idea what goes on out here. Never has. That is our biggest problem. I would go as far as to say that the greatest problem this colony has is balancing the needs of the city and the country.'

'Why do you think that God took Mr. Blackwell away,' asked Merlin. 'Was he like Enoch in the Bible because he walked with God?'

'No, of course not,' replied Rouse, visibly irritated. 'I just find his disappearance a mystery. These towns as you know are gossip mills, especially in the church. I thought there might be someone who would know why Blackwell left, but there isn't. It is as if he just vanished.'

'What is your impression on these matters, Mr. Lyons?' Chambers asked.

Lyons stared at him for a moment and then smiled slightly. 'The ways of God are often mysterious Mr. Chambers,' said Lyons. 'Who knows the providential hand of God when it appears? Our lives can all change in an instant. Things simply happen and we are often left wondering why. The Psalmist often cried out to God asking him why he suffered, but it was Saint Paul who answered the question 'my grace is sufficient for you, for we are made perfect in weakness.'

'At the time, it is difficult to understand the will of God, but sometimes we need to walk through the mist until the dawn breaks to make sense of it all. I am reminded of what Jacob's son Joseph said to his brothers at the end of the book of Genesis: 'you meant it for evil, but God meant it for good.'

Lyons looked at Chambers seriously.

'Are you suggesting that some good might have come from my brother's death?' asked Chambers. 'I wish I knew what happened to him. His death has brought me closer to him than I have been in decades. I have met all you fine people and caught up with old friends, such as Richard and Emma, whom I knew years ago when I was a much younger man. My hope was that Blackwell might have provided some light on my brother's passing, but as he is gone, alas, those answers will never be found.'

Merlin interrupted them. 'I remember what you said in Gulgong about friendship Mr. Chambers, how did you put it, friendship is the most important thing in the world,' he said. 'I would concur with that, and he smiled at Elsbeth.

'Greater love has no man than this than to lay down his life for his friends,' said Mrs. Rouse.

'Indeed Madam,' said Lyons, 'but I would go further and say that the love of our heavenly Father for his Son is a deeper love, one that truly transcends all life experience. In the same way, the love that a human father has for his son is truly a wonderful thing, and there is nothing, absolutely nothing a father would not do for his son. I am sure as a father, Mr. Rouse, you would concur. Your children are your treasure, not greater than God, but a different kind of treasure. They are your legacy to the world. I see the love of fathers for their children as a picture of the love our heavenly Father had for his Son. Such was the cost of salvation, that the Father gave up the Son out of love for us all so that we might live.'

'A transaction,' asked Chambers, 'his death for mine?'

'Absolutely,' said Lyons. 'He died for you so that you might live and become a child of God.'

'Are you trying to convert me?' asked Chambers.

Lyons laughed. 'I am always looking out for the spiritual well-being of those in my parish wherever I am. For the next few days, Gulgong and Guntawang are part of my parish.'

'I've had many friends over the years who died for me,' said Chambers, 'I'm well-versed in Christian theology, I guess I am weary of all the years of war. I've found religion to be less useful to me than a simple faith, that I am alive because others died in my place. I call them my 'cloud of witnesses,' and I can tell you I have many witnesses.'

'In the old days Mr. Chambers,' said Mrs. Rouse, 'we used to meet under the tree for our Sunday services, and to be honest with you, I am more at home with God under the tree and playing the piano than I am sitting in a cold, dusty church building. We are farmers. We see the change and decay all around us, but there is beauty in all of that too, the changing of the seasons, and surely God is there in all of his universe.'

'I couldn't agree more with Mrs. Rouse,' said Elsbeth. 'If God is really God, then he is everywhere, and all the world is his.'

'Did I hear you mention a piano?' interrupted Merlin. 'I would be absolutely delighted to see it.'

'We might have a cigar and some brandy Mrs. Rouse,' said her husband, 'and Mr. Merlin and Elsbeth can hear you play.'

'I would love a cigar as well,' chimed Elsbeth, but Merlin stopped her.

'I need you to hold the song sheet,' he insisted.

Lyons, Chambers, and Rouse moved to the smoking room. It was carpeted in red, and the walls were full of family portraits. The room looked out to the paddocks. Rouse gave the two men cigars, and they lit them. Rouse offered them both a glass of brandy.

'This is real brandy,' said Rouse. 'I do have a small supply of homemade liquor made by Mr. Constantine of Gulgong, which is also good, but not for the faint-hearted.'

'Do you have an alcohol problem on the goldfields?' asked Lyons, showing deep concern. 'It is truly a vile substance when abused, but even St Paul told Timothy that he might be permitted a drop for his poor stomach.'

Chambers just held his cup politely but didn't drink.

'To whom shall we offer a toast, gentlemen?' asked Rouse.

To the Queen,' said Chambers. 'God save the Queen.' The others assented. Chambers sipped his brandy faintly, just allowing it to touch his lips, and put down the glass on a side table.

'I'm afraid I have something to say that concerns both of you,' said Lyons, holding his leather satchel bag tightly. 'May I sit down Mr. Rouse?' he asked politely. Rouse pointed to one of the armchairs on the side of the room and Lyons slowly sat down.

'I must admit I am still weak from Sunday Mr. Rouse, but I have had no ill effects from your wife's excellent food, so I am sure that all will be well.'

Rouse and Chambers remained standing, Rouse in front of the painting of his grandfather, and Chambers by the window looking out to the paddocks. Lyons looked nervous, quite unsure of where to begin.

'I fully understand if you have to return to Sydney as soon as practically possible,' said Rouse, trying to anticipate Lyon's train of thought. Lyons smiled briefly.

'It has nothing to do with my short-term tenure in Gulgong,' he protested.

'Well, man, out with it!' insisted Rouse. Lyons sighed deeply.

Lyons leaned forward, holding the satchel tightly.

'As you know, last Sunday, a few of us became ill because of something in the food prepared by the late Mrs. Knox, though it was hardly her fault, and I am not laying any blame at her feet. I am saddened by her death, and that of her station manager, Mr Maxwell, who was a rough diamond, as they say, but quite a gentleman in his own way. I too was greatly afflicted as you know. I spent all of Sunday in agony in Rev. Blackwell's old lodgings near the current church building. I was beset by bouts of the most intense internal pain, the likes of which I have never experienced before. Mr. Smyth came to minister to me on Sunday, and Monday, and then this morning, just before I came to have lunch with you all here at Guntawang.'

'You are not telling us anything we do not know Mr. Lyons,' said Rouse. 'I ask you to tell us plainly what you want to say. You are among friends here, and nothing you say will leave this room, I can assure you of that.'

Mr. Lyons took off the cross that was around his neck. It was quite beautiful. It seemed to be made of copper or bronze, and it seemed rather heavy in his palm.

'I have prayed to God most earnestly these last few days, wrestling with him in prayer, wondering what to say to you when I found what I did. I think that the Saviour whose body was slain on the cross would tell me to tell you the truth plainly. On Sunday, when I was laying in agony, I rolled off the bed onto the wooden floor of the bedroom. I did not mind, a few bruises were nothing to compare with the agony I felt, sharp, biting pains from one end of my body to the other. As I was rolling around on the floor, my undergarments caught on a piece of timber that was lying on the floor, jutting out slightly. I played with it for a while, while lying on the floor. I found if I lay in a particular position, the pain would lessen slightly. So, for a long time, I simply stared at this piece of wood. But curiosity got the better of me, and I moved it. It came away relatively easily and underneath the floorboards, I found two things which I did not expect to find.

'I have them in my possession now. One is relatively self-explanatory and will resolve some questions concerning the property dispute between Mr. Knox and Mr. Chambers, the second is more problematic, and seems to provide evidence of several serious crimes conducted in the area by important people.'

Lyons reached into his satchel and produced a small cotton bag, tied with string. He indicated to Chambers that he was giving it to him, and so Chambers came over and took it. He opened it. He was astonished.

'It is gold, pure gold,' he exclaimed looking at Rouse.

'It is not only gold,' said Lyons.

Chambers looked in the bag, and saw something else in there, and pulled it out. It was a necklace.

'This belonged to my mother,' he said exasperated. 'This was my mother's. I can only assume Henry took it when he left us all those years ago. What was Mr. Blackwell doing with it? Did he steal it?'

The priest held his cross, sighed and closed his eyes. 'I think the evidence is that Blackwell stole both the gold and the necklace the night Henry died, and brought them home, but guilt over his actions forced him to hide them both under the floorboards.'

'Then, where is he?' asked Rouse.

'I believe him to be dead,' replied Lyons. 'Guilt can sometimes destroy a man. Blackwell, from what I have heard around here, was not a good man. He had his temptations and he indulged them. But this theft of the money and your mother's necklace must have driven him to his end. To be honest, I believe that when he disappeared a short while ago, he went somewhere familiar he knew and wrestled with himself over what action to take. This struggle might have lasted a few hours at best, but then, I believe, he has taken his own life, out of shame for what he did.'

Rouse turned away and looked at the portrait of his grandfather.

'What do you mean?' asked Rouse, surprised. 'What did Blackwell do?'

Lyons looked over to Chambers and pulled from his satchel a book, with old, worn pages. 'I believe this to be your late brother's journal,' pronounced Lyons, and gave it to Chambers.

Chambers took it in his hands and his eyes filled with tears. He held the book, its pages dirty, and smudged, its entries written in ink, dating back years, occasionally entered, and all the pages are worn.

'I have only read the last few pages,' admitted Lyons. 'I know it was not my journal or my place to do so, but I am a priest, and at first, I thought it was Blackwell's journal and it took me several pages to discover that it was not.'

'It doesn't matter at all, my dear friend,' said Chambers. 'What you have done cannot be measured in words, for you have brought my dead brother to life again, and we will hopefully find some clues about his last days.'

'I am sad to say that it is all there in black and white Chambers,' said Lyons sympathetically, 'especially the last two pages. I am sorry that you need to read those pages. I truly am.'

Chambers looked at Lyons and then at the journal. He knew that what he was about to read was going to change his life, and probably not for the better, but he opened the journal at the end and read the last two pages. Rouse stood patiently in front of his portrait smoking his cigar pipe while Lyons sat quietly on the seat, his eyes closed.

As he read, Rouse could see Chambers was deeply upset by every word that he read, and that it was like a man in deep anguish of spirit. He could tell that Chambers was a good man and that he needed to do all he could to keep him in the country. The land needed more men like him.

Chambers did not take long to read the final two pages of the journal. He closed it and put it on the table and then walked to the window, looking out at the paddock.

'A man could find peace here,' he said. 'A place to settle, live, raise a family. I could be a farmer.'

Rouse was pleased to hear that.

'But I'm not,' continued Chambers. 'I am a soldier, and I am always fighting one war or another. I honestly long for peace, to lay down my sword, and find a little patch of God's earth to call my own. Gordon said that he knew that he would die a soldier doing God's will. I fear that God has that planned for me a soldier's death as well.' He sighed and turned to the two men.

'Lyons is right. The last two pages tell me everything I need to know. The rest belongs to Mary, for she is already his wife, which makes her a widow.'

'What?' asked Rouse incredulously.

Lyons nodded slowly.

'According to his journal, Mary and Henry were married secretly a few days before his death in the new Wesleyan Chapel in Gulgong, by a visiting minister arranged by Mr. Samuels, the Catholic priest. They could not get married in either the Church of England or in the Roman Catholic Church, so they were married by the Methodists. This money is hers, as is the necklace, and the horses you are looking after.'

'Why did she not say anything?' asked Rouse.

'Mary was terrified of the man who most likely was responsible for Henry's death: John Knox,' replied Lyons.

'I was afraid you were going to say that very thing,' replied Rouse.

'Mary was always the key,' said Chambers. 'My brother was with Biddy, the half-aboriginal girl, but he broke it off when Mary wanted to marry him. This would explain the strange conversation I had with Biddy the first time I met her. Henry alludes to this relationship in his journal and his regrets about it.

'Henry had decided to sell the farm to Knox so he could work with Mary and Shamus in Gulgong. Henry writes that he was about to sell, but suddenly, he changed the deal and asked for a much higher amount. Shamus told him that gold had been discovered on his land by George, Biddy's brother.'

'Another seam of gold?' asked Rouse.

'George apparently saw gold one day on Henry's farm, and he reported it to Knox. Mrs. Knox overhead the conversation and knew that her husband was going to diddle Henry out of a proper deal if there was indeed gold on the land, and she told Shamus, her old friend from childhood, that Henry should increase his asking price. Henry writes that Knox was livid and only paid him on the condition that their friendship was over.'

'So, what happened to George?' asked Rouse.

'Well,' said Chambers, 'according to Henry, he, Jed Barton, Blackwell, and George used to go fishing at a waterhole along Cooyal Creek. The last entry in Henry's journal recounts that he was supposed to meet George to go fishing, but he was running late, and he saw Jed Barton shoot George dead by the river. He waited until Jed left and then he buried the body. The last thing Henry wrote was: 'I must keep Mary safe. I wish Nate were here, he would know what to do."

'It is a good thing that I asked Joe Mitchell to go and get Powell and Hannan,' said Rouse.

'When was that?' asked Chambers.

Rouse said that it was yesterday morning.

'They should be here by now,' said Chambers. 'It is only a short ride. Something must have happened.'

Rouse went and poured himself another brandy and drank it. 'I hope nothing happened to Joe. I am sure they are just running late,' he said optimistically.

'This journal is enough to convict Jed Barton, or at least have him arrested for the murder of George,' said Chambers.

'One aboriginal?' asked Rouse. 'I don't think so. I wish it were not the case, but the life of an aboriginal man is not worth much out here.'

'Why don't you take revenge?' asked the priest. 'You have fought in wars all your life.'

'Not even for Henry,' replied Chambers. 'I believe in the law. Without it, there is just chaos, and we just end up like China. We should be free to make our decisions, to say what we want, live where we want, and have that little piece of happiness your God keeps promising us.'

'I am impressed by your attitude,' said Lyons. 'Most soldiers I have met, fight only for themselves, some for their friends, but most have a price tag attached.'

'Where is Cooyal Creek?' asked Chambers.

'It is the creek behind your brother's farm,' replied the farmer.

'I thought that was Crooked River,' said Chambers. Rouse shook his head.

'That is the name of Knox's farm. Someone told him that it is the English meaning of the word 'Gulgong,' but it actually means 'deep waterhole."

'Where is the waterhole?' asked Lyons. 'I don't see any body of water near the town.'

'There isn't one,' said Rouse.

'So why is the town called Gulgong?' asked Lyons, puzzled.

'I am not sure. I think the name referred to a waterhole along the Cooyal Creek somewhere, and over time as the gold was discovered, the location of the town moved as well. In ancient times, many of these creeks were probably larger rivers, and we see that from all the gold being dug up. No one knows for sure.'

'Don't you have a 'Crooked R' brand as well?' asked Lyons.

'My Grandfather's brand, yes,' replied Rouse.

'I will leave at dawn,' interrupted Chambers, changing the subject. He handed Rouse the journal and the money. 'Please keep these for me if you will Rouse until this is all over. They are the property of Mary Kelly or should I say Mary Chambers.'

'You have my word,' replied Rouse. 'Whatever I can do to help, then you have it.'

'I am going to look for George's body and when I find it, I think I will speak to Jed Barton, and try to convince him to confess to murder.'

'What should I do?' asked Rouse.

'This is a bad business,' replied Chambers. 'I don't think you or your family should be involved. Let me talk to Jed. If the detectives are not here by tonight, ride to Mudgee and fetch them but tell no one you are going.' Rouse nodded.

'Had Jed spoken to you?' Chambers asked Lyons.

'I cannot reveal to you anything said in confidence,' replied Lyons. 'I dare not violate my vows, but I can tell you that Jed spoke to me last Sunday at length about the atonement of our Saviour, asking about the manner of Christ's death on the cross, and the pain and suffering he experienced on it. I believe that the poor boy is in turmoil over what has happened.'

'Where is my horse?' asked Chambers.

'It is in the stables,' replied Rouse. 'Richard brought it up after the accident.'

The sound of a piano could be heard in the other room.

'Shall we join the ladies for some song and music?' asked Rouse.

After the music had ended, Merlin was feeling weak and so Elsbeth and Lyons helped him to his room. Rouse and Chambers chatted for a while, mainly going over the plans Chambers had for the following day and the necessity of Rouse to get help as quietly as possible. Soon,

Chambers was left alone in the room. He stood by the window and looked out into the darkness. He thought of Henry writing his journal at Eliza, and the turmoil of his brother in that last week of his life. He remembered Mary and how she gripped the veranda so tightly that he could see the whites of her knuckles, and he thought of George, Biddy's brother, whose body he intended to find in the morning. Death had indeed followed him to Gulgong, and peace had eluded him once again.

The next morning, Chambers left before dawn, reaching Eliza, rode past the farmhouse where his brother was found, and went straight for the creek. It stretched in both directions.

'Which way shall we go my girl?' he asked the horse. 'We might try the easy way first and then come back, what do you think? Henry would not have gone far.'

Chambers looked to the left. The creek meandered along through the bush and away from the town of Home Rule towards the growing town of Mudgee. It seemed an easier path to follow. It was also away from the Knox homestead, so it might have been where Henry and his fishing friends went. He crossed the stream and turned left, following the paddock all the way until the end. When he reached the edge of the paddock, the terrain became rugged bushland, and Chambers apologized to the horse.

The bush was thick, and the horse found it too difficult to move safely, so Chambers decided to go forward on foot. He quickly found the river and waded in. It felt cool on his legs, and he bent down and washed his face. He looked up the river. Chambers reasoned that it would be best to wade along rather than go by the bank. He tried this for about ten minutes, but the creek bed suddenly fell beneath him, and he sank down to his shoulders. He pulled himself up and swam to the side of the river. It was then that he smelt it. The odour hit him like a stone on the face. It invaded his nostrils. He knew that smell. He had experienced it hundreds of times before. He reached into one of his pockets and pulled out a bandana. He soaked it in the water and then wrapped it around his neck and walked slowly towards the source of the smell.

It was then that he saw the body. It was face down in the bush. He knelt and turned it over. It was the corpse of a man in clerical clothes, and the remains of a Bible next to him, soaked and torn. Chambers reasoned that it must have been the body of Mr. Blackwell. Chambers looked and tried to find the cause of death. Parts of the feet and some of the chest was missing, obviously eaten by dogs or other animals. He was not sure of the time of death. The weather was hot, and this would have accelerated decomposition, but Chambers guessed that it might have been a few days at best. Lyons was probably right. It was quite possibly suicide. He decided not to linger too long. He retraced his steps and found the horse. He took a spade and returned to where the body lay. He dug a shallow grave further up the bank in the scrub. He dragged the corpse of the priest into it. He covered the body with dirt and stones and then leaves. He fashioned a cross with two pieces of wood, tied together with a little cloth he tore from the bandana and pushed it hard into the ground. He looked up at the trees around the grave. They all stood still, and Chambers felt that he was standing in church, rather than the bush, God's cathedral, not the hideous stone mausoleums he knew, run by men of power and brutality. He looked at the cross and realized that it was simply respect that made him do it. It was the first time that he was not offended by the crucifix since his wife's death.

Chambers went to the creek, took off all his clothes, and bathed in the creek. The water was cool and refreshing, and he just sat there by the side of the creek, naked until he dried off in the sun. His wounds still hurt, but the more he moved, the less painful everything became. These were only rope burns. They would heal. His heart was weighed down by grief with wounds that he felt would never heal.

He thought of Mei. She was smiling at him. He dressed again. He realized that he was sitting next to a very tall eucalyptus tree, its branches reaching into the sky. A few parrots sat in its branches chirping. It was then that he saw the other grave, the one Henry must have dug to bury George. He was surprised that he missed it. It was on the other side of the creek, and a little cross was still sticking out from the ground. He knew what he had to do. It was not pleasant. But it was not the first time he had to ascertain the identity of the dead.

Suddenly, he felt a wave of emotion wash over him. Tears welled up in his eyes, and he could not contain himself. Deep in the Bush, away from others, Chambers wept. He wept for George, whom he had never met. He also wept for all those he knew who died before him, those who died before their time. He wept for those who died in his arms, those who died with him in battle, and those who died alone. There were so many, his 'cloud of witnesses.' He ached for peace, a time when he could sit like Rouse in a chair and look out at the horizon, and not have the ghosts and spirits of the departed accuse him for still being alive. They were always with him, his fallen comrades, whose names he had never forgotten. They would never leave him, and he knew he would never find peace. He rose to his feet and crossed the creek towards the grave, with the spade in his hand.

23.   THE CURSE

The Canadian Hotel in Home Rule, and the Royal Hotel in Gulgong

Chambers rode as fast as he could to Home Rule. The street was relatively busy in the late morning. Most of the men were at their diggings, while sulkies were going up and down the main street from Mudgee on one side to Gulgong on the other. He had in his pocket George's ring, and he intended to give it to Biddy when he found her. It was the only mark of identification he could find on the rotting and decomposing corpse of the young man. He arrived at the spot he had arrived at the previous Thursday night. It seemed like a long time ago, but it had only been a few short days.

He had wondered on his journey from Shanghai what he might find in the little town of Gulgong. He had assumed something relatively simple, a clear case of foul play, but instead, he found a series of riddles enveloped by a mist, in the middle of darkness. He still smarted from his rope burns, and even though he had washed again in the Cooyal Creek, the smell of decaying flesh stuck in the depths of his nostrils. It made him think of the wars he fought in China, and all those terrible memories had returned. He wondered whether it would be ever possible to have a life like Rouse, sit out on a veranda in the evening and watch the sun fall behind the horizon. He didn't think so.

Rouse and the priest did not understand his reluctance to use a gun or carry one. They were not soldiers. They had never served in battle. They were civilians, and despite all their anxieties and troubles, neither of them knew the life or the mind of a soldier. Neither of them had faced an enemy on the field of battle. Anyone could be a bully or a thug, but even the strongest of men quaked in front of a full volley of fire, or a bayonet charge. Fear was a constant companion and dearest friend. The bold and the confident always died first.

He certainly desired to kill Knox and Jed Barton, but for other reasons. Knox had put fear into Mary's heart so that she grasped the wood so hard, he could see the whites of her knuckles. She was so scared of Knox that she kept her marriage to Henry a secret. She also knew that Jed most likely had murdered her brother, but she was so overcome with fear that she kept quiet. This was evil. If Chambers had a gun, then he would most certainly shoot and kill Knox without a moment's remorse, but this wasn't China, and this was a time of peace. He would also gladly kill Jed Barton for shooting poor George. He could kill both men with his eyes shut. Murders by civilians were done out of rage and anger, and a tsunami of emotions built up in the sinews and hearts. Not so the soldier. It was all as natural as waking up in the morning, the training, the habits, the calculations, and the risks. For the sake of Mary, Biddy, and even Rouse, he needed to get Jed to confess publicly and then force Knox to the end of himself.

As he approached the Hotel, he could see Mary on the veranda in front of The Canadian. She looked worried.

'How are you?' she asked with genuine affection.

'I am fine Mary,' he replied, getting off his horse and tying her up on the riling. Mary came over to him and stood close to him. He looked at her. She had let her hair hang low and it sat on her shoulders.

'Thank you for visiting me at Guntawang,' he said. She blushed.

'I know that you and Henry got married,' he said. 'I also know that Shamus told you who stabbed him.'

Mary's eyes widened and she fled back to the door of the hotel, holding onto the frame tightly, staring back at him. Chambers followed her and stood close to her.

'I am a dead woman,' she said softly. 'Shamus told me it was Jed. He said that George had found gold on Henry's property a few days before, just after we got married. He said that Mrs. Knox didn't want Henry to lose money in the house sale. This meant that Mrs. Knox betrayed her husband. If he knew, then he would have killed her.'

'Why didn't you tell anyone?' asked Chambers.

'But who?' she exclaimed angrily. 'Who can you trust out here?'

Chambers pulled Mary off the door frame and tightly held her.

'I will not let anything happen to you Mary,' he assured her, taking her inside the Hotel. It was surprisingly empty.

'Where is everyone?' he asked her.

'There was a fight down the street before between two prospectors. Everyone went down there, and I think they started gambling. They will be back soon.'

'I need to find Biddy,' said Chambers. 'Where is she?'

'Why do you need to find Biddy?' asked Mary.

'I found George, or what was left of him,' he said.

Mary was speechless, but took his right hand, and led him out to the back of The Canadian, and next door to the back of William and Sarah Fung's shop. She thumped on the door.

Sarah answered. 'Come in,' she said to them.

When they entered, Chambers saw the body of a man on the floorboards, with a blanket over him. 'Who is this?' he asked.

'Joe Mitchell,' said Sarah.

'What happened?'

'We don't know exactly,' said Sarah. 'Biddy came in this morning with the body, crying, and covered in blood. She said that Cooper had shot Joe dead on the road to Mudgee yesterday afternoon.

'Where is Cooper now?' asked Chambers.

Sarah said that she didn't know where he was, and that Biddy told her that she waited for Cooper to leave until she retrieved the body.

'Where is Biddy now and where's your husband?' asked Chambers, kneeling, and uncovering the blanket to reveal Joe's face.

Sarah said that William had ridden to Guntawang to get Rouse and had not yet returned. As for Biddy, she was outside somewhere.

'Sarah,' said Chambers. 'I have found George's body by Cooyal Creek.'

'So, he is dead, after all,' she replied calmly. 'I thought maybe he just left and went somewhere. His people often do.'

Chambers shook his head. 'I need to speak to Biddy and then I need to see Jed Barton.'

'I saw him this morning,' said Sarah. 'Jed said he was going to help Richard and Emma at Happy Valley. Why do you need to see him?'

Chambers looked over to Mary. 'Jed Barton murdered Shamus Murphy, George, and probably Henry.'

The two women stood there in the back room shocked and silent. Chambers left, walked through the shop, and out onto the street. He saw Biddy next to his horse. She was feeding the horse an apple.

'I am afraid Biddy that I have some news about George,' he said.

Chambers looked at the woman. Her eyes showed that she had been crying for hours. He reached into his pocket and pulled out the ring. She was astonished when he produced it, took her right hand, and put it in her trembling and shaking palm.

She looked up at him. 'You found him?' she asked.

'At Cooyal Creek, near my brother's place.' Biddy took the ring and held it up.

'I was never allowed near that part of the creek, near the Knox farm,' she said. 'It is forbidden for our people; you wouldn't understand anyway. I am deeply saddened they buried George there. The ancestors would be furious. It is a terrible thing.'

She sighed and looked at the ring again.

'This was George's pride and joy,' she said. 'It was from our mother, and the only thing we have of her that is still here, apart from our memories.'

'George, Henry, Jed, and Blackwell used to go fishing along the Cooyal,' said Chambers. 'From what I can work out, George discovered gold on Henry's property. George was killed so he would not tell anyone what he found, but it was too late. Mrs. Knox overheard what George had said. She told Shamus, and Shamus told Henry. Henry in turn demanded a higher price for the farm.'

'But there was no gold there,' said Biddy.

'What do you mean?' asked Chambers.

Biddy sighed and walked out to the middle of the road looking down to Gulgong.

'George came and told me about the gold. He was excited. He thought he had seen gold shimmering in the creek at Henry's place. I could see the creek from Henry's place, and I had a look. It must have been the sun on the water, and there was no gold. George was a good brother Chambers, and a hard worker, but he had the mind of a child, he was always a little kid in his head.

'My mother said that I had to look after him and so I was glad that he found a job with Knox even though he was a very unpleasant person. George just helped around the place, didn't do too much, and did nothing that required much thinking. Knox knew that, and for all his faults, he accepted George, and let him work. But George talked too much. He would blabber and tell people the strangest things. A few years ago, he told everyone that he saw a bunyip in Gulgong and that it was wandering around the area looking for food. He would say things like that all the time. I suspected the discovery of gold was another one of his imaginative inventions. He wanted to be important. He did not want to be ignored and so he just invented things.'

'So, there was no gold at all on my brother's farm?' asked Chambers.

Biddy nodded.

'There is always gold in the rivers, little pieces here and there. This whole area is full of gold, but enough gold for a claim or a mine shaft or a lead? No, not at Eliza. Knox had a few claims on his property, but none amounted to much. As luck would have it, all the leads seemed to bypass his farm, as if the entire world conspired against him. The curse of Crooked River was always John Knox and what he brought from Ireland, his hatred for life and everyone in the world. He is the curse, and he infects everyone around him.'

'Do you think he murdered his wife as well?' asked Chambers, 'and little Millie?'

Biddy nodded again.

'Yes, of course,' she said. 'If Gulgong was Sydney, then Knox would have been hung for murder long ago, but this is the country, where people get away with all kinds of crimes all the time. If one of my people were even suspected of doing one percent of what Knox has done, they would have been shot already. There is no law out here.'

'So, what happened to Millie?' asked Chambers.

'Jed could kill a man, but a young girl?' she asked. 'He has been living in torment these last twelve months because of what he did. Only Knox could kill a child. He has love for no one, but everyone praises him because he goes to church.'

Biddy looked up at Chambers. She reached out with her hand and touched his cheek. It was soft to touch. He did not move away.

'You are a man with two faces,' she said. 'One face was that of a bully. That man used to go hunting my people with his friends and shoot them like animals. I knew this even when we were together. What kind of woman does that make me? I craved friendship and Henry was there for me, at least for a while. Your face is that of an outsider, a man without a home. I don't think you have ever found a place to rest your head, have you?'

She caressed his cheek and then removed her hand. She turned back towards the Canadian and saw Mary standing there.

'What I am going to say is what I should have said years ago, but I have been hiding from who I am for too long. These words are not for you or for Mary. The ancestors need to hear them, and I need to say them. Please take her away from here, away from this terrible, horrible place of death.'

She looked at Mary once more and started walking down the street.

'What did she say?' asked Mary.

'I am not entirely sure,' replied Chambers.

A sound pierced his ears. It was like the cry of the land itself. He heard Biddy scream at the top of her lungs and fall to her knees. Mary went to go to her, but Chambers stopped her.

'No, this needs to be said,' urged Chambers. 'These words need to be uttered. Too much blood has been spilled here and there needs to be an atonement.'

'What are you talking about?' she asked.

Biddy screamed again, and again. It was a deep, guttural wailing as if her entire body was in agony. Shopkeepers came out of their stores, People stopped what they were doing and stared. Sarah came out of her store and stood on the veranda.

'I curse this land!!' screamed Biddy, and pounded the ground with her fists, digging her fingers into the dirt and scraping up the soil. She groaned in pain, and lifted the soil above her head, dropping it on her hair and face.

'I curse this land!' she cried out again. 'I curse the soil, I curse the people, all my family is gone, all my family murdered. My mother, George, all my family, Henry, all dead. All the voices are silent now. They are silent. They are still. The land hears their cries. The land remembers. My land.'

'I curse all of you, all the people here, may this town die, and never rise again. It will linger like a dying man, but it will never rise again. Its name will be forgotten. No one will remember it. All that will remain will be a road, and paddock and all that is here will go to dust.

'I curse Gulgong and all the people there. May darkness shroud it forever. May it always look back to the past, may it be chained to the past, enslaved to the past. May it always linger in obscurity, and never find peace.

'I curse Mudgee, that land of death, where so many of my people died, and were butchered. May my curse be over it forever, over its people and its riches and wealth.

'I curse Bathurst, and all the towns and farms and waterholes and valleys where they slaughtered my people like cattle, like sheep to the slaughter, and then went to church and prayed to the God from whom they had turned away.

'I call to my people now dead, the spirits of my ancestors and to the God of heaven, the blood of my people is soaked into the soil, it is in the earth, hear my cry and my pleading. I pray for vengeance, I pray for justice, I curse the land!'

Chambers went to his horse, untied it, and mounted it. The horse reared up in the air, unsettled by the screaming of Biddy, as if the ground was too hot to tread upon.

'I am going after Jed Barton,' called Chambers to Mary, who looked up at him. 'This ends today!'

'Don't confront him!' she pleaded. 'He is too dangerous for you. He has already killed people Nathaniel, and you are a good man!'

Chambers ignored her and rode away down the main street of Home Rule, the horse kicking dirt into the air. He turned around to see Biddy still weeping in the middle of the street. It was the last thing Mary said that stuck in his mind as he rode quickly to Gulgong via Happy Valley.

Chambers knew that Mary was wrong. He was not a good man. He had killed too many people. He had too many of his witnesses passing judgment on him in his mind every night as he slept. There were times on the battlefield when he wrestled with thoughts, temptations, and ideas that should not be thought by any decent man. All he heard were the accusations of his cloud of witnesses. He tried to shut them out, yelling at him, accusing him, of leaving them, betraying them, killing them.

He quickly made his way to Happy Valley. Some of the miners who were there recognized him and said hello. He asked them where Jed Barton was, and they told him that he was probably at the Royal Hotel in Gulgong.

Chambers set off for Gulgong. He knew that Biddy had shot Cooper dead. He could see it in her eyes. There was bravado there, a new air of confidence, and the absence of fear. She had shot him dead and dumped his body somewhere. It didn't matter. Cooper was filth. He didn't deserve to live. He was a thief and a liar, who sold his commission for whatever he could get. He was unworthy of the uniform and a disgrace.

Chambers was going to make a Judas out of Jed. He was going to beat him until he confessed, even if he had to bring him to the edge of death. What he did in the mining shaft was unforgivable, trying to hurt him while he was rescuing his brother so he could get the locket. What a wretch of a man! He was not going to kill Jed. He needed him alive. He needed a confession.

Gulgong was packed with miners when he arrived at the Royal. The main street was thronged with people, coming, and going, stagecoaches going up and down the street, traders talking, men chatting, and boasting. Music was being played across the street in another hotel. Chambers tied his horse to a railing. He ran up to the hotel. Emma was serving drinks, and he nodded in her direction, asking her whether she had seen Jed Barton.

"He is over there,' she said, pointing to a man standing facing away from them, talking with a few other men. Chambers picked up a bar stool, went over, and smashed it over his head, bringing Jed crashing to the floor. He struggled to get to his feet, and Chambers helped him.

'I will show you the same courtesy you showed George when you shot him in the back,' he said angrily. He picked him up and threw him through the front window of the Royal Hotel.

Jed's three mates turned on Chambers, but he was too fast for them. The first swung wildly, and Chambers punched him in the stomach, pushing him against the second man. Both fell to the floor. The third tried to rush him, but he moved aside and threw the man onto a table, and it collapsed under his weight. Chambers stormed outside, to find Jed climbing to his feet, pieces of glass sticking out of his arms and legs.

'Why did you shoot Millie?' yelled Chambers, while Jed shook his head, struggling to stand.

'I didn't,' protested Jed holding his face, with one hand.

"You killed my brother though, didn't you,' answered Chambers and kicked Jed roughly in the ribs. He was thrown onto his back and cried out in pain.

'You killed Shamus Murphy!' shouted Chambers. 'The reign of John Knox, the tyrant is over, you do not have to do his bidding. You are not his slave. Why do you let him run your life? Knox will walk free, but they will hang you Jed, and what will Mrs. Pete Barton do then? Or little Ralph. Pete will not walk again Jed, you know that. They need you. I know you are a good man. It is never too late to make the right decision.'

'It is too late!' screamed Jed, 'I have done too much!'

'You coward!' shouted Chambers and kicked Jed again, this time deeply in the side. Jed began to vomit. He spat and wiped his mouth.

Richard appeared at the doorway and came over, his rifle in his hand. 'What are you doing?' he demanded.

'Jed murdered my brother, he murdered Shamus, he murdered George, and he probably murdered Millie,'

'Get away from him,' ordered Richard.

'Are you going to shoot me too Richard?' asked Chambers.

Richard was angry. The front window to the Royal was smashed, and Chambers had caused costly mayhem in the hotel. He had every right to be furious. He looked back at Emma who was standing nervously in the doorway.

At this moment, Lyons arrived on a horse, dismounted quickly, and rushed over to the three men. Jed looked up at him and turned his face away.

Chambers decided to kick Jed one more time, but Lyons stopped him, holding him back. 'It's enough for one day,' he cautioned.

The three men stared at Jed, who lay on his back in pain, moaning. He vomited again, and a foul stench filled the air. Other miners began to pour out of the Royal, and a crowd began to gather.

'All right!' Jed called out in pain. 'I give up! I can't do this anymore! I am so tired of it all. I cannot live in this daily hell of guilt and shame!'

He crawled to his feet and looked up at Chambers, Richard, and the priest.

'I didn't kill Millie,' he said. 'I didn't kill Mrs. Knox, that was John, he murdered them both.'

24.   MILLIE

The Church of England Chapel, Church Hill, Gulgong

Jed confided in Lyons he would not say anything more until he sat in the church. Lyons said that it would be a good place for everyone to go. Cooler heads would prevail, noted the priest, in God's house. By then, Mary and Sarah had arrived from Home Rule but William had still not returned from Guntawang. Richard helped Jed to a wagon and put him on it. He took his rifle with him and made sure he had his pistol as well. He was not going to take any chances. Emma stayed behind at the Royal. Lyons and Chambers rode with them, with Sarah and Mary, joining Richard and Jed on the wagon. Few words were spoken as they ascended Church Hill towards the church. When they reached the building, Chambers remembered the awful events of the previous Sunday. They all stepped out of the carriage and walked to the church.

'I must admit,' said Lyons. 'It is strange to be back here after the events last Sunday. I did not think I was going to live through the night.'

'Was Smythe right then?' asked Chambers.

'I don't know Chambers, 'said Lyons. 'I must admit that I was not feeling well on Sunday morning before church. I felt nauseous. I don't think poor Henrietta knew how to cook properly. It was the worst food I have eaten. I think the meat was off.'

Chambers looked over to the place where Henrietta Knox dropped dead. The area was empty now.

'What is it?' asked Mary, wondering if something was wrong.

'It's nothing,' said Chambers. 'Henrietta Knox died just over there,' pointing to the place.

'She was a horrible woman,' said Mary. 'Full of bile, venom, and spite. All the malicious gossip of Gulgong was spread by that woman. She will not be missed by anyone. She ruined the lives and reputations of many people, especially women. Maybe God killed her stone dead that day for her sins.'

'I don't think God works like that,' said Lyons who was listening.

Are you so sure?' asked Mary. 'Didn't God say vengeance was his, he would repay?'

'Indeed,' replied Lyons. 'But I like to think that there is always the road back to redemption that anyone can take provided they turn back to God.'

'It is that forgiveness of God I wish to claim,' insisted Jed. 'I know I have done wrong. I know I have sinned. Please let me explain to you all why I brought you here and what really happened that terrible night.'

He turned and stroked the church door with his hand.

'This is my church, my church,' he said fondly. 'This is where God is.'

He stepped inside and bowed to the altar and walked towards it. Lyons and the others followed him in. Lyons stopped Richard and told him that he would not allow a rifle in the house of God. Richard reluctantly leaned the rifle against the wall of the church near the entrance, but he did not tell the priest about his pistol. Barton stopped at the altar and put his hands on it. He reached for the chalice and held it in his hands. He then fell to his knees. Lyons came up and put his hand on his shoulder.

'Unburden your soul my friend, tell us what you know,' said the priest.

'I need a moment,' he said and stood there quietly.

Mary and Chambers sat together in a pew with Sarah and Richard on the other side of the aisle.

'I didn't know for sure that Jed killed Henry, but I knew he had killed my brother,' she said. 'I was too terrified to tell anyone. Who can you trust around here?'

'If you can't trust anyone, why stay here?' asked Chambers. 'We all need someone we can trust, someone who is there for us.'

'Who is there for you?' she asked.

'I have my cloud of witnesses Mary, the men I left behind on the battlefield. I am never alone,' replied Chambers.

'But someone real, Nathaniel,' insisted Mary. 'You need someone whose heart is still beating. I am sure your cloud of witnesses or whatever you want to call them, wanted the best for you, and you do not need to punish yourself for being alive. That would be the last thing they would want.'

'I am still haunted by the death of my wife Mary,' said Chambers. 'I was not there for her when she needed me.'

'She was a victim of war,' said Mary. 'And today you were here for Biddy, and most of all, you were here for me.'

Mary reached across and placed her hand in his.

'I'm ready to say what I need to say,' said Jed, looking over to Lyons who nodded.

'It is true what I said back at the Royal,' said Jed. 'I accidentally shot Henry that awful night. I killed him with one shot from my rifle. It went right through him, and he died on the spot. I thought it was young Millie Thorpe who had seen John Knox poison his wife. John shot her as she tried to escape, and he sent me after her. She made it all the way to Henry's farm, across Cooyal Creek, but I think she died before she reached the homestead. I saw some movement in the grass, and I fired my rifle. I thought it was Millie, but it wasn't.'

Jed looked over to Mary.

'I think you already know the rest,' he said.

Lyons came and put his hand on Jed's shoulder.

'You should tell the rest, Jed. It is important to make a full confession.' Jed looked at the priest, and he nodded reluctantly.

'Lee Peng, the Celestial gave me the poison. He had a little still making illicit whiskey, and I suspected that it was there he was also dabbling in herbal medicines and poisons. He had a shed deep in the bush. Only he knew where it was. But Lee Peng gave me the poison after I threatened to report his illicit whiskey still to the detectives Hannan and Powell. I didn't know that administering the poison would have caused Mrs. Knox such incredible pain. She was in agony for hours before she died.'

'Why did John Knox kill his wife?' asked Sarah.

'He caught her fraternizing with Shamus. I mean that they were not doing anything inappropriate, just talking. They knew each other in Ireland, in fact, they were old friends apparently, and they were astonished to meet each other again. John is a very jealous man and saw them talking together one day at Gulgong. It was then he started beating his wife. I heard her cries every night. So did poor Millie. We were both terrified.

'Anyway, Henry told John that he was going to sell the farm so he could marry Mary and help out at the Shamrock and Thistle in Gulgong. They were about to shake on it a few days later when Henry said that he had been told that gold had been found on his property. John knew that only two people aside from himself knew that. George, the aboriginal boy, and me. This meant that Mrs. Knox had overheard us talking about the gold and she went and told Shamus to tell Henry. When we confronted Mrs. Knox about it, she admitted it, and she said that she didn't want Henry to lose money due to her husband's deception. For John, who came here to Australia to raise money to pay off his family debts in Ireland, this was the last act of betrayal. Mrs. Knox had to die.'

There was silence in the church for a while.

'What I don't understand Jed,' said Mary. 'Why did you continue to work for Knox if he was such a monster?'

'He was blackmailing me,' replied Jed. 'He saw me kill a prospector a few years back and he used it against me. I often tried to get free, but it was the guilt that trapped me, and the guilt that prevented me from leaving. I became entrapped further and further into a web of my own sins.'

Jed sat down on the pew and put his head in his hands. Everyone sat silently for a while.

It was Sarah who spoke eventually. 'What are we going to do?' she asked.

'I feel numb,' said Mary to Sarah. 'I feel completely numb. I don't think anything has really sunk in yet. I feel like they are just words now.'

She looked up at Chambers. 'What should we do Nathaniel?' she asked.

'Well, I think that we need to bring Knox in, quietly if we can, if that is indeed possible,' he replied.

Jed looked up. 'He will not listen to you. He hates you,' he said. 'He will kill you the moment you set foot on the farm.'

'I will go,' volunteered Lyons. 'I am a priest in the Church of England. If he respects anything, he will respect me. I am not even from around here. I have never been here before. I don't know anyone here. I am thankful to God that in these few days, I have been able to do some good. It was providence that Rouse met me in Mudgee last Wednesday, I spent a few days in Guntawang, then I endured that awful night at the Knox residence, and most of my time recovering in bed here in Gulgong, but I think that John Knox will listen to me. I feel able to talk to him.'

'That is a good idea,' said Jed. 'He has spoken highly of you the last week. He really wanted you to stay on as our priest. I am sorry that you have decided to move on. I only wish we knew what happened to Blackwell. His disappearance is the only remaining mystery for me.'

'He is dead,' announced Chambers.

Everyone was shocked.

'I found the body today.'

'So much death for such a small town,' said the priest.

'Jed,' said Chambers. 'You took the locket from me when I was out of breath on the rope the other day didn't you?' Jed nodded.

'I have it here,' he said and reached into his pocket. He pulled it out. He placed it on the altar.

'I don't think Jed is finished, are you,' said Richard. 'You could have told us all this in Gulgong, at the Royal. Why bring us all to the church and make your confession here?'

'This is the house of God,' said Lyons.

'Shut up priest,' spat back Richard, 'You don't care about Jed. This is just another soul for you to win on your way to heaven.'

There was silence.

'I'm sorry,' said Richard, 'that was unfair. I am just angry.'

'Don't even think about it, Mr. Noble,' replied Lyons. 'It is a sad day, a sad day.'

Chambers stood up and moved away from Mary and towards the altar. He was horrified by what he was thinking, but a thought had come into his mind, something so awful, but so true, that it was astonishing.

'You were confessing to Millie,' he said. 'You are confessing to her because she is here.'

Jed said nothing, but his face told Chambers everything. He turned away from the altar, whereas Chambers turned his attention to it. It was made of packing cases with a flat board of wood on the top, with two brass candlesticks on either side. He lifted the wooden board and wrenched it free. It wasn't even nailed down on the packing cases. The candlesticks and chalice fell off the table onto the floor. Chambers tossed the wooden altar table across the room, and it smashed in the corner. Everyone was so shocked at what he had done that nobody said or did anything. Even Lyons just stood there, speechless.

Chambers kicked over the packing cases. They tumbled over

themselves and fell silent. He looked and saw that the wood had been recently moved and repaired by someone. He looked down and he knew that he was standing in front of Millie's final resting place.

'This is the house of God Mr. Chambers,' said Lyons, visibly upset that Chambers had desecrated the altar.

'God left here a long time ago,' retorted Chambers. 'I am pretty confident he is not going to come back to this wretched place.'

He pointed to the floorboards. 'Millie is under there isn't she Jed?'

Everyone looked at Jed horrified.

He said nothing.

'You buried her under the altar?' asked Chambers. 'You did not even give her a Christian burial? What kind of devil are you?'

Jed burst into tears. 'I burnt her body the night of Henry's death because John told me to. I put her remains together in a hessian bag. John wanted me to bury her near the river, but I could not do that. I burnt the remains again the next day and put what was left in a small box and buried her here under the altar. I am the groundskeeper of the church and so I am always here.'

Chambers was furious but he turned to Lyons.

'Take Jed and bring Knox back if you can. We will wait a few hours for you, no longer. Go quickly.'

Lyons nodded, pulled Jed up and they started to walk down the aisle to the door. Mary stood up and walked over to Chambers, asking him to sit with her.

A figure stood at the doorway.

It was Knox. 'You Judas!' he yelled at Jed, 'You bloody Judas!'

He was holding Richard's rifle.

'Back into the church all of you,' he ordered. 'Going to come and get me to come back quietly?'

He told them to gather at the front of the church, near where Chambers had destroyed the altar.

'You desecrated my church,' he said, pointing the gun at Chambers. 'I hated you the moment you turned up.'

Richard was shielding Sarah behind him and gently urging her to stand behind the pew, not in the open. Jed and Lyons had their hands up and they were walking back toward the others. Jed turned to face Knox.

'I will not let you kill any of them,' Jed said firmly to Knox. 'I have confessed everything John, everything. The only thing waiting for us is a rope.'

Knox was furious, but then he smiled at everyone. 'There may be a rope for me,' he said slyly, 'but not for you Jed.'

He discharged the rifle. The bullet struck Jed in his chest, and blood sprayed out over the remains of the altar. The moment the shot rang out Chambers pulled Mary down and shielded her with his body. Richard did the same with Sarah. Lyons didn't move and was covered with Jed's blood.

Jed stood for a moment, then held his chest, with a surprised look on his face, staring at Knox before falling to the floor. Knox turned the rifle towards Chambers.

'I have wanted you dead since the moment we met,' he said.

'I don't care who you want to kill Knox!' shouted Richard, pulling out his pistol. 'My rifle has one shot, and you have used it up.'

Knox threw down the rifle and reached for his pistol.

'Touch that pistol and I will shoot you dead,' said Richard.

Knox immediately withdrew his hand and started to back away.

It was at this moment, that Lyons, still drenched with blood, stepped between the two men raising his hands. Jed's blood ran down Lyon's face, but he didn't flinch.

'I will not allow further bloodshed in this church!' he sternly ordered both men. 'What is wrong with you people? This is a church. A girl is buried without proper rites under the altar, and you have no qualms about shooting a man in the aisles. Is there no honour in this town?'

'I am sorry Mr. Lyons,' apologized Knox, clearly distraught over what he had done looking down at the body of Jed Barton, now lying in a pool of blood. 'What have I done? Oh my God, what have I done? God help me!'

He started to sob and began wiping his eyes, backing away towards the door of the church. 'I will crucify the first man who turns up at my place, do you hear?' he yelled.

'I will set up three crosses, one for each of you men if you dare to come after me, and I will leave the one in the middle for the great Messiah, Nathaniel Chambers. If you stayed in China, Jed and Joe would still be alive. Their blood is on your hands.'

Richard aimed his pistol, but Lyons stopped him.

'Let him go,' he said with great weariness. 'I will not allow any more shooting in God's house.' The priest sighed. It seemed a pointless thing to say, but he sounded desperate.

'Remember what I said,' said Knox. 'If you follow me, I will crucify all of you.'

He turned and stormed out of the church. As soon as he left, Richard, Chambers, and Lyons moved the pews out of the way to get to Jed. He was barely alive.

'Mary!' Chambers called her over. He knelt and lifted Jed's head onto his lap.

'I'm here Jed,' said Mary, sitting next to him, holding his limp hand. He looked up at her, his eyes full of tears.

'I'm sorry,' he said gasping, coughing up blood. 'I wanted to tell you that I shot Henry.'

Mary was crying. 'I always knew Jed,' she admitted. 'I could tell from your eyes you had done it. You were always carrying around this burden of shame. You could never speak to me after Henry died. I knew.'

'Can you forgive me?' he asked.

She nodded, weeping softly.

He tried to look up at Chambers, but the light faded from his eyes, and he died.

Lyons said a few prayers over the body of Jed, but no one was paying attention. He slowly wiped the blood from his face and neck. Everyone else sat quietly in the pews, except Richard who went outside to smoke a pipe. Emma arrived soon after the shots were fired, and so did quite a few people, but none went inside. They all gathered outside, milling around quietly. Chambers and Mary were sitting together, not saying anything. Sarah had quietly and slowly repaired the altar that Chambers had smashed and returned the chalice and candlesticks to their original place.

Lyons saw her do this and smiled.

'Thank you, dear Sarah,' he said quietly. 'Please tell William that he is not to blame for anything. It is God's will that things happen the way they do.'

A few moments later, Chambers saw him leave, mount his horse and ride away.

'Where did the priest go?' asked Mary about an hour later.

Chambers sighed. 'He has gone to bring Knox in,' he replied sadly. 'He is a determined man, that priest.'

'I'm afraid that he will not be coming back,' said Richard. 'Only

Jesus rose from the dead.'

In what seemed an eternity later, Rouse stormed into the church, followed by William, Hannan, and Powell, the two detectives whom he brought from Mudgee. Chambers and Hannan laughed when they saw each other and shook hands warmly.

'You are still alive I see,' laughed Hannan. 'I knew trouble would find you, Chambers, it always does.'

'You didn't tell me you knew Chambers,' exclaimed Rouse.

'I don't have to tell you everything Rouse,' replied the detective, 'I work for the government, not for you.'

He patted Chambers on the back warmly. He then noticed Mary standing there behind him, shrouded in darkness.

'This is your wife?' he asked. 'Did you finally decided to settle down, the great adventurer Nathaniel Chambers?'

Chambers laughed. 'No, this is my late brother's wife, Mary.'

'Oh yes,' said Hannan, 'I didn't see you clearly,' realizing who she was. She glared at him with contempt.

'So,' interrupted Rouse, 'what is the situation?'

He looked down and saw the body of Jed lying on the floor. Chambers explained to the men what happened.

Hannan was furious. 'You let the priest go?' he asked.

'If you all go up against Knox,' said Chambers, 'the way he is, the way that farm is located, out in the open, he will take a few of you out before you can get within a hundred yards of the place. Give the priest some time.'

'I think Chambers is right,' said Rouse. 'There is a large clearing between the farm gate and the front door, and dusk is approaching. He has the upper hand. We will be out in the open for a few hundred meters. He knows that place well.'

'I disagree,' said Powell, stepping forward. 'The problem with some priests is that they think they can appeal to a man's better nature, but as an officer of the law, I can tell you, that a man's better nature is often difficult to find, even on a good day. We need to ride out to Crooked River as soon as possible with as many of men you can trust as possible Rouse.'

'Do you think that the priest will be in trouble?' asked Mary.

'No, Mrs. Chambers,' said Powell. 'I think he will already be dead.'

It took several hours for Rouse to gather his men and others together. They came to the front of the Church of England building on the top of Church Hill at dusk, mostly with torches. Some were from the Catholic Church, others were Methodists, and many were miners. Robinson the jeweller was among them, and Constantine the miner.

Rouse addressed them all when he had mounted his horse.

'Friends,' he said loudly. 'For those of you who do not know the facts, Jed Barton was murdered in this church a few hours ago by John Knox. He died in the aisle surrounded by his friends, and whatever we thought of Jed, he died a good man. It was cold-blooded murder and Jed was unarmed.

'As you know, there have been many strange deaths in Gulgong in the last twelve months, and I have suspected the involvement of John Knox in many of them: the suspicious death of his wife last year, the murder of Shamus Murphy here in Gulgong, and the tragic death of Lee Peng. Jed Barton confessed that John Knox poisoned his wife and shot young Millie Thorpe.

'But we failed him, and I know I did. He was a man in pain, and we just ignored it. If we are to survive as a town, we must pull together, we must work together, and we must not ignore each other. We are now paying for our lack of concern for our brother John.'

'You didn't fail him,' said Hannan. 'We are all responsible for the choices we make.'

'Be that as it may,' continued Rouse looking at all the men gathered.

We are riding to Crooked River. Knox said that he would kill anyone who tried to arrest him. Knox is well-armed. We expect to meet resistance. There is a wide paddock between the bush and his homestead. He will have us in the open, and therefore we ride into great danger.

'But my friends know this. If we are to survive as a town, then we must come together and stand for what is right, uphold the law, and protect the vulnerable. The arrest of John Knox will mark a new beginning for Gulgong and hopefully the end of a darkness that has hung over this district like a plague. This curse began at Crooked River, and I will make sure that it ends there tonight. That is my hope, and it is my hope for all who ride with us.'

Rouse turned his horse and with Powell and Hannan beside him, lead the riders towards Crooked River. Chambers was the last to get on his horse and he turned back once more to see Mary standing there.

He smiled at her, tipped his hat, and rode off, saying nothing.

'Richard,' said Mary, as the men rode off into the distance. 'You know Chambers more than most here. Who is he, really? Don't tell me he is just an old friend.'

Emma laughed. 'He is lots of things dear Mary,' she explained, frowning.

'Mrs. Chambers,' interrupted William. 'I admit I know a little about him. I was not honest with you before. Chambers is a kind of detective in his own way, but he doesn't work for the police. He is not like Powell or Hannan, though they are also good men.'

'For whom does he work?' asked Mary, intrigued.

'Nobody knows for sure,' said William. 'He is always on the side of good, that is what I have heard over the years. He is relentless in pursuit of justice, no matter the cost.'

'I don't understand,' said Mary. 'Why doesn't he just settle down?'

'He is a good man, Mary,' said William. 'I have seen the way you are together. I hope I am not speaking out of place, but a man like Chambers is always on the move, he is always off on a new adventure. Nevertheless, he was ready to settle down in China, so maybe he would be ready to settle down again, but don't pressure him to decide.

'Men like Chambers could face an entire regiment of mad Taiping warriors singlehanded, believe me, I know he has done that, but he will be tongue-tied if he tried to say anything of significance to the woman he loved. That is the way of the warrior, in China too. It is remarkable how men are, the good ones. You know a man by his good deeds, not by his empty promises.'

'Thank you, William,' said Mary genuinely. 'I think I know what I need to do, and I will know what his thoughts are, even if he does not speak.'

'You summed up dear Chambers perfectly,' added Richard. 'He is also a good friend.'

Meanwhile, Chambers and the others were riding slowly towards Crooked River.

'Are you convinced that Lyon's made a deadly mistake?' Rouse asked Hannan.

He nodded in agreement. 'I don't think that we will be bringing Mr. Knox back for a trial. I think he will want to settle this the old-fashioned way, to go out in a blaze of glory.'

'Then he will be in for a big surprise,' said Powell, riding up to the two men. 'I want to send some of you around a different way, so we don't have everyone coming in the same direction if he is waiting for us.'

'My brother's farm is across the creek, I can take Robinson, Constantine, and a few other men and we can come across the paddock,' said Chambers.

Powell nodded and called out to those men to go with Chambers. They headed off towards Eliza, while Powell, Rouse, Hannan, and the other townsfolk of Gulgong went on ahead towards Crooked River.

It was about dusk when Chambers reached the entrance to Eliza. He could smell the smoke as the wind changed and blew toward them.

'Smells like something is on fire,' yelled Constantine.

'It smells like a house burning,' said Chambers, and prodded his horse forward. The four men crossed Cooyal Creek onto Knox's land and then they saw it. The Knox estate was indeed on fire. It was burning to the ground, and smoke enveloped it.

'It was lit some time ago,' said Robinson. 'But since there is no wind tonight, it has not spread far. It will hopefully burn itself out, otherwise, we will have a bushfire.'

'Have your rifles at the ready gentlemen,' said Chambers. 'I don't want us to take any chances in case Knox tries anything.'

'Do you think he is still alive?' asked Constantine.

'I don't know anything,' said Chambers. 'That's why we need to be ready.'

As they approached the estate and the burning house, they were met by many cattle moving away from the property, some of them singed from the flames. All the other buildings on the property were aflame and there was chaos. Chambers could see in the distance the other men. They had all dismounted and were walking slowly up the path toward the house. He could not see anything clearly in the smoke. It burnt their eyes, and they could not see the shape of the house. Suddenly the wind picked up and for a moment, Chambers couldn't see the house and what the men were looking at in front of the house.

'What are they looking at?' asked Robinson.

'I don't know,' replied Chambers, and rode his horse closer to the burning Knox estate. He began to feel a sense of dread deep in his chest, and his mouth went suddenly dry. As Chambers reached the edge of the homestead, through the remains of the fence, he could not believe what he saw.

Knox had done exactly what he said he would do. Rouse, Powell,

Hannan, and the others were simply standing next to their horses, watching the blaze consuming the house, but they were also watching something else.

There were three wooden crosses in front of Crooked River, all aflame. Two had what looked like the remains of men on them, now thoroughly consumed by the fire, their limbs stretched out revealing their last moments to be ones of terrible agony. The middle cross was empty, but it was still burning, probably because it was so close to the others, and because at the base of each cross, there were bonfires burning piles of wood. In front of the middle cross, lying on the ground, face up, and a gun in his hand was John Knox.

'It appears,' yelled Hannan to Chambers and the men with him, 'that John Knox shot and killed Mr. Lyons and some other poor devil we cannot identify, from what we can tell. There are the remains of the priest on the left, I believe.'

'Who was the middle cross meant for?' asked Chambers, his mind dizzy.

'I think it was meant for you if you came Chambers,' said Hannan. 'But since you didn't show up, Knox killed himself.'

Chambers stumbled off his horse and found it difficult to stand up. He fell to his knees in shock and distress, clutching his head. He didn't know what was happening. He thought for a moment that he was not in Australia anymore but in China. He tried to ignore the thought, but it came back to him. The more he pushed it away, the more vivid it became until he opened his eyes, and he was no longer standing in front of Knox's farm, but he was back in his village in the mountains of China. He was staring up at the hill and the burning crosses that littered it, dozens of burning bodies, in the night. He was staring at the remains of his wife, in front of her home, a woman he failed to protect, a woman he loved, and was going to stay with for the rest of his life. He looked, and all he knew and loved, was on fire.

Chambers then saw the strangest thing. He felt he had drifted back to the Knox Estate. He was back at Crooked River. But he saw his dead wife standing in front of him. She was beautiful.

'What are you doing here?' she asked him, smiling.

'I thought you were dead,' he said to her, as she took his right hand.

'My poor darling,' she replied. 'I came back for you. We are all here, all your friends, all your cloud of witnesses. We were just talking about you.'

Chambers looked back at Rouse and the others. They seemed so far away, like he was in a dream. They were talking amongst themselves. They did not see that he had walked up to the crosses and passed them. He was standing in front of the burning house, so close that he could feel the embers flying into his face. It was incredibly hot.

'Just a few more steps my love, and we can be together forever,' said Mei to Chambers.

He looked at her. He had longed to see her face for so long.

'I am sorry I was not there for you,' he said. 'I am sorry that I failed you.'

'It doesn't matter anymore Nathaniel,' she said, taking his hand. 'It is time to leave all of this behind, all those bad memories, and step with me into the flames.'

Chambers was about to take one step into the fire, when he felt an incredible surge of pain at the back of his head and he found himself falling sideways to the ground, where all he saw was darkness.

25   FAREWELLS

Guntawang

Chambers stood on the front veranda of Guntawang looking out across the garden, the fences, and the paddocks beyond. Rouse stood next to him, smoking a pipe.

'Are you sure I cannot convince you to stay Chambers?' he asked.

'A man could find peace here,' said Chambers. 'Without any doubt I am sure of it. You and Charlotte have done a fine job here. You should get more involved in local society. Have you thought about politics?'

'Politics?' asked Rouse. 'Can you imagine me in Parliament House in Sydney Town, walking around with the Governor?'

'Yes, I can, said Chambers. 'I think you would make a fine representative.'

He turned to Rouse and offered his hand. They shook hands warmly.

'It has been an eventful time,' said Rouse. 'I hope you enjoy a quiet journey home to China.'

'Thank you for all your kindnesses and hospitalities Richard,' replied Chambers.

He turned to enter the house once more to make his farewells. His horse was packed and ready. Rouse had even found a satchel of fresh apples for the horse to eat on the journey back to Sydney, and then hopefully to Shanghai.

Chambers was also grateful to Rouse for the rough knock on the head that night on Knox's farm at Crooked River. He was only a footstep from death when Rouse stepped forward and stunned him with the butt of his rifle. Rouse said he didn't need any explanation. He suspected that Chambers was suffering a severe delusion, with the burning crosses conjuring up the nightmares of his past in China.

Powell and Hannan heard Chambers call to his deceased wife he thought was in the burning house. It was Hannan who alerted Rouse and Rouse stepped forward and stopped Chambers from accidentally committing suicide. For Rouse also, the deep secrets of a man belonged to him and him alone, in his relationship with God. It was not for public viewing. The men who were there accepted Hannan's explanation that Chambers was still suffering from the loss of his wife and family in China, and everyone agreed to leave the strange incident there.

On their journey back to Guntawang, Hannan informed Rouse that Chambers had met up with the two detectives in Mudgee before he arrived in Home Rule, to become acquainted with the facts of his brother's disappearance and inform them of his intentions to find Henry's killer.

The death of Lyons and Rogers, Rouses' informant, and the manner of their deaths hung heavily with the men as they returned home early that following morning. It was not something they wanted to talk about, nor did they want to sensationalize. The three men were buried at Crooked River, and everyone agreed on the official story: the men died in a tragic house fire set by Mr. Knox as the culmination of the bitter events the previous week. Nothing would be gained by talk of burning crosses and burnt corpses. This would only scare the townspeople and threaten the gold rush. Nothing would be gained if it were widely known. There were a few rumours over the years about that strange night at Crooked River, but they vanished as quickly as the gold and by the end of the decade, both were but distant memories. The only regret Rouse had was that he had the unhappy duty of writing to Lyon's family who was in New Zealand. Priests did not seem to last long in Gulgong.

Chambers quickly recovered from the blow to his head, and the following day said his farewells in Gulgong, spending the evening with Richard and Emma Noble as they drank malt whiskey while Chambers enjoyed a few pots of freshly brewed tea, laughing and talking about the old days. The next day he spent with Mary, walking quietly along the river near Home Rule, before returning to Guntawang with her in the afternoon.

Chambers saw Hannan in the corridor and shook his hand.

'It has been good to see you again Chambers,' said the detective. 'It is a pity you have to leave so soon. I guess life goes on, but we could always benefit from your insights into detective work. I still remember our adventures years ago with great fondness.'

'As do I, Hannan, as do I,' said Chambers. 'Where is everyone else?' he asked.

'Listening to Mrs. Rouse and Merlin play a duet on the piano,' replied Hannan. 'I am more of a harmonica man myself.' Both men laughed.

Chambers walked into the music room. They had all enjoyed a lovely dinner provided by the Rouse family. There had been much conversation, and Chambers felt a strong urge to stay, and that's why he felt he had to leave. Elsbeth was at the piano holding the sheet music, while Merlin thumped on the keyboard, much to the surprise of Mrs. Rouse who tried to keep up. Mary was standing talking with Sarah and William in front of a landscape painting of Guntawang, and they were laughing about something. It was time for him to leave. It was a nice final memory.

That night, on the front veranda looking out across the paddock, Chambers had given the gold and the horses to Mary as she was, legally, the rightful heir to Henry's estate. She protested strongly and only relented when Chambers accepted a necklace that was with the gold, stolen from Henry's home by Blackwell the priest. When he held it in his hands, he realized this was the only thing of his mother's that he owned.

He wanted to say much more to Mary, but the words would not come. Every time he tried to speak, he felt confused and decided to stop talking and leave the words unsaid. Mary told him that she was going to leave Home Rule, to go with Sarah and William to Sydney to help them set up their new tea rooms in one of the more fashionable suburbs of the city. Chambers was glad she was leaving. He and William had even spent a few moments together, earlier in the evening, speaking about the Nemesis quietly in the smoking room. Both men toasted absent friends, sharing tea together, and talking about China.

Chambers walked to the front door, waved to Rouse who was still smoking on the veranda, and went to his horse.

'Are you leaving without a word of goodbye?'

Chambers turned and saw Elsbeth there.

'What would you like me to say to you?' he asked.

'Not to me, you fool,' replied Elsbeth. 'To Mary, how could you leave without saying goodbye? If you do not say anything, then I will never speak to you again.'

Chambers sighed, relented, and walked back up the steps, past Rouse who stood resolutely on the veranda smoking slowly and walked back into the house.

'Wait!' ordered Rouse. 'A rider is coming.'

Chambers turned and there was indeed someone riding quickly towards Guntawang. He wasn't prepared to wait and walked with Elsbeth back into the house and into the music room.

'Here he is,' she announced.

Everyone stopped talking and looked at him, waiting for him to speak.

'I just wanted to thank you all for your kind hospitality,' he said. 'I am not good at farewells. Life is full of unexpected surprises, some of them good, some of them bad. I count meeting all of you a great privilege.'

He was about to continue speaking when he was interrupted by Rouse who was standing next to a very exhausted rider. He was dressed in military uniform.

'There is a rider here for you Chambers,' said Rouse, 'I think he has a message for you.'

Chambers looked at the soldier. He was young, not twenty-five, well-dressed, and bearing a letter that he held in his wavering hand.

'I bear a message for Colonel Chambers, from the Governor of the Colony of New South Wales. Are you he Sir?'

Chambers nodded, saluted, and took the note.

The young man stood to attention.

'Get this man a drink Rouse, I think he is in need of refreshment,' he said.

He looked over to Mary. 'Can you read this note? I do not wish there to be any secrets between us.'

She walked over slowly, took the note, and opened it. Her eyes opened with surprise.

'It is a handwritten note,' she said. 'To the attention of Dr. Nathaniel Chambers, Colonel.

I am requesting your urgent and immediate return to Government House, Sydney. Yours sincerely, Hercules Robinson, Governor of NSW.'

'Who are you?' asked Rouse, surprised. 'I assumed that you were in the British Army, long ago, and Hannan intimated as much, but you are still Colonel Chambers, on active duty, and on a first name basis with the Governor of NSW?'

Mary stood there looking at him. He was unsure of her response or attitude. She neatly folded the letter back into its envelope and handed it back to him with a smile.

He smiled back at her and turned to leave.

'Goodbye Richard,' he said to Rouse, and left them all in the house, walking once again out to the front, down the steps, and to the horse. He sighed. He was not ready to say goodbye. He turned around and walked back into the house again, down the corridor, and to the room where they were all gathered. Nobody had really moved from where they were standing.

'Mary!' he said loudly, walking over to her. She looked at him, unsure of what to say. He reached into his pocket and pulled out his mother's necklace, the one Mary had returned to him. He looked at her, and proceeded to put the necklace around her neck, slowly, and carefully, gently moving her hair and speaking to her softly.

'This is the only thing I have that belonged to my mother,' he said. 'I want you to have it. In fact, I would be happy if you wore it.'

'I am happy to wear it,' replied Mary. 'What about your sister in London, I hope she doesn't mind.'

'My sister?' asked Chambers. 'Oh I think, if I told her that I gave you the necklace, she would be happy for you to have it because she would know what it means.'

'What would she say to another woman wearing such a precious heirloom?' asked Mary.

'My sister?' laughed Chambers quietly. 'She has inherited more heirlooms from her husband than Rouse has sheep and cattle combined. She married a bishop. They have ten children.'

'I don't want ten children,' replied Mary quietly with a smile.

'I think that is wise,' replied Chambers. 'How many did you have in mind?'

'Three,' said Mary. 'One to be like his father, an adventurer, one to be a farmer, like Henry was, and one to be like Biddy, a good friend to everyone she meets.'

Chambers looked at Mary. They were standing close to each other without touching.

'I have to go,' he said. 'Walk with me to the door.' She smiled and they walked slowly down the corridor together. He stopped at the front door. He turned to leave, but she grabbed his arm.

'What do I call you?' she asked.

'What do you mean?' he inquired.

'Is it Chambers, or Nathaniel, or Nate, or Dr. Chambers, or Colonel Chambers how should I address you?'

Chambers stopped and thought about it.

'I have never told anyone my middle name. I do not like my first name. I usually go with Chambers, but you can be the first, aside from my parents, to call me by my middle name. It is Edward.'

'Edward,' said Mary.

Chambers smiled.

He turned, walked down the steps, and got onto his horse. When he looked up, he saw that a dust storm was approaching in the distance.

'Come girl,' he said to the horse. 'Let's try to get ahead of the storm. I do not want to get caught in it.'

The horse galloped down the path away from Guntawang and towards Sydney.

They had not gone far when they reached the edge of Home Rule. He passed the Hotel where he had been a week before, the night he arrived, met Biddy, and argued with Mary. He was reflecting on it all when he saw her. She was standing alone in the middle of the road, as the red dust swirled around her. It was Biddy. She was leading her horse across the street heading for home.

She looked up at him as he went past her and stared at him. Biddy had called him an outsider, but she could have been talking about herself. This was her land, and yet she was alone, walking in the dust storm, while Mary, Sarah, William, and others were entertained at Guntawang.

Biddy and her people would not have been welcome there. She was a stranger in her own land, an outcast, and another reminder to Chambers of the hollow words of freedom he heard at Eureka all those years ago. It was freedom for some, and exclusion for others. Even Fung needed to change his name to be accepted and become someone he was not. Australia was a nation of secrets and lies where only some could walk boldly in the open, while the rest cowered in the shadows.

Part of him wanted to stop and talk with her, but he had heard her curse the towns and the land. Chambers knew the power of words, especially those spoken in anger and fury, drenched in tears. Those words could stop an army, even raise the dead. When he saw Biddy, he was ashamed of his brother Henry and he felt for poor George, the man with the mind of a child, eager to impress, naïve and innocent in the ways of the world, cruelly and brutally murdered, and then forgotten. He knew she was angry and upset. Biddy was right. The land was cursed, but it was cursed long before either of them had arrived. Too much blood had been spilled.

Their eyes met as he rode past slowly. Chambers nodded in respect but said nothing. She tried to smile, and she wanted to say something, but he had already left. She wanted to thank him again for finding George, and for saving Mary, but something held her back as well. As he rode into the dark and was enveloped by the storm, it was as if the land had reclaimed him, as if he returned to the darkness. Biddy shuddered and all her skin tingled. Twice she had touched death on the cheek. Twice death came with a human face. She looked again into the darkness that lurked on the edge of Home Rule. She would never see Chambers again, but she would never forget him.

Chambers rode through the evening, along the road. He wanted to arrive in Sydney as soon as possible. The letter from the Governor seemed urgent, and he was glad that he had something else to think about to distract himself from the turmoil he felt within. He reflected on the week that had passed. He had come for vengeance and found love instead, but was it all a dream? The night of the fire was the first he slept soundly. If Rouse had not struck him, he knew that he would have walked to his death. He had been haunted by images of Mei taunting him ever since her death in China. His every step was plagued by guilt. He survived, once again, while others died. But maybe Rouse had also knocked some sense into him and he, for the first time in years, thought about the possibility of settling down.

But Chambers also left Gulgong and Home Rule with a heavy heart. The maelstrom around John Knox resulted in the deaths of at least ten people, most of them completely innocent. Knox brought the spectre of death to all the lives he touched and put fear and dread into many more. In some ways, the insanity behind the three wooden crosses outside Crooked River was a fitting end to the life of a man of violence. But it was seeing those crosses which broke Chamber's fragile state of mind and took him to China, forcing him to relive the death of his wife. Chambers felt responsible for the tragic death of Mr. Lyons who gravely misjudged the evils lurking in Knox's heart.

But some good came of his visit. He found answers to the riddle behind his brother's death. He was able to push Rouse towards a more active role in the town of Gulgong. He rekindled a friendship with his old friend Richard Noble and was reconciled to his estranged former lover, Emma. He was inspired by the life of Elsbeth and her eccentric companion Merlin, and he was encouraged by the example of William and Sarah Fung.

It was early the next morning when he realized that his horse needed to rest, and his eyes were also weary. At this time, his thoughts had returned to Mary, and wondered how they might meet again in Sydney. He hoped that their paths might once again cross. He also realized that, for the time being, his adventures in China were at an end. He made a small campfire to warm himself. He had almost run out of apples for the horse, and so he was rummaging around in the satchel when his hand came across a letter. He pulled it out, walked over to the fire, and saw that it was addressed to him. He quickly opened it.

It read:

'My dear Chambers,

I once said to you that there was nothing a father would not do for his son. I told you that at Guntawang. There was nothing I would not have done for my son. What amazed me was that I sat opposite you at Guntawang, and you did not recognize me. When I discovered you had turned up at Home Rule looking for your brother's killer, I had to hasten my plan. I had already kidnapped Blackwell the priest, tortured him, and obtained from him all the information I needed which explained how my son died, was falsely accused, and who was responsible. I kept him drugged on opium in my son's shack in the middle of the bush where he had the little distillery. I knew it was a risk, but no one came, and Blackwell was not discovered.

Only Fung knew my real identity. We both thought you would be onto us, given your stellar reputation as a spy for Her Majesty, and Fung told me that he was not going to lie for me. I thought I had given myself away when I accidentally called Mrs. Fung Sarah in the church as there was no way for me to know her on such an intimate basis, but you must not have noticed.

Do you really think that you were the only white man to find a Chinese wife?

Do you really suppose that Queen Victoria has only one spy in the

Orient?

She has many. Why else do you think Britain rules the waves?

Lee Peng was my adopted son.

His father was killed in that wretched Taiping Rebellion. I saw him as my own, as my other children died years ago, and Lee Peng was the one I would see grow into a man. We were delighted when he wanted to go to Australia to find work. When William wrote to me that he had been killed, and told me about the wretched circumstances, I was overcome by rage. I wanted vengeance.

I wanted not only to kill John Knox, but destroy him, and take away every single joy in his life, before killing him personally. I put a little something in Henrietta's scones on Saturday evening. A single scone was enough to make one bilious, but Maxwell must have eaten a dozen of them. He would have died in agony. I poisoned Henrietta during the Church Service. How did I do that? I put poison on the wafer for Communion. I also laced one for myself, just a little bit, enough to make me genuinely sick. I also put a little on the wafers for Mr. and Mrs. Clarke, two of the witnesses who damned my son and said that he was arguing with Shamus Murphy. My son was not even in Gulgong the day the Irishman was killed. I returned later to serve Communion to the Clarkes in their beds. They are both dead now.

'Old Bert Palmer was the third false witness who betrayed my son, this time for money. I lured him into the bush and strangled him. I also walloped the solicitor the night of the storm and made it look like an accident. He covered up the death of my son and protected John Knox and his corrupt business practices. I threw a snake at the good doctor, who squirmed and squealed all his way to hell. He failed to accurately diagnose the death of Mrs. Knox and I enjoyed the irony of his demise, staying in his house and watching him die.

'My original plan was simply to kill Jed and Knox and make it look like a house fire but when Knox announced to everyone that he wanted to crucify people, I decided to be more creative. I did indeed meet Knox. I even managed to convince him to take Communion, which we did, but I laced the wine with a sedative this time, which gave me the opportunity to dig up the decaying and smelly Mr. Blackwell. Thank you for burying him. I killed him on Saturday night and made it look like suicide. Mr. Knox had already built the beautiful crosses in front of his homestead and that was very obliging of him. It did not take long to put the late Mr. Blackwell, or what was left of him, on one of them, and my cross around his neck for identification, the one I drew attention to at Guntawang. I am sure Rouse used it to identify me. The other body was that of a man called Rogers, who turned up unfortunately at the same time to confront Knox. He was just in the wrong place at the wrong time. He had to die. You should have seen the look on Knox's face when I roused him and revealed my identity.

My dear Chambers, you might think me a monster. But you took revenge for the death of your wife in China. You lived through the insane madness of the Taiping Rebellion, tens of millions of dead, hundreds of millions displaced, and unbelievable suffering and no one in Australia even knows about it. They don't even know who Ward was, and no one cares about Gordon anymore, or what we did, what we accomplished. We changed the world. I am surprised you didn't recognize me. Our paths crossed a few times in China over the years.

We are both victims of war Chambers, as was Mei, and in some ways Lee Peng, who grew up in a prison camp, experiencing terrible suffering. I can only assume that the horrors of incarceration drove him blindly onto the street that fateful day when he was falsely accused by Constable Cooper.

Why did I choose to assume the role of a priest? My identity was a difficult and delicate matter to resolve as I needed to go incognito. I had decided on my disguise before I left Shanghai, buying some clerical garments, a Bible, and various ecclesiastical documents from an associate of mine in the Church of England. In his letter, Fung had told me that the priest responsible for Gulgong, was in his words, 'a vile man with debased appetites.' I knew immediately that this was a perfect opportunity. I searched for the priest and feigned interest in him, luring him to the distillery in the bush with all kinds of inducements. The rest you know.

It is easy to copy a religious hypocrite. As you know, the West is all about appearances, not the heart. But even I needed a template, and to his eternal regret, my father was mine, like you, a good man. He was deeply disappointed in the choices made by his son, but he would have been impressed by my religious doctrine during my brief tenure as a priest. I would like to think that I made a positive impression on Rouse, and all the people of Gulgong with my words of encouragement, as I simply echoed what my father taught me. I also hope that my life and death in Gulgong might lead the town to appoint a more suitable man in the future, with a purer heart, but you and I both know how corrupt the Church of England is, so that is unlikely.

On a lighter note, I saw you with Mary and the way she looked at you. She loves you. William told me that Mary and Henry respected each other, but there was no real love there. You should marry that woman and settle down. As for me, we just have different methods and different ways of doing things. You are a gentleman spy. You have a moral core; and are what we call a good man. I am not. It is that simple, but I love Britain as much as you do, and I loved my family and my son. Don't worry about the man who murdered Mei, I will kill him for you. I know about him, and I know about your wife. It is my promise to you, one man to another.

You are not so different from me, I must admit, after all. I am heading back to China to do some work for the Chinese, but secretly working for the Queen, as do you. Consider it a wedding gift from one spy to another. Settle down, my friend. Say farewell to China and the past. Give Mary that beautiful necklace that she returned to you today at Guntawang.

Yours with every best wish, Mr. Lyons.

P.S. Not my real name.'

Chambers froze, and the letter fell from his hands to the ground. He stared into the embers of the fire, unable to fully comprehend what he had just read. He rubbed his eyes and looked down at the pages at his feet, reaching for them again.

He carefully re-read the letter, and as he read it for the second time, what astonished him at first was now horrifying him. Not only had he been deceived, but he was also guilty of the same prejudice he saw in others, a prejudice he was confident he had repudiated.

He was just as narrow-minded as poor Pete Barton and just as blind as Elsbeth and Merlin. He assumed that Lee Peng's stepfather was Chinese, and everyone had, except William Fung, who tried to provide clues for Chambers to follow. He was one question away from the truth, and yet the only one he cared about was his brother Henry.

Fung told him that Lee Peng's stepfather was a former soldier. Why did he not simply ask his name? Why did he assume that he was Chinese? He was so close to the truth, it was shouting at him from heaven, but Chambers was too arrogant to dwell long on the life of one Chinese man in the colony of New South Wales.

He was right in his first assessment of the poisoning at the Sunday luncheon. It was indeed the work of a man well versed in the art of death, but again, for some reason, he convinced himself that it was not possible. Why did he do that? Was he distracted by the search for Henry's killer, or still wallowing in self-pity over the death of his wife? Elsbeth, Mary, and Lyons were all right. He was a victim of war, and still lived in its terrible shadow, unable to see anything clearly.

Then it struck him. It was not what William said or failed to say, nor was it anything Lyons said in the church. Jed Barton was shot at close range and his blood covered the remains of the church altar, but it also showered Lyons who was standing behind the poor man. Lyons did not flinch even for a moment, nor did he try to move away. When he stood between Knox and Richard, it was as if the blood did not bother him in the slightest. A normal man, a civilian, would be horrified by the situation and at least try to wipe off the blood. It never occurred to Chambers that the reaction of Lyons at that moment was the first and only time the priest showed his real identity, a man well acquainted with blood and death. When the shot rang out, Richard and Chambers pulled the women down out of harm's way, but Lyons did not even move.

How did Lyons know about the necklace unless he was there at Guntawang, pretending to be one of Rouse's many workmen? He must have written most of the letter beforehand and then written the postscript on the spot, placing the letter with the apples.

But Lyons was wrong about one thing. The fake priest too was living in the shadow of the war, that terrible slaughterhouse that was China. Even Lyons had a choice. He could talk all day about good men and bad, but the way he killed all those people, and the manner of their deaths, this was all born in the madness of the Taiping Rebellion, and Lyons did not send those men to hell. He was living in hell, each day, in pain, alone, and suffering.

But Chambers was not alone. He had people who cared about him, people he hardly knew, but who stood with him on some of his darkest days. His cloud of witnesses was no help to him, all they did was accuse him, but Richard and Emma, Sarah and William, Mary, Biddy and Richard, and Charlotte Rouse, they in their own way, shone a light into his heart that helped to dispel the darkness he carried around with him. For the first time in years, he had hope.

Chambers had pity on Lyons and was saddened that the man did not confide in him. They might have worked together, and Knox and the others would be facing real justice, not summary executions in the middle of the outback. But Lyons was right about Mary. It was time to settle down. The time for war was over. The days of peace were coming, or at least, he hoped and yearned for them. Maybe the dawn would bring a new beginning.

Chambers gradually stood up and tossed the letter into the fire. What was done, is done, he thought. Life was too short for regrets. He wanted the dead buried but he knew they would always be his cloud of witnesses. He was ready to continue his journey. He looked up into the sky. It was full of stars.

HISTORICAL NOTES

The Curse of Crooked River is a work of fiction. The names, characters, events, and incidents mentioned here are the product of my imagination, and any resemblance to actual persons, living or dead, or actual events, is purely coincidental. Nevertheless, it is set in history. This book is historical fiction. My methodology is to weave a fictional narrative that does not affect or alter reported events or biographies of real people, whose presence in the novel anchors the fictional characters with authenticity.

Crooked River takes place in real-time, a period of just over one week, in real places (Gulgong, Home Rule, and Guntawang) among historical personalities. Within these historical boundaries, it is entirely possible that the events could have taken place in Gulgong and Home Rule in 1871 and 1872. This was a dark period for Australian crime in the colony of New South Wales, and many people died, were murdered, or disappeared on the goldfields. The police, as few as they were, had considerable responsibilities.

Historical characters such as Richard and Charlotte Rouse of Guntawang, Henry Beaufoy Merlin the photographer, Robert Hannan, and Charles Powell, the detectives, exist within their timelines, and known personalities. Above this foundation were placed composite characters, based on historical personalities such as William and Sarah Fung, and Biddy. William was based on the famous early Australian businessman Mei-Quong Tart (1850-1903). The fictional characters of Chambers, Knox, Mary, and Jed were placed on top of these two layers.

Trove was an essential resource, and I studied all the newspaper articles I could locate on Gulgong, Home Rule, Guntawang, and the surrounding district from about 1866 to 1872, to provide an accurate picture of the setting, buildings, personalities, and issues of the time.

Richard Rouse (1842-1903) and Charlotte Emily Rouse (-1902) lived at the newly built Guntawang estate during this period, and I made sure Richard's character was as close as possible to what we know of him as a prince among the landed aristocracy in the colony of New South Wales. His hospitality was generous and well-known, his brand was the Crooked R, and he bred sheep, cattle, and horses for carriage transport. He was the main shareholder in his Guntawang Freehold Gold Mining Company. He became mayor of Gulgong and served as a representative for Mudgee in the NSW Parliament in 1876-77 and 1879. Guntawang was a veritable oasis in the bush and a contrast to the filth and squalor that was Gulgong in the 1870s, one of the main causes of the high rates of infant mortality due to typhoid epidemics.

Henry Beaufoy Merlin (1830-1873) was a photographer of late nineteenth-century Australia, a showman and a magician. His many photos of Gulgong and Home Rule in 1872 captured the sense and excitement of a gold rush town in its heyday. He visited Gulgong, Home Rule, Hill End, and the Central West for much of 1872, his photographic collection becoming the heart and soul of the Holtermann Collection. His tragic death in 1873 of pneumonia in Sydney is alluded to in the novel and reflects the fragility of life in those days. Merlin had an assistant, Mr. Charles Bayliss. Elsbeth, sadly, is a fictional replacement, as is the opium episode to provide colour to the insanity of seeking to photograph the outback, which led to his untimely demise. Merlin was one of Australia's greatest photographers.

For the plot, I placed the detectives Robert Hannan and Charles Powell in Mudgee for the week in question to allow the corruption of Constable Cooper to reach fruition. I also removed the other detectives with illnesses typical of the time. Gulgong was notorious for violent crime during the gold rush years. The government failed in its duty of care to the growing township of Gulgong by investing not only the role of gold commissioner, but police magistrate in the sole hands of Arthur Hannibal Macarthur (1830-1871), the grandson of Governor King. Macarthur also regularly conducted church services, and it was after one such service he suffered a stroke and subsequently died. Following his death, the enormous workload undertaken by one man was given to many, including the provision of detectives, and other police constables. Powell and Hannan were successful in their pursuit of the many criminals that took advantage of the flow of gold from Gulgong, Home Rule, and Mudgee. Bushrangers plagued the roads from Mudgee to Gulgong, shoot-outs were commonplace, as were drunken brawls, and street fights.

What of the Anglican clergy? There was so much darkness and evil associated with the Church of England and the role that institution played in early Australian history. While there were a few exceptions, Church of England priests supported the wholesale destruction of an indigenous culture or defended those who did. The Church of England up until the early post-war era, was the church of the landed aristocracy, of pew rentals, the church of the establishment, conservative, white supremacy. There were few in Australia that this denomination did not despise. They did all they could to discriminate against, marginalize and persecute other Christian denominations, especially Roman Catholics.

The Church of England in Australia in country towns was never loved, never well attended, and needed constant patronage from wealthy farmers who rented the pews. This meant that only the wealthy who had paid for their family pews could attend services. The church literally 'belonged' to those who paid for its upkeep and everyone else was excluded.

The original church building in Gulgong was built in December 1871 and was described by one contemporary as 'the shabbiest place of worship ever built.' It was poorly attended, had an altar and pulpit made of packing cases, and was a constant fire hazard, built on the top of Church Hill, a desolate, moon-like landscape bereft of trees and any signs of life. It was difficult in the early township of Gulgong (and many other rural towns) to secure priests for any length of time. The early priests came and went quickly, especially from 1871-1873. The Rouse family had their own church St James at Guntawang, as was the custom of large rural families in that era. Guntawang had several hundred people living and working there at the time. The old church in Gulgong was torn down in 1874, to be replaced by the Edmund Blackett-designed structure, with pew rentals, but by the time it was built in 1876 the gold rush had ended, attendance collapsed, and the money dried up. The Church of England never played a significant role in the life of the town, except as the church of the wealthy landowners.

What of Mr. Blackwell and his murderous trips into the bush? When I lived in Mudgee, I heard people say that one of the priests used to ride into the bush to kill aboriginal people. I could not corroborate this with any evidence, but the character of Mr. Blackwell seemed a natural one, his ominous name chosen to mean Black or Dark River, tying into the title of the book. Rev. Jakob Gunther (1806-1879) the first Church of England rector at Mudgee (with oversight of Gulgong) was a dreadful racist, and his aboriginal mission in Wellington in the 1830s (where Biddy, George, and their mother resided for a time) was a complete failure. Gunther despised aboriginal people, their culture, and their lifestyle, which he saw as an affront to Christian values. This view was common among the clergy. The main massacres of the local tribes around Mudgee, Rylstone, and Gulgong took place much earlier (around the 1820s and 1830s).

As for the towns themselves, I constructed Home Rule from various photos from Merlin's collection, and from Merlin's photographs I found on Trove. Home Rule came into being after May 1872 and rivalled Gulgong for a few years, reaching about 20,000 people. Herbert Street in Gulgong stretched for several kilometres from the Adams and Black Leads, with hotels at the top, and Chinese market gardens and brothels further down the street. The Shamrock and Thistle (run by Shamus and Mary) was the name of a real hotel in Gulgong at the time, and Samuel Bibb's Hotel in Home Rule became 'The Canadian,' as a nod to the Canadian Lead, the origins of the Home Rule Lead. The centre of cultural life in Gulgong was what became the Prince of Wales Opera house in 1872. Henry's estate was a typical miner's cottage (four rooms) with a veranda.

The character of Biddy was inspired by a real aboriginal woman called Biddy Giles (1820-1890s), a member of the Dharawal people in Sydney, who farmed goats, tended fruit trees, organized bush tours, and was widely respected. In my novel, Biddy is half-aboriginal, reflecting the harsh realities of that period, namely the raping of aboriginal women by farmers as well as rampant syphilis among the landed aristocracy. William (and Sarah) Fung are based on the famous Chinese Australian Mei Quong Tart (1850 -1903) and Margaret Scarlett, who opened a tea house in the Queen Victoria Building in 1898. John Knox was so named in honour of the presbyterian leader John Knox (1514-1572) who wrote in 1558 his book against women called 'The First Blast of the Trumpet Against the Monstrous Regiment of Women.' Enough said. John Knox in my novel embodied the typical religious bully who preyed on the vulnerable, despite all his praying to God.

I came up with the idea of Nathaniel Chambers after reading about the life of Frederick Townsend Ward (1831-1862). Ward was a remarkable American adventurer who helped create the 'Ever-Victorious Army' in 1860, a mixture of Chinese government troops and foreign mercenaries to fight the religious zealots of the Taiping Rebellion led by Hong Xiuquan, a man who believed himself to be the brother of Jesus Christ. I then studied the lives of other foreigners who worked for the Manchu Dynasty during the tumultuous final decades of the nineteenth century. Chambers is inspired by the lives of all these men who fought, died, and often fell in love with China at a time when the West was flexing its xenophobic muscles.

Nathaniel Chambers was born in China in 1820. His father worked as a shipping agent for the British East India Company. In 1839-1842, he served under the British against the Chinese during the First Opium War. He studied some medicine in London in the 1840s, becoming 'Dr. Chambers,' and then travelled around Europe and the Middle East. In 1854 he arrived in Australia, and he was involved in the Eureka Stockade in December of that year when he met Richard and Emma, among others.

He returned to China and worked as a gentleman 'spy' for the British and served during the Second Opium War (1856-60). He was sent by London to Australia in early 1861 and was caught up in the Lambing Riots of June 1861. He returned to China and fought alongside Ward, then General Charles Gordon in the militaristic efforts to defeat the Taiping Rebellion throughout the following decade. This book details the beginning of Chambers' last visit to Australia. The second in this trilogy will see our hero up against the Church of England and Sydney's class war, and the final book will see him do battle with politicians and the ghosts of the past.

 Chambers is in China what William is in Australia – an outsider trying to fit in. He speaks Chinese, he prefers Chinese food, and he has an open mind regarding China's place in the world. This reflects his long experiences in China. He realizes that he is still deeply prejudiced and still living in the shadow of his experiences. Such is life. He is also the antithesis of Mr. Lyons, himself a spy working for the British, but the fake priest has no moral core.

Despite all his anguish and suffering, traumatic experiences in China and Australia helps to place Chambers firmly in a world where right choices can be made. Unlike Lyons, Chambers brings people together. Despite his religious scepticism, there is an authenticity to his life that the horrors of life have polished, not eroded. 'The Curse of

Crooked River' was not Chambers' first mystery to be solved, nor his last, but it is the first novel to be written in this series.

ABOUT THE AUTHOR

Michael J. Sutton grew up in Sydney, Australia, before moving to Japan to lecture in economics and International Relations. He has been a political economist, a professor, a priest, a pastor, and now a publisher and author. He is the CEO of Freedom Matters Today, looking at freedom from a Christian perspective. He has a PhD and First-Class Honours degree in Economics (Social Sciences) from the University of Sydney, a Master of Divinity from the Australian College of Theology, and a Diploma of Bible and Ministry from Moore Theological College. He discovered the remains of Home Rule while acting as priest for the Edmund Blackett-designed Anglican Church in Gulgong in 2017. For two years he presided over Mass with the cockroaches, mould, and rising damp in that place, outdoing its predecessor as the shabbiest church in the nation. He is the author of five books.